MILE HIGH MURDER

Recent Titles by Marcia Talley

The Hannah Ives Mysteries Series

SING IT TO HER BONES
UNBREATHED MEMORIES
OCCASION OF REVENGE
IN DEATH'S SHADOW
THIS ENEMY TOWN
THROUGH THE DARKNESS
DEAD MAN DANCING *
WITHOUT A GRAVE *
ALL THINGS UNDYING *
A QUIET DEATH *
THE LAST REFUGE *
DARK PASSAGE *
TOMORROW'S VENGEANCE *
DAUGHTER OF ASHES *
FOOTPRINTS TO MURDER *

* *available from Severn House*

MILE HIGH MURDER

A Hannah Ives Mystery

Marcia Talley

Severn House Large Print
London & New York

This first large print edition published 2018
in Great Britain and the USA by
SEVERN HOUSE PUBLISHERS LTD of
Eardley House, 4 Uxbridge Street, London W8 7SY.
First world regular print edition published 2017 by
Severn House Publishers Ltd.

British Library Cataloguing in Publication Data
A CIP catalogue record for this title is available from the British Library.

ISBN-13: 9780727829061

Typeset by Palimpsest Book Production Ltd.,
Falkirk, Stirlingshire, Scotland.

*For Linda Sprenkle, longtime friend
and partner in crime, who will know why.*

Acknowledgments

Thanks to my husband, Barry, who, in spite of his better judgment, totally went along with the research on this one.

And to Susan and Saul, who will try anything once.

I'm grateful to Cybele Merrick, whose generous bid at a fundraiser for Lyme Elementary School in Lyme, NH allowed her mother-in-law to check-in as a guest at my fictional B&B.

No charity is dearer to my heart than Every Child Counts in Marsh Harbour, Abaco, Bahamas. Thanks to Marilyn Prosa and her daughter-in-law, Heather of the Hope Town Coffee House, whose generous contribution to help these special needs kids gave 'Bell House' a clever Italian chef.

1,000,000 thanks to my colleagues in the Writers' Circle in Hope Town on Elbow Cay in the Bahamas, and to my partners in crime back in Annapolis, Maryland – Becky Hutchison, Mary Ellen Hughes, Debbi Mack, Sherriel Mattingly, Shari Randall and Bonnie Settle. They read it all first.

To friend and fellow writer, Sujata Massey, for the 'ah-ha' moment.

And, as always, to Vicky Bijur.

'Beware! Young and old – people in all walks of life! This may be handed to you by the friendly stranger. It contains the Killer Drug 'Marihuana' – a powerful narcotic in which lurks Murder! Insanity! Death!'

(US) Federal Bureau of Narcotics poster, 1935.

One

Why is my verse so barren of new pride,
So far from variation or quick change?
Why with the time do I not glance aside
To new-found methods and to
compounds strange?
Why write I still all one, ever the same,
And keep invention in a noted weed . . .

William Shakespeare, 'Sonnet 76'.

I had a wet rag in one hand and a wizened green pepper in the other, when I realized someone was calling my name.

'I can't hear you,' I called out, addressing a carton of pulp-free orange juice. 'My head's in the fridge.'

Paul tapped me lightly on the shoulder. 'What are you doing?'

I eased my head past the vegetable crisper drawer and turned, hoping that after thirty-some years of marriage he'd be able to read the 'duh' look on my face. 'Isn't it obvious?' I indicated a plastic-wrapped block of . . . something. Could have been cheese in a former life – organic butter, maybe. 'I'm trying to decide whether to throw that out. Could be a cure for Alzheimer's.' I picked up the baggie between thumb and fore-finger and handed it over. 'You decide.'

Paul scrunched up his nose adorably. 'No, thank

1

you, Hannah.' He pitched the mystery object into the trash can I'd set out to the right of the refrigerator in order to make my job easier. 'Don't you have your breast cancer support group today?'

I swiped an errant strand of hair out of my eyes with the back of my hand. 'Yes.' Suddenly, it occurred to me why he might be asking. 'Golly,' I said. 'What time is it?'

'If you hurry, you'll just make it.'

'Here,' I said, handing him the soapy rag. 'You take the helm.'

'Thanks heaps.'

I struggled to my feet. 'You can start with this spaghetti you insisted we save, when was it? Two weeks ago Monday?'

'I'll have it for lunch.'

I surrendered a Ziploc container, its contents flocked with a greenish-black mold. 'Go for it, Professor.'

He made a face. 'I see what you mean.' He tossed the spaghetti, container and all, into the trash.

My deep, puritanical New England roots recoiled. I rescued the container, ripped off the lid, tapped the revolting contents into the garbage disposal and placed the plastic tub, now empty, into my husband's hands. 'That's why God invented dishwashing liquid,' I said.

Leaving Paul to ponder the medicinal potential of the disgusting green map on the inside of the blue plastic lid, I raced for the shower.

Seven minutes later, wearing a red-and-white striped, long-sleeved T-shirt over a pair of white jeans, I tore down the stairs, scooped up

2

my handbag and car keys from the table in the entrance hall, then paused at the door. 'Where did you leave the car?' I yelled.

Parking on Prince George Street in Annapolis, where we live, is at a premium; it's a rare home in the three-block section of eighteenth- and nineteenth-century houses that has off-street parking. Paul had made a run out to Home Depot the previous evening – a bathroom faucet needed replacing – so I hoped I wouldn't have to walk all the way to the downtown waterfront before locating the family Volvo. Fortunately, he'd managed to squeeze the vehicle into a tight spot opposite the historic William Paca House, just a short trot away from our front door.

Sometimes the traffic gods are with you, sometimes they're not. By some miracle, I made it to the Anne Arundel Medical Center campus on Jennifer Road in less than ten minutes, hitting all the traffic lights on Bestgate Road green.

Reach for Recovery, the cancer support group that I facilitated on a rotating basis with several other long-term cancer survivors, met every Tuesday afternoon in the Belcher Pavilion, one of eight named pavilions in the sprawling hospital complex.

The Doordan Institute occupied the entire seventh floor of the Belcher Pavilion, offering an outdoor terrace with a commanding view of the Annapolis skyline. In addition to a state-of-the-art auditorium that could seat up to 400 people, there were five smaller classrooms. I was headed for one of them.

I knew from experience that Parking Garage E

in the hospital complex would be so full that I'd probably have to wind my way up to the top open-air deck before finding a spot, so I pulled instead into the garage adjacent to the Sajak Pavilion. I eased the Volvo into a corner space on the second deck and took the stairs down to the sidewalk at street level.

As I rounded a corner between the two pavilions, a familiar odor – a heady combination (at least to my mind) of hops, fresh-cut grass and burning palm fronds – stopped me cold.

'Senator Thompson!'

Maryland State Senator Claire Thompson leaned back against the dense hedgerow that separated the hospital campus from the Annapolis Plaza mall. In spite of the warm weather, she was dressed in blue jeans and an oversized hoodie that read, *Go Navy, Beat Army*. The hood was up, covering her short-cropped pale blonde hair.

Claire didn't reply at once. As I stood there, transfixed, she took a deep drag, inhaled, held it for a long five seconds, then exhaled a thin stream of smoke into the spring air. She opened her eyes. 'Hello, Hannah.' Her eyes drifted from me to the smoke, following it as it dissipated, mingling with the pollen from a nearby row of Bradford pear trees, their branches heavy with white blossoms.

'Do you realize how many laws you're breaking?' I scolded. 'To begin with, this is a smoke-free campus.'

If I could detect the distinctive smell of marijuana, I knew others could, too. From the stump of the joint she held between her thumb and

4

forefinger, I figured she'd been standing in that spot for a while. I expected the DEA to come whoop-whoop-whooping around the corner at any minute. Marijuana was still a Schedule 1 drug, according to Federal law.

Claire shrugged. 'I have a prescription.'

I knew that Claire – a breast cancer survivor – had been prescribed marijuana to help mitigate the side effects of her chemotherapy. 'How's the nausea?' I asked, remembering what she'd told the group at the previous week's Reach for Recovery session. Claire took another drag, exhaled and managed a wan smile. 'Better,' she said. She stubbed the joint out on the bottom of her jogging shoe and tucked the butt into her pocket. 'I've got the munchies, though.'

'Isn't that the whole point?' I said, thinking back to my own chemo experience more than a decade earlier. The nausea medication the doctor prescribed had turned me into a drooling zombie, so I'd made an executive decision. I'd quit taking it. After that, I'd spent several weeks hugging bowls of chicken noodle soup and praying for death. I'd been so sick, in fact, I'd spent most days on the sofa in front of the television, and watched all of *Killer Klowns from Outer Space* because I'd been too ill to crawl out from under the afghan and locate the remote.

I'd also lost twelve pounds.

'You gotta eat,' I told Claire, remembering how weak and exhausted I had felt. 'As diets go, chemo is way low on the totem pole.'

'We're gonna be late,' Claire said, ignoring my comment.

'So, what do you do?' I asked, trying to keep the discussion going as we headed into the building. 'You can't just sashay down to CVS and pick up a prescription.'

'Actually, I get it in DC. Maryland's medical marijuana dispensaries don't open until July.' She paused. 'If then. It's been a bumpy road.'

'Why?' I asked as we passed through the automatic glass doors and walked into the lobby. 'I haven't been following the news closely, but I thought medical marijuana was legalized here in 2015.'

We reached the bank of elevators and Claire punched the up button. 'It was, but since then we've been wrestling with the grow licenses – how many, who'll get them, yadda yadda yadda. What a clusterfuck! I thought we had it sorted,' she said, stepping into the elevator ahead of me. 'And then we got sued because *somebody* forgot to factor in racial diversity among the permit holders.' The way she emphasized the word 'somebody,' I knew she didn't hold herself to blame for the oversight. 'We were even forced to hire a diversity consultant.' She rolled her eyes.

As the elevator doors slid shut, she said, 'If you have a few minutes afterward, I'd like to talk to you about something. Coffee in the cafeteria?' she asked. 'My treat.'

'Sure,' I said, genuinely curious about what the topic of conversation might be. I opened my mouth to ask for details, but the elevator doors opened on the second floor and three women flounced in, two of them clutching bags from the hospital's Bayside gift shop.

'Oh, hello, Hannah,' one of the shoppers chirped.

It was hard to be depressed around Heather, our yoga instructor, an energetic bundle of radiant good health, wrapped up in pink-and-black Spandex exercise duds. She wore her infectious, almost pathological cheerfulness like a badge. Somewhere in the attic was her portrait as an ax murderer.

We started each Reach for Recovery session with a fifteen-minute yoga routine, after which Heather would flip her blonde ponytail and disappear with a wave and a chirpy, 'See you next week, ladies.' It invariably evoked a 'So what am I? Chopped liver?' comment from Bob, the only gentleman in our group. Men can get breast cancer, too.

Following Heather's workout and a round-robin of updates – Bob's blood work was totally clean (yay!), Jeannie's kids were taking her on a Caribbean cruise (I wish!), and the sonofabitch who Brendalee married, a Lutheran minister who should know better, was cheating on her with the parish secretary (divorce his sorry ass!) – we segued into a discussion of an upcoming fashion show sponsored by the Reingold-Yasinski Foundation in cooperation with MICA, the Maryland Institute College of Art. 'They're looking for a couple of dozen survivors as models,' I informed the group. 'If you're accepted, they'll pair you off with a promising young fashion designer.'

'Like *Project Runway*?' Ellie wanted to know.

'Exactly,' I said. 'They've even lined up one of the Project Runway finalists as emcee.'

'Oh my gosh, I love that show!' Tammy gushed. 'Who did they get?'

'I can't remember,' I confessed. The show had been on the air for what, fifteen seasons? As an off-again-on-again viewer, the contestants tended to blur in my mind.

'Oh, who cares, Tammy? It sounds like fun.' Ellie turned to me. 'Where do I sign up?'

I distributed a printout with details about the event, including the foundation's contact information. 'The show will be at the Visionary Arts Museum,' I continued. 'It's an awesome venue.'

I didn't tell the group that I was planning to apply to be a model myself. The American Visionary Art Museum, located at the foot of Federal Hill overlooking Baltimore's Inner Harbor, featured an eclectic mix of permanent and rotating exhibits by free-thinking, self-taught artists. I'd visited several times, and it was always an 'Oh, wow!' experience.

After everyone left, I finished closing up and hustled across the pedestrian bridge to the Garden Café on the first floor of the Clatanoff Pavilion.

Claire had already gone through the cafeteria line and was sitting at a wrought-iron table on the patio outside, nursing a bottle of iced tea. I waved, went through the line myself, snagged a cup of coffee and two oversized blueberry muffins, and joined her.

'Gosh, the sunshine feels good,' I said as I pulled out the chair opposite her and sat down. 'Here.' I pushed my plate across the table. 'For internal use only.'

'Thanks,' she said, selecting the smaller of the two muffins. 'I do believe I will.

'So, what's on your mind?' I asked.

Claire plunged right in. 'How would you like a free trip to Colorado?'

I choked on the coffee I'd just swallowed, and coughed. 'Colorado? What's in Colorado?'

'Denver, to be specific,' she said.

'You're kidding.'

Claire took a bite of her muffin and chewed it slowly, thoughtfully, as if willing it, once swallowed, to stay put in her stomach where it belonged. 'There is a catch, however.'

'Isn't there always?'

'You'd have to testify before the Maryland State Senate about what you'd learned.'

'Learned about what?'

'Recreational pot.'

Colorado, I knew, had legalized recreational marijuana several years before and, by everything I'd seen in the news, was making a huge success of it. 'I'm totally the wrong person for the job, Claire. I haven't smoked since graduate school.'

She waggled her eyebrows.

I had to laugh. 'Well, not cigarettes, anyway.' After a pause, I added, 'Smoking killed my mom.'

'I hadn't realized,' Claire said, her face instantly serious.

We sat in silence for a while. 'Congestive heart failure,' I explained. 'I'd give anything to have her back.' I shook off the chilling memory of my mother's final days. 'Edibles, however? That's a more recent story.'

Claire brightened. 'Naughty girl! Do tell.'

'Paul and I took one of those Viking River cruises you see advertised on PBS. It was fabulous,

9

by the way. The cruise ended in Amsterdam.' I shrugged 'When in Rome . . .'

As I paused, wondering how much to tell her, Claire said, 'What happens in Amsterdam stays in Amsterdam, am I right?'

I relaxed. 'We wandered around a bit, looking for the specific coffee house our daughter, Emily, had recommended. We didn't realize how hard that would be.' I leaned forward. 'She was rather vague on directions, and Amsterdam is a big city.'

'They sell marijuana in coffee shops? How very Starbucks of them!'

I shook my head. 'Not coffee shops, coffee *houses*. Big difference. In Amsterdam, you can buy a cappuccino or a latte at a coffee shop or a café, but weed is available only at coffee houses which, oddly, rarely sell coffee.' I shrugged. 'Go figure. I was on a caffeine high,' I continued, 'before a helpful barista explained that coffee houses can't advertise because *weit* isn't strictly legal, just tolerated, but we should be on the lookout for places that display one of those red, green and yellow Rastafarian flags in the window. So, long story short, that's how we ended up in a funky place called the Bluebird not far from the Rembrandt Museum. Have you ever been to Amsterdam?' I asked my friend.

She shook her head, then pressed a hand against her chest, covering the spot where her left breast used to be. 'This is all new territory for me.' After a moment of silence, she flapped her hand, urging me to go on.

'I don't know how they do it in Denver, Claire, but in Amsterdam you simply walk into the coffee

10

house, study the menu, make your selections and pay the budtender.'

'Budtender!' She laughed.

'Helpful guy, we found.' I chuckled, joining in. 'How else do you find out that the cheap joints are usually cut with regular tobacco?'

'How much *does* it cost?' she asked.

'Eight to ten euros for pure weed,' I said. 'The cheap shit? Half as much.'

'So . . .?' She paused, eyebrows raised.

'As I said earlier, I wasn't about to pollute my lungs, but edibles? We decided to sample something they call "space cakes."'

'Alice B. Toklas brownies, you mean?'

'Like that, only better,' I said. 'Alice's were more like fruitcakes with not a speck of chocolate in them.'

I picked up the second muffin, slowly peeled off the paper wrapper and, using my hand as a saucer, placed the muffin on it. 'They look exactly like this, but they're made, I'm told, using hemp butter.' I set the muffin down. 'Space cakes come with operating instructions. *Had too much? Do not panic! No need to call a medic! Baked fresh daily.* In four languages, no less. *Ingestion de spacecakes à vos propres risques*, you know. Anyway, I took a bite, waited a bit but nothing happened. I figured we'd been ripped off. So I went to bed. When I got up in the middle of the night to go to the bathroom – whoa! – the party in my head was already in full swing! Paul found me rummaging through the minibar for cans of Pringles and giggling my head off.'

'I knew you were the right gal for the job.'

11

Now she had my attention. Maybe I should have quit blabbing while I was ahead. 'What job?'

'You've been working with cancer survivors for a long time, Hannah. You offer a unique, long-term perspective.'

Claire was still talking in riddles. 'Perspective for what?'

'I've co-sponsored a Cannabis Legalization bill for Maryland. Legalize marijuana across the board. Regulate and tax, that's our motto.'

'Tax revenue,' I said. 'That should help sell the idea to skeptics.'

'Indeed, but it goes way beyond the money we know legalized pot would bring into Maryland – more than one hundred and fifty million dollars per one estimate. We want to study best practices and lessons learned from other states. One of the highlights of the trip is a day-long tour of an up-and-coming weedery outside Denver. You can be my eyes and ears there, focusing on growing techniques and commercial operations, while I concentrate on the legal aspects of the business. I'll need to offer evidence that rates of crime, black-market drug dealing, teenage heroin abuse and highway fatalities while driving under the influence actually go down after legalization.'

'Do they?' I asked.

'In Colorado, Washington and Oregon, so far, yes. The other five states and the District of Columbia, it's too early to tell.'

She drew a quick breath and hurried on, smiling confidently as if I'd already agreed to whatever she was proposing. 'You'd be part of a small, fact-finding task force. You, me and Representative Mark King from the Eastern Shore. You know him?' When I shook my head, she continued, 'Used to play for the Ravens. Retired after five or six seasons due to injuries.'

'Dangerous sport, football,' I commented.

'Especially for offensive linemen,' Claire said. 'But he landed on his feet. Married a cheerleader. Bought a tobacco farm in Dorchester County and they seem to be making a small success of it.'

'Maryland's climate should be ideal for cultivating pot.'

She grinned. 'It is.'

'Sounds like you speak from personal experience.'

'I do.'

That made me smile. I recalled a certain potted plant on a certain graduate student's fire escape . . . but I digress.

Something Claire had said earlier about introducing the bill didn't make sense. I knew that the Maryland General Assembly met for only three months each year, from mid-January to mid-April – ninety days precisely. It was already early April. The trip Claire proposed would have to be taking place *after* the assembly adjourned for the year. I pointed this out.

'We're taking a different tack this session, Hannah. Instead of offering a single, comprehensive bill, we've filed two pieces of legislation, one to address the criminal justice aspects of legalization, the other to deal with taxing and regulating the drug. Dividing the legislation into two bills allows different committees to delve

13

more deeply into the technicalities of setting up a regulated marijuana market for Maryland.'

'I get that,' I said, 'but time's running out. Do you really expect either bill to pass this year?'

'Frankly? No.'

This surprised me. 'But, surely I read in the *Baltimore Sun* or *The Washington Post* or somewhere that more than sixty percent of Maryland voters were in favor of legalized pot.'

She nodded. 'There has been a sea change, for sure. From recent public testimony, it seems clear that Marylanders have moved beyond the question of legalization and are now focused on the best way to do it. All the hoo-hah surrounding the rollout of the medical marijuana dispensaries did us no favors, though. If we get the dispensaries up and running this July and all goes well . . .' Her voice trailed off.

'I have a solution for you,' I said.

'What's that?'

'If it's working so well in Colorado, why not take the Colorado law and search and replace, "Maryland" for "Colorado."'

Claire laughed. 'Don't think I haven't considered it.' After a moment, she added, 'So, you'll do it?'

I stalled for time, finishing the last of my muffin, wiping sticky fingers on my napkin.

'All expenses paid,' Claire added, sweetening the pot.

Claire Thompson was a single woman. In the off-season, she ran a consulting firm specializing in small business development. She had no husband or business partners to convince and work around.

14

'Depends,' I said at last. 'Are you talking about a trip or a *trip*, if you know what I mean?'

Claire raised both hands in mock surrender. 'You won't get into any trouble, I promise.' She leaned across the table and lowered her voice. 'Unless you want to.'

'The last time I got roped into helping a friend,' I confided with a grin, 'it was my college roommate. I ended up at a Bigfoot convention in Oregon.'

'I saw that on CNN! Somebody murdered that debunker guy from *Don't You Believe It*, what's his name . . .?'

'Martin Radcliffe,' I supplied.

'I forgot you were there. Very cool, in a perverted sort of way.' She paused. 'You can tell me all about it on the plane.'

I still hadn't made up my mind. Thinking about Martin Radcliff, Kendall Barfield and a few other folks who'd had the bad luck to be murdered when I just happened to be in the neighborhood, I said, 'I have to warn you that I come with more baggage than a 747.'

She flapped a hand, dismissing the concern. 'Say yes.'

'I'll have to think about it, Claire. When do you have to know?'

'I'm not going anywhere until April the eleventh, when the session ends. And it will have to be after April twentieth because Colorado will be swarming with cannatourists around then.'

'What's so special about April twentieth?' I asked.

'Long story,' she said, 'and I've got to go. Another damn meeting.' She stood and snagged the strap of the handbag draped over the back of her chair. 'Google Four-Twenty,' she said. 'Then give me a call. You have my number?'

'It's on the recovery group list,' I reminded her.

She tipped an imaginary hat. 'I'm counting on you.'

Two

The Scythians put the seeds of this hemp under the bags, upon the burning stones; and immediately a more agreeable vapor is emitted than from the incense burnt in Greece. The Company, extremely transported with the scent, howl aloud.

Herodotus, *The History of Herodotus*, translated from the Greek by Isaac Littlebury, London, D. Midwinter et al., 1737, p.381.

I returned home around three-thirty, eager to discuss Claire's unusual proposal with Paul, but he'd already left for the Naval Academy where he taught advanced calculus to midshipmen. I decided to fix myself a glass of iced tea and do what Claire suggested – Google Four-Twenty.

I opened the fridge and was momentarily blinded by the pristine, Arctic whiteness of its interior.

Anyone looking casually over my shoulder would have assumed that the Ives family subsisted on milk, half and half, tub butter, orange juice and baked potatoes. A lone egg rested in solitary splendor in a custard cup. Soda cans were lined up on the bottom shelf with military precision. Not even the freezer had escaped my husband's attention. We still had steaks and chicken parts, but the foil-wrapped packets of leftovers had vanished. Next time my spice shelf needed organizing, I had the man for the job.

The iced-tea pitcher, too, had disappeared, so I grabbed a can of Coca-Cola, headed down to the basement office and powered up the family computer.

Four-Twenty, or April the twentieth, had become a counter-culture 'high' holiday for pot aficionados, I learned. According to Google, in 1971, five high-school students in San Rafael, California calling themselves the 'Waldos' – because their usual hang-out spot was a wall outside the school – invented the term to refer to the meeting time for their post-class smoke sessions: four-twenty. It was at one of those sessions that they cooked up a plan to search for an abandoned marijuana crop they'd heard about based on a treasure map – 'X' marks the spot and all – given to them by the supposed grower, a coastguardsman stationed at Point Reyes. The boys never located the stash. Eventually the term was picked up by followers of the Grateful Dead and became a code word for marijuana smoking in general.

I read on, clicking through from the Google entry to the various articles it cited. The term had

17

become so ubiquitous that California had named its marijuana bill SB420, many of the clocks in the movie *Pulp Fiction* were set to four-twenty, and people on Craigslist advertised for 'Four-Twenty-friendly roommates.'

I was chuckling over one particular article when Paul came downstairs and joined me.

He leaned over my chair from behind and brushed my cheek with his lips. 'What's so funny, sweetie?'

'I'm researching Four-Twenty,' I explained. 'Do you know what that means?'

'It's four-twenty,' he quoted. 'Do you know where your bong is?'

I turned to look up at him. 'Smarty pants!'

He shrugged. 'When you work with twenty-something students, you need to be aware of what's going on.'

'This is hysterical.' I tapped the screen. 'It says here that Colorado had to replace the 420-mile marker on Interstate 70 east of Denver with one reading 419.99 because the sign kept getting stolen. Idaho, it says, simply gave up on the marker on Highway 95 south of Coeur d'Alene. Painted the number 420 directly on the pavement.'

'Why this sudden interest in marijuana?' Paul asked. 'I love you, Hannah, but I have the funny feeling you're about to complicate my life.' He paused, then added for emphasis, 'Again.'

'I'll explain over dinner.' I stood and turned into a welcoming bear hug. 'Super job cleaning the fridge,' I mumbled into his blue, Oxford-cloth, button-down shirt. Even after a long day in the classroom, it still smelled clean and Tide-fresh. When he released me, I said, 'But because of your admirable efficiency, there's no food left in the house, unless you propose that we share a boiled egg. How about Galway Bay? If we hurry, we'll make happy hour.'

Galway Bay, an Irish pub and restaurant around the corner from us on Maryland Avenue, was our go-to place for dinner, particularly when I didn't feel like cooking. Paul, expressing a craving for corned beef and cabbage, readily agreed. Thirty minutes later, we sat opposite one another at a table for two near the back, relaxing in the familiar red-brick and dark-wood rustics of the place and sharing a plate of fried calamari. 'Cheers,' I said, tapping my glass of Sauvignon blanc against his pint of Guinness.

He sipped his ale. 'So, what's the story?'

As I told him about my conversation with Claire, I watched his face, looking for signs of disapproval. They weren't long in coming.

He pursed his lips, skewed them sideways.

I forged on.

He propped his elbow on the table, rested his head in his hand.

I continued to plead my case.

As if studying the placemat, his head began to wag, slowly, like an oscillating fan.

'Besides,' I concluded, 'unlike you, I've never been to Colorado.'

Paul looked up, his eyes dark as chocolate in the subdued lighting. 'Giving a lecture at the Air Force Academy in Colorado Springs doesn't exactly count, Hannah. I saw the inside of a

C-147 transport plane and the air base at Peterson. And a very sketchy view of the Rocky Mountains through the windows of a military bus.'

'Boo hoo,' I said, sawing my index finger across my thumb. 'World's smallest violin.'

Paul laughed and waved our server down. After the young man left with our order, I had a brainstorm. 'Why don't you come with me?'

Paul leaned across the table, took my hand firmly in his and said, 'I'd like to keep my job, thank you very much. Cannabis is against federal law, in case you've forgotten, and the academy has a zero-tolerance policy.' He lowered his voice and added, 'All I'd need is one unannounced whiz quiz and I'd be grubbing for work at the community college.'

'They make *faculty* pee in a cup?'

'Not yet, but in the current political climate, anything is possible. I need to keep my nose clean.'

I reached out and tapped the aquiline nose of which he spoke. 'It's so clean it positively squeaks.'

He batted my hand away. 'Behave,' he said with a good-natured grin.

I sipped my wine obediently.

The world would not end if I decided to decline Senator Thompson's invitation – I knew that. Claire would find somebody else for the job. But with each sip of wine – cool, crisp, grapefruity – I grew more jealous of that Somebody Else. I used to work in Washington, DC. I had experience dealing with bureaucrats. I was a silver-tongued information specialist. A professional twister of arms. Somebody else would goof it up for sure, and then how would I feel? I could see the headlines

20

now: *Recreational Marijuana Bill Fails in Maryland Senate After Close Vote.* And it would be my fault! Stoners state-wide would revile my name. Could I live with that?

That's how I reasoned at the time, anyway, as the wine made a beeline from my empty stomach to my brain.

'I warned Claire that people had a tendency to drop dead around me,' I said in what turned out to be an ill-considered attempt to lighten the mood. 'She didn't take me seriously.'

Paul snorted. 'She should.' He began to tick names off on his fingers. When he got to Jennifer Goodall, he paused and winced. The young naval officer's attempts to break up our marriage and ruin my husband's reputation and career still rankled. 'Melanie Fosher,' he continued, 'Masud Abaza, Kendall Barfield . . .'

I batted his hands, cutting him off in mid-sentence. 'It's not *my* fault those poor people died. What is it that you used to say about synchronicity, Professor?'

He thought for a moment. 'Correlation does not imply causation?'

'There you have it.'

He speared a calamari, one of the many tentacle bits. 'If you keep it up, you'll rival the on-screen body count of Gimli in *Lord of the Rings*.'

'That's not funny, Paul.'

He shrugged. 'You brought the subject up, sugar pie.'

I opened my mouth, but no clever repartee fell out. Fortunately, our dinners arrived just then, bringing the conversation to a screeching halt.

21

As I savored my shepherd's pie – ground sirloin and veggies swimming in a rich brown gravy I wish I had the recipe for – I watched Paul tuck into a generous plate of corned beef and cabbage. A bright orange mound of carrots mashed with parsnips sat to one side. He reached for the malt vinegar and sprinkled it liberally over the cabbage. 'So, when is this patriotic, fact-finding mission for the state of Maryland supposed to take place?'

I swallowed a forkful of vegetables and mashed potatoes. 'She's going to let me know. Sometime in May or June? Definitely after April the twentieth, though. We didn't get as far as the planning stage.'

Paul applied a knife to his corned beef, but it was so tender it fell apart immediately. He laid the knife aside and continued with his fork. 'And what am I supposed to do while you're away?'

'So, you're OK with it, then?' It wasn't an argument, exactly, but I was surprised to have won it so easily.

'As the Borg say on *Star Trek*, "Resistance is futile."'

'Do what you usually do in the summer, sweetheart,' I suggested, getting back to his original question. 'Coach sailing. June, July . . .' I waved a well-buttered slice of soda bread. 'When you go offshore with the mids, I'm practically a widow. Not that I begrudge you the time at sea.'

Paul smiled. 'It's how I keep my boyish figure.'

That was certainly true. A grandfather three times over, yet Paul remained the same tall, lean, athletic guy I'd married. These days, his dark curls were laced with gray but, to my mind, that was an enhancement.

'There's a new horse in the stable,' he said after a moment.

I must have looked puzzled because he quickly added, 'A Swan 56.'

Swans, I knew, were beautifully built, budget-busting sailboats. 'Donated to the Naval Academy fleet?' I guessed.

Paul nodded. 'Last fall. A sweet, fifty-six footer formerly known as *Neva*. A proven offshore racer. She's called *Apollo* now.'

'Isn't it bad luck to rename a boat?' I asked.

'Not if it's done properly,' he said. 'It involves petitions to Poseidon and incantations to the four winds,' he explained. 'And lots of champagne.'

I laughed. 'Some of it might even splash over the bow.'

'Indeed.'

'So, how are you involved with *Apollo*?' I asked, trying to remember if he had mentioned the boat before.

'Shake-down cruise,' he said. 'If all her systems check out, we'll race her to Newport in early June.'

'There you go!' I said.

'What?'

'Most likely you won't even be here when I'm gone.'

'But, if I am, I will miss your sweet, sweet loving. And your cooking, too.'

'That's why God invented the hot food bar at Whole Foods, Professor.'

Three

It is one of the happy incidents of the federal system that a single courageous State may, if its citizens choose, serve as a laboratory; and try novel social and economic experiments without risk to the rest of the country.

US Supreme Court, Justice Louis D. Brandeis, dissenting, *New State Ice Company v. Ernest A. Liebmann,* 1931 (285 US 311).

Six weeks later, at the crack of dawn, I stood in front of the full-length mirror in our bedroom, chanting, 'Mirror, mirror on the wall,' and wondering what to wear when traveling with a Maryland State senator. Claire had warned me that state government employees always flew coach, so I wouldn't be hobnobbing with the rich and famous on the flight, but still. My grandmother Alexander wouldn't have dreamed of traveling wearing anything less dressy than her Sunday-Go-To-Meeting clothes – a suit, hat and gloves, not to mention stockings and fashionable shoes. The way folks dressed for commercial flights these days would have given Granny palpitations.

I decided to split the difference, choosing the

24

middle ground between Grandmother's navy-blue Lilli Ann suit and short shorts with flip-flops. I pulled a pair of black slacks off a hanger, paired them with a pale peach top, added a colorful jacket from Chicos and accessorized the outfit with a scarf and a chunky silver chain that Emily had given me one Christmas. With my longish brown curls drawn back into a low ponytail, and a splash of makeup, the woman staring back at me from the mirror looked like she was heading to a job interview, something I hadn't done in years, thank goodness. But, sadly, the necklace had to go. It would set off every bell and whistle at airport security. I tucked it back into the jewelry box and retied the scarf a bit more jauntily around my neck, then went to find my iPhone.

My Uber driver, a chatty young Nigerian with exceptionally good taste – he complimented me on my outfit – told me he was working his way through an undergraduate degree in animal care and management at the University of Maryland. An hour later, joining the line that snaked through the security checkpoint at BWI, and despite the Uber driver's approval, I felt woefully out of place among the tracksuits, skin-tight leggings and tank tops worn by many of the female travelers. And men! Whoever wrote the law making saggy-baggy jeans, team jerseys and neon-colored athletic shoes the uniform of the day should have been lynched. But at least they were prepared to sleep in the airport should their connecting flight be delayed for a couple of days.

My boarding pass was stamped TSA Pre, so I

didn't have to unpack my laptop or slip out of my pumps to pad barefoot on the cold concrete through the metal detector. Once on the other side, I found Claire easily, sitting in the departure gate area of Concourse D, a cup of coffee in one hand and an Auntie Anne cinnamon pretzel in the other. 'Morning,' I said, taking the seat next to her.

'You have time for a coffee,' she said, bobbing her head in the direction of the Chesapeake Bay Roasting Company kiosk nearby.

'I'm already wired,' I said. 'I haven't set an alarm for four a.m. since I worked in Washington. Without caffeine, it isn't pretty.'

Perhaps that's why I started when the public address system crackled to life: 'Passengers Thompson and Ives, please see the United agent at gate D4.'

I frowned. 'Uh, oh. What'd we do?'

Claire stood, grabbed the handle of her carry-on bag and said, 'C'mon. You may be surprised.'

Still puzzled, I followed.

'May I see your boarding passes, ladies?' the agent asked.

We handed them over. The agent gave me a quick up-and-down glance, smiled and began tapping at her keyboard.

'What's she doing?' I whispered.

The agent looked up. 'I'm upgrading you to first class.' A dazzling smile. 'I trust you have no objections.'

I held up both hands palms out in a gesture of surrender. 'No, ma'am.'

I watched in happy anticipation as our new

26

boarding passes spewed out of the printer. 'In spite of what you told me earlier, I always assumed state legislators flew first class,' I said when the agent handed them over.

Claire wagged her head. 'Only if we pay the difference. Forty-eight thousand dollars doesn't go that far.'

'That's your salary?' I asked. Seemed pretty generous for three months' work, but I didn't say so.

'Plus expenses,' she said. 'Miles, meals, lodgings. Per *diem*, it can add up to another ten thousand or so.'

'So, how did you wrangle this?' I asked, waving my new boarding pass like a victory flag.

'My government ID sometimes does the trick,' she said with a grin. 'That and my charm, good looks and perspicacity.'

'A pleasure to be travelling with you, ma'am,' I drawled.

And indeed it was.

It felt odd being in the first group to board, to stroll leisurely down the ramp, to settle comfortably into wide leather recliners, each with its individual 'flight entertainment system.'

And that nonsense about not serving drinks until well after takeoff?

Rubbish.

Our flight attendant – an attractive, thirty-something man who introduced himself as Dave – appeared almost immediately, balancing a tray of mimosas in champagne flutes. How could I refuse?

'This is so civilized.' I took a sip and melted

27

contentedly into the upholstery, grateful not to be sandwiched between two muscle-bound weightlifters on the three-hour flight. I mentioned the experience to Claire. 'I was flying to a library conference in California. After our meal trays arrived they inhaled theirs, then loomed hungrily over mine. The food wasn't good enough to worry about, so I simply handed it over.'

'No worries on this flight. Have you seen the menu?' Claire said, passing one over.

When dinnertime came around, we would have a choice of three entrées. After careful consideration, I decided on the red pepper quiche with tri-colored potatoes and sundried tomato and mozzarella sausage, followed by a cup of dark-roast Illy coffee.

Life was good.

I'd fallen asleep in the middle of the in-flight movie when something jolted me awake. Next to me, Claire was dozing, too, her Kindle open, drooping from her hand at an unreadable angle.

'For what I pay, you'd think you'd have decent whisky aboard.' A man's voice, dripping with disgust, came from behind me.

Ice tinkled against glass. 'Dump this out and bring me something decent.'

I twisted in my seat and looked back, but the blue of the flight attendant's uniform blocked my view.

'Cutty Sark?' the attendant asked, his voice surprisingly calm.

'Rot gut,' the man snapped. 'I don't know what you're trying to pull – Dave, is it? But this . . .' Ice tinkled again. 'This is not Glenfiddich. Think

28

I'd fall for the old switcheroo, did you? What's in it? Four Roses?' A long, exaggerated sigh. 'You'd think I was flying Southwest or something.'

'I'll see what I can do,' Dave replied in a customer-is-always-right tone of voice.

The altercation had awakened Claire, too. 'Who is that asshole?'

'Don't know,' I whispered back. 'He must have come aboard after we got seated.'

'Bring me a Bloody Mary, then,' the asshole demanded. 'And it better have the whole garden in it.'

I snorted. 'Garden?'

'Celery, carrot sticks, pickled green beans . . .' Claire shrugged. 'Good luck with that, bozo.'

I wondered if passengers should be bracing themselves for a temper tantrum. If, after his drink order arrived and it failed to meet his unreasonable expectations, he'd begin kicking the back of my seat like a petulant three-year-old. If, when all was said and done, we'd have to wrestle him to the floor and duct tape him to his seat until the authorities arrived to escort him off the plane at an unscheduled stop in the middle of Kansas.

I fumbled for my iPhone, made sure it was fully charged, then slipped it back into my pocket. I unbuckled my seatbelt and leaned toward Claire. 'I'll be right back.'

I wandered forward, gave a sympathetic smile to the flight attendant fussing over the man's drink in the compact first-class galley, then popped into the restroom. After spending a respectable amount of time there, I wandered back to my seat.

The guy sitting in the seat directly behind me looked like a prosperous businessman. He wore a dark-blue custom-tailored suit, a conservative striped tie in the new, longer length popularized by the President, and the shoe on the foot that protruded into the aisle gleamed from the efforts of a shoeshine professional. Dark hair, slicked straight back. A stylishly scruffy mustache and a short, neatly trimmed beard. Then his face had disappeared behind a copy of the *Wall Street Journal*.

'What?' Claire mouthed when I returned to my seat.

'Wall Street banker, I'd guess. Straight out of central casting.'

'Entitled S.O.B.,' she muttered.

The Bloody Mary must have met the guy's high standards because we didn't hear any more out of him – except the rustling of his newspaper, and, eventually, snoring – for the duration of the flight.

At the Denver airport, the guy couldn't get off the plane fast enough. By the time we had gathered up our carry-on luggage and disembarked, the back of his blue suit was just disappearing through the door at the top of the ramp. 'Good riddance,' Claire said as we hustled down Concourse B and waited for the people-mover tram next to a life-sized statue of Jack Swigert, an Apollo 13 astronaut. A few minutes later, on our way to baggage claim on level five of the main terminal, I grabbed Claire's arm, pulling her to a halt next to one of a series of apocalyptic murals. On the wall, brightly-clad children huddle in a basement while the Angel of Death, wearing a gas mask, looms over them like an evil Nazi, brandishing an AK-47. The scimitar he holds skewers a dove of peace. 'What were they thinking?' I said, feeling chilled.

'It's called "Children of the World Dream of Peace," Claire informed me. 'By a Mexican-American artist named Leo Tanguma. He's somewhat of a social activist.'

'Tell me about it,' I said, taking in a weeping Madonna cradling her dead infant at the end of a long line of refugees.

Next to me, someone muttered, 'Swell. So my flight is delayed, like, for all of eternity.'

I had to laugh.

Claire shook my hand free. 'This is creepy. Let's get out of here.'

'Maybe there's another mural somewhere with a happy ending,' I said as we hurried past the image of a lad – clearly German by his lederhosen – who was using a hammer to beat a sword into a plow.

Tanguma's mural just outside the baggage claim area was only marginally more cheerful. 'In Peace and Harmony With Nature' featured children grieving over the wanton destruction of the environment. Behind them, seas churned and fires raged. Birds – an auk, a passenger pigeon and a quetzal – gazed out of glass cases with dead eyes. The sea turtle ensnared in a fishing net particularly got to me. I swallowed hard and moved along.

For the final panel, at least, the artist dressed the children in their native costumes and allowed them to celebrate the rehabilitation and rebirth of the planet. 'Too little, too late, if you ask me,' I muttered as I hurried by.

Once in baggage claim, I kept having the feeling I was being watched. And no wonder. Nothing says 'Welcome to Denver' like a demonic gargoyle, the size of my ten-year-old grandson, crawling

31

out of a bronze suitcase. And there were at least two of them leering at me from overhead, disapproving of my every move, daring me to touch a bag that wasn't mine.

Finally, carousel fourteen spewed out our luggage.

'Are we taking a cab?' I asked Claire as I hauled my bag off the conveyer belt.

'Nope. We got a limo.'

'Oooh, I'm impressed.'

'Don't be,' she said. 'It comes with the package.'

'What package?'

'You wouldn't want anything less than the total experience, would you?' she said.

'Certainly not!'

'Then stick with me, girlfriend.'

Four

Marijuana smoking at women's bridge parties has become frequent, the parties usually ending up in wild carousals, sometimes with men joining the orgies.

The Union Signal, Women's Christian Temperance Union, 1934.

We'd been waiting outside the terminal for no more than five minutes when a long, white limousine that had been idling a few hundred yards away swept into an opening created by the departure of a yellow Hertz van and eased soundlessly to a stop. The vehicle seemed to go on forever, so long that its hood would reach our B&B hours before its trunk. I counted five windows, back to front. A logo painted on the passenger-side door read Happy Daze Tours, its letters curved in a semi-circle under a colorful graphic of a five-fingered marijuana leaf superimposed over a bell.

'Let me guess,' I said.

Claire laughed. 'Our chariot awaits.'

'What's with the bell?' I asked, referring to the logo.

'That's the name of the B and B we're staying in. Bell House.'

In Colorado these days, B&B stood for 'bud and breakfast' more often than not. Serious canna-tourists flocked to such private establishments, the only ones where smoking, weed or otherwise, was permitted on the premises.

We watched as the chauffeur climbed out carrying a whiteboard that read *Thompson* in black marker pen.

'That would be me,' Claire yelled above the noise of the traffic, thumbing her chest.

The driver grinned, revealing a row of impossibly white teeth. 'Welcome to Denver,' he said.

'You must be Austin Norton,' she said.

'It's the shirt. It always gives me away.'

Under an embroidered leather vest that flapped loosely at his sides, Norton wore a black T-shirt that read: IT'S 4:20 SOMEWHERE. He'd belted the shirt neatly into a pair of blue jeans that had been pressed into a sharp crease. I guessed he was around fifty. An aging hippie, I thought. His hair, prematurely silver, was tied back in a low ponytail.

'Are we waiting for anybody?' I smiled into his eyes, but saw only my own reflection in his mirrored sunglasses.

'Nope,' he said. 'You're the last.' He took our bags and somehow managed to fit them, like pieces to an intricate puzzle, into a trunk already crammed with luggage. Then he held open the door, stood aside and invited us in.

The last time I'd been in a stretch limo had been with a guy named Ron at my high-school prom. This limo, too, had a bar – stocked with designer water – and circular bench seating. But there the resemblance ended. In the Happy Daze limo, LED lights pulsed green, like Kryptonite, turning Claire's red jacket a dirty shade of gray. A wide-mouthed glass jar containing frosty buds of marijuana took pride of place on a low, central table.

A young guy holding a glass pipe scooted over to make room for us. 'Welcome to the Mile High City,' he said as we cut our way through the smog. He wore a Hawaiian shirt and a captain's hat, soft and faded from repeated laundering, perched at a jaunty angle over his crewcut.

Claire eased into her seat, inhaled and sighed. 'Ah, this is what I'm talking about!'

As for me, I tried not to breathe too deeply. All my fellow passengers seemed to be smoking something: the guy with the glass pipe; a young couple, their blond heads touching, sharing a hookah like a cream soda with two straws; two women sucking on vape pens. I understood about people going on wine tours of Napa or Sonoma, but they're not opening bottles of merlot the minute they leave baggage claim. Still, it must be a relief to get high without being hassled by the cops.

'You trip out early in Denver,' the young guy said, as if reading my mind. He took a hit from his pipe, held his breath and closed his eyes.

Claire wasted no time welcoming herself to Denver. I watched her pinch some weed out of the jar, crumble it between her fingers and line it up neatly in rolling paper. 'Hard to believe this is legal,' she said. She ran the edge of the paper over her tongue, then gently pinched the moistened edges shut.

I thought the kid with the bong was out of it, but he must have been watching Claire through half-slitted eyes. Before she could locate her matches, he whisked a butane lighter out of his breast pocket, flicked it on and held it out.

'Thanks,' Claire said, lighting up.

I settled into my seat, trying to blend into the leather upholstery, grateful to leave the strange airport – looking like an assembly of bright white Native American teepees – in the rearview mirror. The limo headed west. Just when I thought we'd made a clean getaway, an enormous blue horse with bulging veins and demonic red eyes reared into view.

'What fresh hell is this?' I asked of nobody in particular.

The answer came immediately over the intercom. 'To your left is a blue mustang by the artist Luis Jiménez,' Austin Norton drawled. 'It's thirty-two feet high and weighs nine thousand pounds.

35

We've nicknamed it Blucifer. In a bizarre twist of fate, the sculpture actually killed the artist when the head fell on him, severing his femoral artery. He bled to death.'

If a day could get any stranger, I didn't know how.

The drive to Denver took about forty-five minutes. As we sped out of the airport on Peña Boulevard, Norton gave a running commentary, but nobody seemed to be paying the slightest attention, except me. He was describing the towering splendor of the Rocky Mountains to the west when a mother and daughter pair – the resemblance was unmistakable – dissolved in a fit of giggling. 'Wait till I call him,' the older of the two said, fumbling for her iPhone.

'This trip is Mom's birthday present,' the daughter explained to us fellow passengers.

'Here, you dial,' the mother said, handing over the phone.

'Dad can wait until we get to the hotel,' the daughter said, tucking the phone back into her mother's handbag.

Mom leaned into her daughter. 'When the moo-oo-oon is in the seventh house,' she sang, followed by another fit of the giggles.

'We're from Texas,' the daughter volunteered. 'Texans are weed-repressed, you know, unless you live in Austin. Which we don't.' She took a drag from her vape pen.

'Not as weed-repressed as they are in Arkansas,' the gal sharing a hookah with her partner chimed in. 'My husband and me? We teach at Stafford U. Everybody there Tweets in Bible quotes, for the love of Mike.'

Her husband scowled. 'Shhh, Lisa. You're blowing our cover.'

'Cover, schmover,' Lisa cooed, cuddling up even closer. 'I don't know about you, but I'm having a *wonderful* time!'

'It's boring as hell, isn't it, if you're not stoned,' the kid wearing the captain's hat observed between tokes.

Actually, I was finding it fascinating.

The limo left Interstate 70, turned left, right, and left again, cruised past a huge medical center and through an upscale area Austin Norton described as Five Points. Near Cheesman Park, the limo parked in front of a modern, colonial-style mansion. After a moment, the door opened. 'First stop,' Norton said.

'Is this us?' I asked, peering through the tinted window at the house. I expected Scarlett O'Hara to flounce down the walkway at any moment, hoop skirts swaying.

'Gorton House only,' Norton said. 'Bell House is next.'

The mother and daughter gathered up their belongings. 'Bye, ya'll,' the daughter caroled, wriggling her fingers. 'Party on!'

I was sorry to see them go. The girl's non-stop patter had been genuinely entertaining.

Bell House, our B&B, was in the 900 block of East 6th Street, about five minutes away. Clutching our handbags, Claire and I were the last to crawl out of the limo, dazed and blinking like moles in the noonday sun. We joined the remaining passengers huddled in a small group on the sidewalk. It was then I discovered that Lisa stood almost a head

37

taller than her husband. She wore slim jeans tucked into a pair of leather boots and three shirts, each layer skimpier than the first, her lacy red bra straps making a clear fashion statement. Her blonde hair hung straight and loose to the middle of her back.

'Gorgeous!' her husband said, referring to the house, not his wife.

I had to agree.

Through a wrought-iron gate and at the end of a long flagstone path stood a turn-of-the-last-century, Tudor-style manor house constructed entirely of honey-colored sandstone.

'A stunner, isn't it?' Norton said. 'Built in 1898 by a prosperous miner, Lucas Bell, as a wedding gift for his daughter, Fannie.'

Clearly, I had chosen my parents poorly. Until Dad retired from the US Navy, long after I'd left home, the finest house we'd ever lived in was officers' quarters at the Naval base in San Diego.

As we stood gawking at our weekend accommodation like six-year-olds at a candy counter, Norton began unloading the trunk and piling our luggage on the sidewalk. 'I'll get these to your rooms,' he said. 'Please, go on in. Desiree will meet you in the foyer.'

Foyer? More like the lobby of a fine European hotel. Oak floors smothered in oriental carpets extended to the right and left of the front door and, just ahead, a grand double staircase of intricately carved oak led to the upper floors. Sun streamed through the leaded glass windows on the landing, casting prisms onto the pale green silk that covered the walls above the wainscoting.

A slim woman with a shoulder-length halo of black, untamed curls stood at the foot of the stairs. This had to be Desiree. As we stumbled over the threshold, we interrupted her in the act of arranging flowers in a massive blue-and-white porcelain vase. The vase sat on a round table directly centered under a crystal chandelier the size of a Volkswagen. 'Welcome to Bell House,' she said, sliding the last tulip into the vase and giving the results a tilt-headed squint and a satisfied pat. 'I'm Desiree. You've already met my husband.'

Desiree invited us to sign the guest book which sat on a sideboard to our right, illuminated by a pair of tall, Tiffany glass lamps. As the others signed, I held back. 'How many guests do you have this weekend?' I asked our hostess.

'Ten,' she replied. 'We can accommodate twelve, but two of the rooms – the singles on the fourth floor – are under renovation.'

'How long have you lived here?' I asked.

Desiree smiled wistfully. 'About ten years. I inherited the place from my father, but it was in pretty bad shape. We seem to be in constant fix-it mode.' She paused for a moment, caressing the tabletop. 'We had a lot of stuff, if you know what I mean, but no money.'

'The house is beautiful,' I told her. 'I particularly love the paneling.'

'Hannah?'

Claire was calling to me, waving the signing pen. When I added my name and hometown to the list, I learned that Mark King and his wife, Cindy, had already checked in, as had somebody named Daniel Fischel from Atlanta. Long, tall Lisa from

Sulphur Rock, Arkansas, was married to Joshua and their last name was Barton. The stoner wearing the Hawaiian shirt was Colin McDaniel and for his hometown he'd simply scrawled, *Planet Earth*.

Before escorting us to our rooms, Desiree led us on a brief tour of the ground floor. To our left was a formal dining room with a table set for twelve. Additional chairs were arranged along the wall, so I imagined the table had leaves and could be expanded to accommodate dinner parties of up to twenty. The centerpiece, a glass and silver pedestal with a tangle of filigree leaves, knocked my eyes out. I couldn't wait to get a closer look in the morning.

'We serve breakfast in the dining room from seven to ten,' Desiree informed us, 'but coffee is available in the kitchen from six o'clock.' She waved a hand toward a door in the far wall which opened, I presumed, into the kitchen.

The opposite side of the entrance hall led to a comfortable sitting room, with brocade-covered sofas and overstuffed side chairs arranged in conversational groups; two armchairs faced a carved marble fireplace in which gas logs were softly flickering. And if one were talented and so inclined, one could tear into Chopin's *Nocturne in C-sharp Minor* on the Steinway grand that angled into the floor-to-ceiling windows that overlooked the garden.

'We ask that you do not smoke in your rooms,' Desiree said, 'but smoking is encouraged in the solarium. Please. Follow me.'

Trellis-like doors flanked by painted panels

opened from the sitting room into the solarium, a spacious, octagonal room with windows on six sides. My eyes widened, wandering from the gleaming white oak floors up to the chandelier that hung from a compass rose painted on the coffered ceiling. Desiree had arranged half-a-dozen white wicker armchairs upholstered in flowered chintz two-by-two around small end tables, and baskets of plants hung everywhere. 'Piano Man' by Billy Joel wafted in softly from somewhere – a speaker installed in the base of a planter dripping with red begonias, I was to discover later.

Smoking is encouraged in the solarium.

For sure.

A glass bowl full of plump marijuana buds sat on a sideboard like Halloween candy. A selection of drinks was also available – water, orange and cranberry juices in single-serving, eight-ounce bottles. Another bowl was heaped with Keebler cookies, two to a pack.

'This is, like, free?' Lisa said.

'It's all part of the Happy Daze Experience package,' Desiree told her.

'Awesome,' Lisa said.

'Happy hour begins in the solarium at four-twenty,' Desiree added as she led us back through the sitting room into the entrance hall. 'That's when we bring out the wine and cheese.'

Wine! Now that was something I could wholly endorse. Until that moment, I'd felt like a Tea Party Republican at a Hillary Clinton rally.

Just ahead of me, Lisa looped her arm through

41

Joshua's and cooed, 'Oooh, happy anniversary, baby.'

I was happy for them. Suddenly, I missed Paul terribly.

Desiree opened the lid on an antique blanket chest and reached inside. 'To welcome you to Bell House, we have a goody bag for each of you.'

The small shopping bag she handed me was jade green embossed with the Bell House logo in gold; green and gold raffia decorated the string handles. Curious, I peered in. I was now the proud owner of a bar of soap shaped like a marijuana leaf labeled *Dope on a Rope*, a sample-size tube of Cannaderm Body Cream and a bite-sized, red foil-wrapped chocolate-peanut-butter *Smack Bar*. From the bottom of the bag, I dug out a cigarette-sized Juju brand vape pen preloaded with a cartridge of cannabis oil. One hundred and fifty hits, the printing on the package claimed. The enclosed brochure stated that Jujus came in three formulations – THC, CBD and a hybrid. My freebee Juju was a hybrid: half and half.

'THC and CBD,' I said. 'Can you explain the difference, Desiree?'

'THC is the psychoactive compound found in the sativa strains,' Desiree said. 'It stands for tetrahydrocannabinol.'

'Tetrahydrocannabinol,' I repeated. 'Say that three times, fast.' I grinned. 'What does CBD stand for, then?'

'Just plain cannabidiol,' she said, pronouncing the word carefully: ka-nah-buh-*dye*-all. 'It's an antipsychotic. Helps you relax.'

'Like yin and yang?' I asked, rocking my hand back and forth.

Desiree grinned. 'Sorta like that.'

'Is vaping safe?' I asked.

'We're stoners, not doctors,' Desiree drawled.

'Is vaping safe?' I asked again.

'Safer than smoking cigarettes.'

'Seriously,' Josh chimed in.

'Nicotine is habit-forming, addictive,' Desiree added. 'Marijuana, not so much. You might *want* to smoke it every day, but if you skip a day or even a week, nobody's going to find you writhing on the floor fending off imaginary demons with a table knife.

'Definitely safer than wearing a Jets jersey to a Patriot's game.' She laughed. 'Let me show you to your rooms.'

Like obedient ducklings, we followed Desiree up the grand staircase, single file, carrying our goody bags. 'Feel free to explore the house,' she added over her shoulder. 'Nothing is off limits.'

As we reached the landing, she turned to the right and opened a door. 'Mr and Mrs Barton, this is your room.'

Joshua bopped right in, but Lisa trailed behind, examining the textured wallpaper with apparent fascination.

Colin was given a single across the hall from the Bartons, while Claire and I had separate rooms overlooking the garden at the back of the house, linked by a shared 'Jack and Jill' bathroom.

Claire paused, her hand resting on the doorknob to her room. 'I saw that Mark and Cindy King have signed in. Are they around?' she asked Desiree.

Desiree pointed toward the ceiling. 'They've got the big double upstairs, but I believe they've stepped out for lunch.'

'I'll catch them later, then,' Claire said. 'Thanks.'

'The weekend schedule is on your desk, ladies. Dinner on your own tonight, but we hope to see you at happy hour.' She bowed slightly. 'If there's anything I can do to make your stay more enjoyable, let me know.'

Free pot? Free wine? Luxury accommodation? How could Desiree possibly improve on that? A massage therapist, I was thinking, or a full-service gym. But, a few minutes later, I discovered Bell House offered those services, too. The weekend schedule on my desk – which came with a personal note that began 'High, Hannah' – offered a comprehensive list of onsite spa treatments by a licensed professional named Anya in the Mind, Body, Spirit Wellness Center in the basement.

'I desperately need a nap,' Claire said once our hostess had gone. 'I'm still on east coast time.'

'And I need a bath,' I said. After the long limo ride, I reeked of cannabis, enough to send a sniffer dog, like my old friend Harley, into conniptions.

'You first,' she said. 'Wake me up in time for dinner.'

I spent a few minutes unpacking my toiletries, then headed for the bathroom, where an antique-style slipper tub awaited me, ensconced in a curtained alcove in white-tiled splendor. Desiree had provided a selection of bath salts, so I sprinkled a generous amount of 'Green Goddess' salts into the tub, adjusted the water temperature and, while the tub filled, took iPhone pictures of my room to send to Paul – the lavender wisteria painted along the molding, the matching valence, the plum-colored drapes and striped Queen Anne chairs. 'Missing you tons,' I wrote on the photograph of the queen-size brass bed, covered with a plump, floral duvet and strewn with decorative pillows.

When I awoke sometime later to the ringing of my cell phone in the adjoining bedroom, I was still in the tub and the water had grown tepid. Damn, I thought. Let it go to voicemail. I soaked for a few minutes longer, contemplating my options. Rather than adding hot water, I got out, grabbed a towel from the heated towel rack – whoever invented that deserved a Nobel Prize! – and dried off. Then, I wrapped myself in the terry cloth robe provided and padded into the bedroom. Paul had texted, *Good night, sleep tight*. I texted a puckered lips emoticon back at him, then crawled under the covers and proceeded to sleep as instructed. When I next awoke, the bedside clock read 10:05 p.m. – after midnight, east coast time. I'd missed happy hour! And dinner! Claire would not be pleased.

But I worried for nothing. On my side of the bathroom door, Claire had left a note: *I'm not hungry either. See you in the morning.*

Five

In many respects, the action of cannabis sativa is similar to that of alcohol or morphine. Its toxic effects are ecstasy, merriment, uncontrollable laughter . . . It is an ideal drug to quickly cut off inhibitions.

Marihuana Tax Act of 1937, statement of Eugene Stanley, district attorney, New Orleans, LA.

The next morning, when I staggered, slit-eyed and sleep-drunk, into the bathroom we shared, I knew Claire was already up because a wet towel lay on the floor near the bathtub, and the mirrors – one for each of us over matching pedestal sinks – were steamed up.

I soaked a washcloth in water as hot as my hands could stand and pressed it against my face, breathing in the moist air. That done, I slathered my face with SPF15 skin cream. I examined my face closely in the mirror and decided no, definitely not a day to go without makeup.

I reapplied my eyebrows – tragically lost to chemotherapy – drew a thin, dark line around my eyes and decided that would have to do. Besides, with everyone around me getting stoned, I might even look like a movie star.

I threw on a pair of jeans and a colorful V-neck T-shirt, slipped my feet into sandals and headed down the long, elegant staircase feeling underdressed. A staircase like that, you needed a ballgown and diamonds, with Rhett Butler waiting at the bottom.

But it was just our host, Austin Norton, who greeted me, wearing the same leather vest as the day before, but this time his T-shirt read: CHEAPER THAN OBAMACARE. He was carrying a short stack of newspapers. 'Good morning, Mr Norton,' I said.

'Please, call me Austin. You're Hannah, right?'

With one hand resting lightly on the carved newel post, I agreed that I was.

'What'cha got there?' I asked, falling into step beside him, indicating the newspapers.

He ticked them off. '*Denver Post, New York Times, Washington Post, Dallas Morning News, Atlanta Journal-Constitution.* We like to make our guests feel at home here.'

'Dallas?' I asked.

We'd paused at the door to the dining room. One side of the carved oak double door stood open. 'Sixty percent of our guests are from Texas,' he explained.

'No kidding.'

'You'd think with all those wide open spaces they could grow their own, but, man, those folks are repressed.'

'They're probably like me, then. They get here and it's all "Whoa, dude, I can't believe this is legal."'

Austin laughed and handed me *The Washington*

Post. I gave him points for doing his homework. Annapolis, where I live, is only thirty-five miles from the nation's capital.

'Thanks,' I said.

'Enjoy your breakfast. The van leaves for the tour at ten.'

The tour, I knew from the schedule left on the desk in my room, was of the Happy Daze Weedery, the 35,000-square-foot cannabis grow facility the Norton family owned on the outskirts of town. Because of Colorado public use laws I knew that smoking – anything! – was not allowed on factory property, so I was looking forward to a clear-headed experience. Claire was expecting clear, concise notes, not incoherent scribbling.

The dining room smelled like bacon and onions. Claire was already seated at the table. She looked up from a plate of scrambled eggs and bacon and paused in the act of drizzling honey over a biscuit. From the way the butter had melted and dripped over her fingers, I knew the biscuit was fresh from the oven. My stomach rumbled.

'I hope you don't mind that I started without you,' she said, smiling. 'But, after missing dinner last night, I was famished.'

With perfect timing, a woman appeared through the swinging door that led to the kitchen, carrying a tray of clean coffee cups. She was shorter than I, no more than five foot three or four, and couldn't have weighed an ounce over a hundred-and-ten pounds. She had coaxed her red hair into a no-nonsense twist at the crown of her head and secured it there with a pearlescent white claw. 'Help yourself to the buffet,' she told me as she set the cups down on the end of an antique side-board the length of a football field. 'I'm bringing fresh biscuits in a minute, as soon as they come out of the oven.'

'Thanks,' I said, and held out my hand. 'I'm Hannah.'

The woman wiped her hand on her apron, then shook mine. 'I'm Marilyn Brignole. I cook.'

'My gosh,' I said, as my eyes drank in the buffet. 'It looks wonderful! I hardly know where to begin.'

Marilyn leaned toward me and whispered, 'Start with the *crostata*, filled with *frutti di bosco*. Old family recipe.'

I didn't need to be told twice. I hit the buffet, snagging the wild berry tart as she had recommended, and passing up the eggs Benedict in favor of carbohydrate loading: a plate of French toast, topped with a fresh strawberry and blue-berry combo, finished with a generous glug of maple syrup and – what the hell – two dollops of whipped cream. Two sausages completed the arrangement. I paused at the basket of muffins and turned to Marilyn, who was adding fresh scrambled eggs to the chafing dish. 'Are these muffins, you know, *special*?'

Marilyn laughed. 'No, the special ones come out later. And we always let you know.'

'The special ones come with operating instructions,' Claire mumbled around a bite of bacon. 'Like the ones you had in Amsterdam.'

I centered my plate on a fringed linen placemat and sat down opposite Claire. 'Where is everyone? Austin says the tour leaves at ten.'

49

'Plenty of time yet,' Claire said. 'It's just eight-thirty. Did you remember to reset your watch to Mountain Standard Time?'

I had to confess that I no longer owned a watch; I depended on my iPhone to tell me the time and it had automatically reset to the local time the moment we'd stepped off the plane.

'Morning, all.'

A man I recognized from ESPN television interviews as Mark King strode, long-limbed, into the room, followed by a petite, painfully thin blonde I figured had to be Cindy, the former superstar's wife. After Claire introduced us, Mark hit the breakfast bar, heaping his plate high. He seemed to be sampling everything, as if preparing for the coming apocalypse. Cindy, by contrast, served herself a small bowl of fruit. 'There's hot biscuits coming,' I said helpfully, thinking the poor waif needed some emergency calories, and quick.

'Thanks,' Cindy said, sliding into the chair next to her husband, who was seated at Claire's left. Mark was studying his fork as if he'd never seen one before.

'Mark?' Cindy said. It sounded like a question.

Mark turned his head. He watched as she speared a pineapple bit with her own fork, slid it into her mouth, wrapped her lips around the morsel then pulled out the fork, rather slowly and seductively, I thought. Mark reached out a beefy hand and stroked her cheek, then dug into his own breakfast like a starving refugee. I wondered if they were already high.

There was no question about the next guest

who wafted congenially into the dining room and weaved his way along the breakfast bar. After he'd made his selections and sat down at the head of the table, Colin McDaniel played with the arrangement of eggs and sausage on his plate until they looked like a happy face. Two lemon slices snitched from the smoked salmon platter were added as ears, then he sat back to admire his handiwork. *'Perfecto!'* he giggled.

'I don't believe we've been formally introduced,' I told him. 'I'm Hannah.'

'Hannah Banana?' he said, and giggled again.

I hadn't been called Hannah Banana since grade school. If he hadn't been so stoned, I'd have punched him in the nose like I did the last ten-year-old boy who dared to try the nickname out on me. I scowled disapprovingly instead, not that he noticed.

We were joined a few minutes later by Josh and Lisa Barton, looking clean and well-pressed, like Mormon missionaries. It was a good thing the doorway was wide, designed for women of an earlier era to accommodate their broad skirts and petticoats, because the Bartons came through it together, holding hands.

I tried to remember Lisa's comment from the day before. 'Honeymooners?' I asked once they'd sat down.

'Sort of,' Lisa said. 'Josh and I were married last August, but because of our teaching schedule, this is the first time we've been able to get away.'

'Really get away.' Josh stroked his wife's arm affectionately, then turned to me. 'It's the fifth anniversary of our first date,' he explained. 'It took me a while to convince Lisa to say "yes."'

'What do you teach?' I asked.

'Biology,' Josh said. 'Lisa teaches modern American literature.'

'To unappreciative brats,' Lisa added.

'Stafford U's not *that* bad,' Josh said. 'Lisa's just coming off a bad semester.'

'Maybe I'll teach *Winnie the Pooh* to the freshmen and be done with it, but they'd probably find talking animals an insult to God and veto that one, too.' She turned to me. 'Did you know that *Alice in Wonderland* was banned in some schools because it had references to . . .' she glanced around the table, then lowered her voice, '. . . sexual fantasies and masturbation, as well as promoting drug use in children?'

'The hookah-smoking caterpillar I get,' I said. 'But masturbation? No way.'

'New Hampshire, early nineteen-hundreds.' Lisa threw up her hands in surrender. 'But what do you expect from idiots who think a dictionary should be banned for defining the term "oral sex"?' She picked up her fork and skewered me with her eyes. 'I am *not* making this up.'

I found myself liking Lisa a lot.

'If Merriam-Webster doesn't define it, maybe it doesn't exist,' I offered.

'Ha! They wish.' Lisa sprinkled salt and pepper on her eggs and tucked in.

I was feeling a bit isolated, with empty chairs to my right and left. Had my deodorant failed? A professorial type wandered in, looking vaguely familiar. I decided that was because he so closely resembled my favorite English teacher, a Shakespeare scholar who could make

52

even Thomas Hardy's dreary *Jude the Obscure* pulse with passion. The new arrival, who by process of elimination had to be Daniel Fischel from Atlanta, Georgia, wore chinos and a striped, button-down shirt. A gray-and-green plaid sweater vest was pulled snugly over his paunch but barely covered his belt. He seemed stone-cold sober, too, and glared through his tortoiseshell glasses at Colin, who had eaten the smile off his happy face by then, without any trace of amusement.

Josh opened his mouth to say something, but Lisa silenced him with a quick jab of her elbow.

This promised to be a long day.

I had gone back for seconds – the smoked salmon was too good to resist – when an elderly gentleman sidled up to me at the buffet, rubbing his hands together. 'Do I smell bacon?' He turned. 'Phyllis, hurry up! Don't keep a boy away from his bacon!'

Phyllis duly appeared, a cheerful woman about the same age as her husband, with short, neatly styled silver hair. Soft waves framed her remarkably unlined face, with bangs swept casually to one side. 'For heaven's sake, Hugh, just help yourself.'

While her husband waffled over the selections, Phyllis made a beeline for the fresh fruit, covered it with several spoonfuls of yoghurt and slid into the chair next to me.

'Good morning,' she said. 'My name's Phyllis Graham. What's yours?'

I introduced myself, as did the others at the table, round-robin style.

'Did you sleep well?' I asked, simply to make conversation.

'Very well,' Phyllis replied. 'We got in late. Slept like a baby.'

'We're from Monson, Mass,' Hugh volunteered in a booming voice from the buffet bar. 'So it was after midnight our time.'

Appearances can be deceiving, but Hugh and Phyllis seemed two of the most unlikely people in Massachusetts – Boston, Quincy, Monson or elsewhere – to splurge on a pot tour. 'Are you with our group?' I asked.

Behind her glasses, Phyllis's blue eyes twinkled. 'Group? What group?'

I indicated the daily program that Desiree had propped up in a plastic holder on the table like an à la carte menu.

Phyllis picked it up, scanned it quickly and smiled. 'Afraid not,' she said cheerfully, 'although by the time this week is over, I might need a little pick-me-up.'

'Not my first choice, this place, I can tell you,' her husband chimed in as he joined us at the table. 'The travel agent screwed up our reservations. By the time we got it sorted out, all the rooms at the Crowne Plaza were gone.'

'There are other hotels, surely,' I pointed out.

'Not with all the Methodists in town, there aren't.' He turned to Phyllis. 'The next time your girlfriend decides to get married, tell her she can do it in the Bahamas during low season.' He grunted, and turned his attention to slathering butter on his biscuit.

'I don't wholly approve of Marjorie Ann,' Phyllis

54

confided to me in an aside, 'but she's one of my oldest friends.'

'Marjorie Ann is careless with husbands,' Hugh said.

She shot him a withering glance. 'It's not Marjorie Ann's fault that Harrison and Stephen passed away before their time, Hugh.'

'At least I knew the other two,' he said. 'This new guy . . .' He shrugged. 'But he must have money because they're holding the shindig at the Brown Palace Hotel.'

'Marjorie Ann always goes first class,' Phyllis said, sending her husband a look that spoke volumes. I suspected they rarely did anything first class. I imagined years of Holiday Inns, Ruby Tuesdays and shopping at Costco.

Phyllis sighed and turned to me. 'I'm the matron of honor,' she said. 'Again.'

'But at least she gives us an excuse for a vacation every four or five years,' Hugh said reasonably.

'There is that,' his wife agreed. 'And I get to shop for . . .'

Whatever Phyllis was planning to shop for remained a mystery because Marilyn Brignole popped in from the kitchen just then to do a quick head count.

'Good!' she said. 'You're all here.'

'Hail, hail, the gang's all here . . .' Colin sang, conducting the performance with his knife.

'Do you ever get used to this?' I asked Marilyn.

'All I care about is that everybody's happy and well-fed.'

Six

*In comparison with changes
produced by many medicinal drugs
and alcohol, [d]rivers under the influence
of marijuana retain insight in their
performance and will compensate where
they can, for example, by slowing down or
increasing effort. As a consequence,
THC's adverse effects on driving
performance appear
relatively small.*

'Marijuana and Actual Driving
Performance: Final Report.' US
Department of Transportation,
National Highway Traffic Safety
Administration, November 1993, p.xi.

After breakfast, I returned to my room to brush my teeth and locate a sweater. I'd never been to a weedery before. For all I knew, it'd be hot as Equatorial Africa inside, but I had been a Girl Scout in an earlier life. Best to be prepared. I picked up my notebook and pen and tucked them into my handbag. Hannah Ives, Ace Researcher, that's me.

Back downstairs, I nipped into the solarium to snag a bottle of water from the drinks bar, where I ran into Phyllis and Hugh, dressed like L.L.

Bean models. Phyllis was tucking the last of the water into her backpack.

She flushed. 'There seems to have been a run on water this morning.'

By the way her backpack bulged, I had a good idea who'd made the run.

'That's all right,' I told her. 'I'm sure they have more in the kitchen. Where are you off to?'

'We're hiking Bear Creek Trail up at Lair o'the Bear Park.' Hugh patted his breast pocket. 'Got the trail map right here.'

I was puzzled. 'I thought you had a wedding to attend to.'

'Not until later tonight,' Hugh said. 'Rehearsal dinner.'

'Wedding's tomorrow. Leave it to Marjorie Ann to get married on a Sunday,' Phyllis explained.

'Well, have a good time on your hike,' I said, turning to go. 'And watch out for bears!'

A minute later, I straight-armed my way through the kitchen door and stopped dead.

Julia Child would have lusted after such a kitchen. Martha Stewart would have killed for it. Brick, tan and grey tiles were laid out beneath my feet in a checkerboard pattern, a perfect complement to the banks of dark wood floor-to-ceiling cabinets. A country sink large enough for me to bathe in was installed in a central island over which hung a pot rack festooned with copper pans and bouquets of drying herbs. On the wall next to the oversized, stainless-steel refrigerator was a long, narrow chalkboard. According to what was written on the board, we'd be having a cold Italian antipasto buffet that evening. Crystal vases of tulips were arranged here and there on the spotless black marble countertops, as if the television production team from the Food Network was expected at any minute.

Marilyn Brignole, Queen of Cuisine, stood to my right in front of an industrial-size Wolf gas range. I counted eight burners. A colorful scarf was wrapped Creole-style over her hair, exposing a fringe of red bangs. Next to her, peering into a steaming pot, loomed Daniel Fischel.

Marilyn noticed me gaping, smiled and said, 'Hi, Hannah, come on in.'

'I'm sorry to interrupt, but I was wondering if there's any more bottled water? The Grahams just swept the sideboard clean.'

Marilyn handed the wooden spoon she'd been holding to Daniel, then wiped her hands on her apron. 'Sure, just give me a minute.' She smiled. 'I'm giving Daniel a cooking lesson.'

Curious, I took several steps forward. 'What's in the pot?'

Daniel laughed out loud. 'Pot!'

I didn't get it at first. 'Pot?' I said stupidly.

Daniel nodded. 'Pot.'

'Pot's in the pot?'

Marilyn took pity on me. 'I'm making cannabutter. Daniel asked if he could watch.'

Daniel looked up from stirring, blinked at me through his steamed-up lenses and said, 'See for yourself.'

On a slow, rolling boil, plopping like the mud pots of Yellowstone Park, was a viscous moss-green mixture. 'Looks disgusting,' I said. 'Like something cooked up by the three witches in

Macbeth.' I screwed up my face. 'What the heck's in it?'

'Water, butter and marijuana leaves. After it boils for a couple of hours, you strain off the leaves, then cool the mixture. The butter rises to the top. You simply skim it off.'

Daniel aimed a disarming smile at the cook. 'I don't suppose you'd share the recipe?'

Marilyn blushed modestly. 'It's so simple, you won't even need to write it down. For every quart of water, I use four sticks of butter and one ounce of marijuana.'

'Is this what you use in the magic muffins?' I asked.

'I do.'

'How do you get the dosage right?' Daniel wanted to know.

Marilyn's eyes seemed to twinkle. 'You going to open a bakery in competition with me, Daniel?'

'No worries there, Marilyn. I'm the son of the world's worst cook. When I went to college and everyone moaned and groaned about the food, I thought, what's *wrong* with these people? This stuff is delicious!'

'How do you tell the difference between the magic muffins and the ones that aren't so magical?' I asked.

Marilyn opened a cabinet, reached in and pulled out a box of frilled paper cupcake liners. 'If it's in a floral cup, like these, you can expect the magic. For the others, we use plain white liners. Not everyone likes the edibles,' she continued. 'I'm super careful about measuring and, even though I use the same ingredients every time, it's hard to calculate the dosage because the THC content of the leaves can vary. That's why we advise eating a quarter of the muffin, wait for twenty or thirty minutes, then eat a quarter more if you're not getting the buzz you're looking for.'

'That's what they told us in Amsterdam, too,' I said. 'The muffins came with instructions.'

Desiree stuck her head through the kitchen door just then and toodled, 'There you are! We're ready to leave!'

Daniel bowed in Marilyn's direction and tipped an imaginary hat. 'Thank you, dear lady.'

Marilyn flapped her hand in a think-nothing-of-it sort of way. 'Get on with you. Shoo! Don't keep the others waiting.'

'Do you mind if I sit up front with you?' I asked Austin in the driveway a few minutes later. 'I don't smoke much these days, and the fug is kind of getting to me.'

'No problem,' he said, opening the passenger-side door. 'But I'm wondering why a non-smoker is interested in the Happy Daze Experience.'

'I'm chief note-taker,' I explained. 'Claire isn't always straight enough to hold a pen, let alone write anything down.'

While the rest of our party sprawled in their seats in the back of the limo, smoking weed as if the Feds were going to raid the van and take it all away at the next stoplight, I grilled Austin about his business.

'It's a family thing, totally,' he began. 'Desiree

and I were barely making it when we inherited an old shoe factory from her dad. It was a big, drafty, tumbledown ruin. They hadn't made a shoe there for over a decade.'

He eased the limo into the traffic heading west on Seventh Avenue. 'After Amendment Sixty-Four passed, we were sitting around Bell House with friends, smoking a little kush, when Desiree suggested turning the factory into a grow house. And the rest, as they say, is history.'

As we headed north on Interstate 25, he continued, 'We planted inside at first, in the area where the sewing machines used to be. Semi-hydroponically, with grow lights. Then Desiree had this brainstorm. We've got three hundred days of sunshine in Colorado, she figured – why waste all that money on electricity? So we built the greenhouses you'll see today.' He took his eyes off the road for a moment to look at me. 'She's brilliant, Desiree. I married well.'

'I read an article, I can't remember where,' I said, 'that one way the Feds track down grow houses in residential neighborhoods is by pawing through utility bills looking for unusual water and electrical consumption.'

Austin clicked his tongue. 'Swine.' After a moment, he added, 'So, screw them! Now we've got one of the biggest operations in the state. Greenhouses, a dispensary, retail shops both for weed and paraphernalia, a rooftop restaurant with an unobstructed view of the Rockies – that's where you'll be having lunch. If all goes well, we'll be breaking ground for a theater and conference center in the fall.'

Austin slowed for the exit signposted 'Westminster' and then steered the limo toward the mountains. 'Almost there,' he said.

We drove silently for a few minutes more, then turned into a parking lot. At eleven o'clock, it was already nearly full. Cars prowled patiently around the lot, looking for the next open slot. 'Business seems to be booming,' I said.

Austin gave the horn a short, celebratory tap. 'Thank you, Governor Hickenlooper.'

He eased the limo into a spot marked *Reserved*. Once parked, he rushed around to my side of the limo, opened my door and bowed like a gentleman as I emerged. Then he released the smokers from the back, although nobody seemed to be in a particular hurry to disembark.

Colin staggered out first, shaking one leg and then the other, as if trying to figure out how they worked. Claire exited in slow motion, too, but had enough presence of mind to offer Colin a steadying arm, which he took. Mark and Cindy tumbled out next, followed by Josh and Lisa, chattering like school children just released from the classroom for recess, which was certainly true, in a way. Daniel followed, and then Desiree, who herded the group, as skillfully as an Australian shepherd, into a neat huddle near a digital sign that read *Next Tour Begins In 10 Minutes*. As we waited for the stragglers, the digital number ticked down to nine.

Austin had been locking up the limo. The number had just moved to eight when he appeared, holding a digital camera. Next to me, Lisa groaned. 'Oh, no. Not the obligatory group shot!'

'For our scrapbook. It won't hurt a bit,' Austin said, waving us into position for the photograph. 'Tall people in back, please.'

'I wish he wouldn't,' Lisa whined. 'My hair's a mess.'

Which wasn't true. It fell clean, lustrous and shimmering in the sun like spun gold, all the way to its roots.

Desiree positioned a dozy Colin in front of Lisa, who was still fiddling with her hair. She shifted Daniel to the end of the first row, next to me. After Daniel got into position, his hand shot into the pocket of his trousers and came out holding an iPhone. 'Here,' he said, thumbing the phone to life and handing it to Austin. 'Take one for me, too. I'll email it to everyone later.'

This elicited another groan from Lisa.

'Say peaches,' Austin instructed as we posed, forcing us to smile.

'Follow me,' Desiree said after the photo session was mercifully over. With a 'Thank God!' from Lisa, our hostess lead us past a long line of scowling visitors to a door marked *VIP*.

Mark confidently followed. Tottering behind, in strappy sandals with three-inch heels – not my first choice for a walking tour – was Cindy. Her legs disappeared under the skirt of her red-checked sundress and continued upward, presumably forever.

At a small reception desk, Mark paused with a look that said, *Hold on a minute! My wife!* and waited for Cindy to catch up.

Desiree killed time shuffling paperwork while we all signed the guest book, and each of us was issued a clip-on VIP visitor badge. 'Ready?' Desiree asked.

Behind the desk, two rustic barn doors hung from overhead rails. Desiree grabbed a handle and slid one of the doors aside. I don't know what I expected to see behind, but an industrial-strength steel door with a security pin pad attached to the wall wasn't it. Desiree swiped the ID that hung round her neck over the pad and I watched the door swing silently open. 'We take security seriously here,' she said. 'This is a water, fire and bomb-proof door.'

We followed our hostess down a long, narrow hallway painted a soothing off-white. Cindy's heels clattered on the hard concrete floor as we passed door after door, before Desiree paused in front of one labeled CLONES.

'It's like something out of *Star Wars*,' Colin muttered in an awestruck voice.

Inside the room, boxes of cuttings, each about four inches high, sat on chest-high tables in rooting trays covered with raised plastic lids. 'After they root,' Desiree explained, 'we let them grow for a week, a week and a half, then they get transferred to individual pots.'

'What kind of medium do you use?' Mark asked.

Desiree smiled mysteriously. 'The nutrient combination is a trade secret, I'm afraid.'

Further along the hallway, we entered a vast space where row upon row of individual marijuana plants were growing in one-gallon pots. Tubes about the diameter of my arm snaked around the room, providing irrigation for the young plants. 'At this point,' Desiree said, 'each plant gets tagged. We take MITS seriously, too.'

'MITS?' Lisa chirped.

'Above your pay grade, honey,' Josh muttered.

She shot shrapnel into the back of his head with her eyes.

Desiree rattled on as if she hadn't heard the exchange. 'It stands for Marijuana Inventory Tracking Solutions,' she said. 'Each tag contains our retail or medical marijuana license number, a product serial number and a secure ID chip that can be scanned by a scanning gun using radio-frequency identification or RIFD technology, similar to that used by a grocery store clerk.' She paused to let that information sink in.

ID chip, I scrawled.

'A true seed-to-sale system.'

'Ah . . .' Daniel said, sounding wise.

'As you can see,' Desiree continued, 'the plants closest to us have been growing for about a week.' She stood on tiptoes, waved an arm and pointed. 'The tall ones in the back there, for about four. At the four-week point, they get replanted in three-gallon pots and . . .' She paused. 'If there aren't any questions, please follow me.'

We straggled after her, with Colin bringing up the rear, touching plants along the way as if to make sure they were real and not made out of plastic. I smiled when he paused, adjusted his cap, held up his iPhone, grinned and took a selfie.

After he'd caught up with us, Desiree led us to another secure door, a double one this time, swiped her ID badge and, as the door swung open on silent hinges, grandly announced, 'Welcome to Disneyland.'

'Good Lord!' Josh exclaimed.

Mark grabbed Cindy's hand and said, 'A preview of coming attractions, cupcake.'

'Shee-it,' Colin breathed.

My feelings exactly.

We had entered the Flowering Room, a vast greenhouse the size of an aircraft hangar, filled with flowering marijuana plants of infinite variety. It was a dense jungle. Some plants were over ten feet tall, heavy with fist-sized blossoms drooping over string netting that struggled to hold them erect.

It was the humidity that hit me at first, like a wet towel. Then came the overpowering odor of skunk I associated with the plants themselves, followed by overtones of damp earth.

'We grow one hundred and thirty varieties here,' Desiree was saying when I tuned in again.

We wandered down a long row. Surprisingly, she allowed us to touch one of the plants, its buds glistening with crystals. My hand came away sticky with resin.

'Marco!' she yelled suddenly. A man popped up from behind a row of five-foot plants. He wore chinos and a polo shirt, and had a shower cap over his bald head, like the guy who makes sandwiches in my local deli. Turning to the group, Desiree said, 'This is Marco, our grow

66

guru. Marco, please explain to our guests what happens to the buds from this point on.'

For the final leg of the greenhouse tour, we followed Marco into the drying room, where harvested plants hung upside down like tobacco for about two weeks before being trimmed and the buds laid out in single layers on screen trays. 'Next stop for these babies is the retail store,' Marco concluded, and led us through another door into a clean, ultra-modern shop.

'Just like Disney,' Claire complained. 'Climb off the ride and it disgorges you into the gift shop.' Grumbling aside, however, she left me in the proverbial dust as she hurried off to check out the Happy Daze wares.

'I dream of the day when we have choice like this in Maryland,' Claire was saying to the budrista when I caught up with her. She sat at a counter on a tall, aluminum barstool. 'Tell me about that one,' she said, leaning in and pointing to one of the bud-filled glass jars neatly arranged on clear-varnished pine shelves behind the bud bar. 'I'm interested primarily in the *indicas* for my nausea.'

While Claire considered a baffling array of *indicas*, *sativas* and hybrids with whimsical names like sour diesel, train wreck, moon rocks, screaming gorilla and the 'legendary' Alaskan thunderfuck, I browsed nearby glass cases where cannabis paraphernalia was displayed, bathed in pale purple lighting. Grinders, vaporizers and vape pens. Body products like oils, salves, soaks, patches, toothpaste, shampoo and lip balm.

Cannabis suppositories for menstrual cramps. I could even purchase cannabis-infused coffee pods for my Keurig. Who knew?

'Skywalker is good for nausea,' the girl was explaining to Claire. 'And stress.'

'Hell with that,' I heard Colin say as he elbowed his way up to the bud bar. 'Give me something that's loaded with THC. I'm here to get high.'

'Excuse me, sir, but this lady was ahead of you,' the budrista scolded. She took a step in my direction. 'What would you like?' the girl asked, looking directly at me.

'I don't smoke,' I said, with an apologetic smile directed at Colin, although he didn't deserve it.

She gave me a suspicious so-what-are-you-doing-here look, so I added, 'I'm the designated driver.' I paused. 'But I might consider the lip balm.'

Claire was still shilly-shallying over the menu, so the budrista unlocked the cabinet in front of me, reached in and handed me a pot of Goodwitch lip balm. 'All organic,' she added.

What else? I said to myself as I took a moment to read the label.

'No way!' Lisa's voice cut above the hum of casual conversation and the soft music wafting in from speakers artfully concealed in the paneling.

I turned. On the opposite side of the room, Daniel stood with Lisa and Josh next to a bank of cabinets, their functional glasswares attractively illuminated with museum-quality lighting.

Lisa cocked a hip and folded her arms across her chest.

Josh's arm snaked around his wife's waist and drew her close. He rose on tiptoe to speak directly into her ear, but whatever he said, she wasn't having it. She shook her head defiantly.

Daniel leaned in, too. His lips moved, but I wasn't close enough to hear.

Again, Lisa shook her head, so vehemently this time that the chandeliers dangling from her ears bounced against her neck. She shook off Josh's arm and stalked away. What was that all about?

'I'll be right back,' I told Claire.

I left the lip balm on the counter and followed Lisa down a long hallway and into the ladies' room. She wasn't in a stall, as I expected, but hanging over a sink, checking her makeup in the mirror.

'Is everything OK?' I asked.

'Just a little panicky, is all. Pot does that to me sometimes.'

'I just saw you talking to Daniel.'

'So?'

'You didn't seem happy.'

She flapped a hand, waving my concern away. 'Oh, *that*!'

'What do you know about Daniel?' I asked.

She dabbed her finger into a small pot of blush and rubbed it into her cheeks. After what I'd seen that day, I wondered if the blush had cannabis in it. 'Not much,' she said.

'What does he do?' I asked.

Lisa shrugged. 'Says he teaches agriculture at the University of Georgia.'

I laughed. 'Marijuana Cultivation 101?'

'Don't know,' she said. 'You'll have to ask him.'

So I was right in thinking he looked like a professor.

'Are you heading up to the restaurant for lunch?' I asked.

'I really need a smoke,' Lisa said, ignoring my question, 'but I guess it will have to wait until we get back to the B and B. Josh bought me some Blackberry Kush. Supposed to help me chill.' She held the blusher between her thumb and index finger, then dropped it into the mouth of her open handbag. 'Don't have a clue what that other shit was.'

'See you later, then,' I said, and headed into a stall.

'Bye!' she said as the restroom door closed behind her.

When I returned to the shop for my lip balm, Claire and Colin had moved on, their places at the counter taken over by Mark and Cindy. The budrista held the couple in thrall, extolling the benefits of a hybrid weed named Girl Scout Cookies. I smiled, and had to eavesdrop. Girl Scout Cookies, it seems, were good for PTSD, but why anyone would consider a combination of sweet pastry, wood varnish and diesel fuel with subtle overtones of lemon Pinesol a plus, I simply couldn't imagine. Still smiling, I paid for the lip balm, then went off to find the restaurant, where I'd been promised organic food, locally sourced. What else?

Seven

The windows were covered with blankets and a single electric bulb flickers through smoke so dense you can barely see across the room. A dozen persons around a penny-ante poker game. They range from boys of 16 to men in their late 20s, all in a state of dazed exhilaration. There are only a few rickety chairs and the table for furnishings and the gang lolls about the room, some chasing cheap whisky with long muggles drags, others content to smoke, laugh vacuously and 'walk on air.'

St Louis Star-Times,
February 4, 1935.

The chance to interrogate Daniel Fischel didn't arrive until later that afternoon, when our merry band of weed pilgrims and medical refugees gathered for happy hour in the solarium.

Slightly more than twenty-four hours had passed since Claire and I had landed in the Mile High City, and the novelty of recreational pot had already worn off, at least for me. At four-fifteen, Marilyn appeared and laid out the *hors d'oeurves*: baked brie, shredded wheat crackers,

71

toast points and paté, assorted olives and frozen seedless grapes. There was Mark loading up his plate as if no supper was in his future. Lisa and Josh were experimenting with the matching glass pipes they'd bought at the weedery that afternoon. Claire was continuing to roll and smoke her own, seeming to enjoy the ritual of it. Daniel was sucking on his vape pen. I was holding a glass of wine. Relax, have a good time, laugh at stupid jokes in a no-shame zone. Wasn't that the point? It all seemed so natural.

Add Desiree in the next room, pounding out Scott Joplin rags on the Steinway.

It didn't get more civilized than that. When I made my report, I hoped I could convince the senate committee to see it that way.

I waited until Daniel got his hands on the wine bottle, then sidled up, held out my glass and requested a refill. After he'd refilled his own glass, too, and taken a sip, I asked, 'So, what brings you here, Daniel?'

'I'm working on background for Georgia State Representative Allen Peake,' he said. 'Bill Sixty-Five recently passed the house and it loosened things up a bit, but some don't think it goes far enough.'

'Bill Sixty-Five?'

'Medical marijuana,' he clarified. 'Recreational's a long way off in Georgia. They still throw you in the slammer.'

'I keep thinking you look familiar,' I said. 'Are you a reporter?'

'Hardly!' He seemed genuinely amused by my question. 'Just a lowly Professor of Agriculture

72

at the university.' He patted his breast pocket. 'I'm taking notes.'

My acquaintance with the man had been short, but I saw no evidence of note-taking paraphernalia. No notebook like the one I carried. No tape recorder, unless he was using his iPhone. The only thing in his breast pocket was his vape pen. I'd just watched him take it out. Maybe he was depending on memory. At Bell House? Good luck with that.

'I noticed you talking with Josh and Lisa back at the weedery,' I said. 'She didn't seem too happy.'

He shrugged, as if he didn't have a clue what I was talking about.

'You look more like a Shakespeare scholar than a corn, wheat and soybeans one,' I said, changing the subject.

He laughed. 'Had quite enough of the Bard in high school, Mrs Ives. "Where the bee sucks, there suck I, in the cowslip's bell I lie" and all that.' He considered the painted ceiling dreamily and sucked on his vape pen. 'Have you ever been face-to-face with a cow, eye to eye?'

I had to admit that I had. 'My sister-in-law raises Dexters in southern Maryland.'

He nodded sagely. 'Ah. Wonderful animals. Trustworthy, honest and straightforward. You never have any doubts about a cow's intentions.'

I flashed back to a summer day, early in our marriage, when Paul and I had taken a picnic lunch to the 'back forty' on the family farm. Fried chicken, potato salad, white wine, crisp and cold. One thing had led to another, then, 'Moo!' How long had she been watching us with her liquid-brown eyes, front hooves firmly planted on the fringed edge of our picnic blanket?

'Non-judgmental, too,' I offered.

'Precisely.'

'How did your hemp butter turn out?' I asked after a moment.

'Superbly,' he said. 'Would you like to see?'

'Sure.'

Taking a temporary leave of absence from happy hour, I followed Daniel into the kitchen, where we interrupted Marilyn in the act of arranging cold cuts in pinwheels on a large silver tray. Daniel made a beeline for the refrigerator. 'Don't mind us,' he called over his shoulder. 'Just showing off my handiwork.' He squatted, rummaged about in a bottom drawer among the cheeses and extracted a waxed paper-wrapped rectangle the size of my usual Kerrygold but chartreuse in color. '*Voila!*' he said, peeling back the paper and holding it out for inspection.

'A thing of beauty,' I agreed.

Like a proud father, Daniel admired his handiwork for a minute longer, turning it this way and that. Then he rewrapped the cannabutter and put it back where he'd found it. 'Wish I could take it home with me.' He sighed. As he straightened his knees and prepared to stand, his iPhone began to gobble like a turkey. He pulled it out of his pocket, checked the caller ID, then said apologetically, 'Sorry, got to take this,' and, with the phone pressed to his ear, hustled off the way we had come.

'Daniel's tickled pink by that butter,' Marilyn said.

'You should teach cooking classes as part of the Happy Daze Experience,' I suggested.

'I already do,' she said, 'but only in the winter when it's not quite so busy.' She cupped one hand and used the other to sweep breadcrumbs off the countertop into it. 'I made a little cookbook as a handout,' she said, tapping the crumbs from her hand into the sink. 'Would you like a copy?'

'I'd love a copy,' I told her.

Marilyn led me down a corridor behind the kitchen that ended in a windowless door with a panic bar – the old tradesmen's entrance, I presumed. Her apartment turned out to be an L-shaped room sandwiched between a well-equipped laundry room and the spacious office (formerly the live-in butler's quarters, Marilyn said) shared by Austin and Desiree.

The cookbook she handed me had been printed from a word-processing file, but someone had known what they were doing. They'd used the column feature, justified the text attractively and inserted color photographs of the finished dishes in all the right places. Even the page numbers – twenty in all – were formatted correctly. I leafed through the booklet quickly. Pot tacos, weed brownies, cannabis caramels . . . Was there anything that couldn't be improved by the addition of pot?

'I can't wait to try the bloody Mary Janes,' I told her. 'Thank you.' I tucked my personal copy of the *Happy Daze Cookbook* under my arm, wondering if I'd have the nerve to try out any of the recipes on Paul – once Claire and her colleagues had legalized pot in Maryland, that is.

As we headed back to the kitchen, a matched pair of musclemen, each wearing black T-shirts belted into slim black jeans, exploded through the back door and passed us in the hallway with only the briefest of nods. They wore sunglasses, even indoors, and no-nonsense athletic shoes bearing the Nike logo. They also wore holstered sidearms and serious, humorless expressions, as if they were about to repo your RV. One of them carried a canvas satchel reinforced with leather straps and handles. 'Who are those guys?' I asked as they let themselves into Austin and Desiree's office.

'Nick and Borys Pawlowski. They're our security guards.'

'Why? Do you think we're going to make off with the family silver?'

Marilyn laughed. 'Oh, no, they are sweethearts, those boys. They just take care of the money.'

Sweethearts? 'Those boys' looked like they were capable of holding you by your ankles, turning you upside down and shaking your pockets empty, down to the last nickel and speck of lint.

'There's money in that satchel?'

She nodded.

'Why aren't they taking the money to the bank?'

'It's complicated,' she said. 'You should ask Austin.'

'I will,' I said. I knew that Claire had scheduled an interview with Austin at nine-thirty the following morning. How to manage the money in what was essentially an all-cash business was definitely high on her agenda.

Marilyn made shooing motions with her hand. 'Out now,' she said. 'Back to the happy hour. The brie will be getting cold.'

I had to laugh. 'Yes, ma'am.'

Daniel had not yet returned to the solarium, but Phyllis and Hugh had joined the group, freshly laundered after their afternoon hike and dressed in their Sunday best.

'Phyl wanted to pop in for a little nip before we headed to the rehearsal dinner,' Hugh said, raising a Martini glass containing a dark chocolate liquid. 'Tia Espresso Martini, shaken and not stirred.' He winked. 'What did you say your name was?'

I introduced myself again.

Hugh looked puzzled and fiddled with his hearing aid. 'Must have gotten it wet,' he said. 'Can't hear a damn thing.'

'My name's Hannah Ives!' I bellowed, using my outside voice. 'I'm from Annapolis, Maryland.'

A clink of his glass against mine, then another wink. 'Here's to you, then, Hannah Ives.'

This was getting awkward. I looked around somewhat desperately for Phyllis, but she was busy chatting with Cindy. I was rescued by Colin, who suddenly materialized at my elbow, looking way too serious for someone who'd been smoking weed all day.

Thankfully, Hugh wandered off.

'Your last name is Ives?' Colin asked.

I nodded.

'From Annapolis?'

'Yup.' Hadn't I just said that?

'You related to Professor Ives? Teaches math at the Naval Academy?'

'Loosely,' I said. 'He's my husband.'

Colin's face paled. 'Oh my God,' he muttered to his shoes. 'I am so screwed!'

'What are you talking about, Colin?'

Then the penny dropped. A clean-cut young man, hair cut high and tight like a military recruit. I set my wine glass down on a table and gave him my full attention. 'Are you a midshipman?'

He nodded grimly. 'A firstie.'

During plebe and youngster years, a midshipman can resign at any time with no military obligation. But after passing the halfway point, like Colin had the previous year, your butt belonged to the United States Navy.

'Damn,' I said. I grabbed Colin's arm and pulled him into the sitting room, past the piano, and parked him next to the fireplace. 'Coming here . . . What were you thinking?'

He slumped against the mantle. 'I used to smoke weed in high school, but I gave it up for the Navy. I knew I'd have three weeks of block leave after exams, so . . .' He shrugged. 'I've had this trip planned for a long time.'

Long time, short time, it didn't matter. If the academy found out, they could boot him out. Make him pay back the money they'd spent on his education. And it wasn't peanuts, unless you had $186,000 burning a hole in your pocket.

'But you *know* they're going to test you, Colin.'

'That's the beauty of it, Mrs Ives. There won't be another whiz quiz until Reform in August, and any marijuana will be out of my system by then.'

'So, I don't get it. What's the problem?'

'All my life I've wanted to be a pilot.'

'Forgive me if I sound preachy, but why on earth would you jeopardize your Navy career for – as my grandmother would have phrased it – a few moments of shabby pleasure?'

'It seemed like a good idea at the time,' he said miserably.

'Famous last words.'

Instantly, I regretted my flippancy; the boy looked like he was about to cry. 'Look, Colin, it may be a cliché, but as far as I'm concerned, what happens in Denver stays in Denver.' I hoped he believed me. Hoped that what I knew wouldn't hang like a specter over his final year at the Naval Academy.

He still looked worried. 'That picture Daniel took? The one he's going to email to everybody?'

I nodded, encouraging him to go on.

'You're going to post it to Facebook, aren't you? Your husband will see it. Everyone will see it! They'll recognize me, and I'm dead.'

I reached out and squeezed his arm reassuringly. 'I promise I won't post it to Facebook. Or show it to my husband.'

His face brightened. 'Really?'

'Really. But, honestly, Colin, you need to clean up your act. Go home. You have a home, don't you?'

He nodded. 'Beaufort, South Carolina.'

He pronounced it like a true South Carolinian: Bew-fud. 'I can never remember which is which,' I confessed, trying to cheer him up. 'In South Carolina it's Bew-fud, but in North Carolina they say Bow-foot.'

He dredged up a smile and pasted it, not very convincingly, on his face.

'Seriously, if someone at the academy finds out you were doing dope in Denver, it will not be from me.'

Colin bowed slightly at the waist. 'Thank you, thank you, Mrs Ives,' he whispered.

After a long day, and still a bit jet-lagged, I excused myself shortly after dinner and headed upstairs. I checked my email, posted nothing to Facebook, then crawled into bed with my Kindle.

Hours later, I awoke to a room in complete darkness, except for the numbers on the digital clock, which glowed red at 3:03 a.m.

I watched the minutes click from three, to four, to five, then threw back the duvet and went to use the bathroom.

As I washed and dried my hands in the subdued light, I noticed that the door leading to Claire's bedroom was standing open. Curious, I peeked in. Gas logs flickered in the fireplace. Her bed was still neatly made.

Claire hadn't come to bed.

I grabbed a terry cloth robe, belted it around my nightgown and crept quietly downstairs to the solarium where I'd last seen her. As I suspected, Claire had curled up in one of the chintz-covered armchairs and fallen asleep.

I shook my friend gently until her eyes opened.

She blinked as if wondering where she was, smiled up at me, then shook her head, clearing out the cobwebs. 'I must have dozed off,' she said. 'What time is it?'

'After three,' I told her.

'Shhh,' she whispered, pointing to the armchair opposite where Daniel Fischel also dozed.

'You two have a big night?' I teased as she uncurled her legs, stretched and stood.

'Ha ha,' she said. 'He was feeling sorry for himself, so I just listened.'

'Glad I decided to skip the after-dinner drinks, then,' I said.

Daniel slouched in the chair, legs extended, his head at an odd angle. 'He can't be comfortable sleeping like that,' I said. 'He'll be sore in the morning.'

'*I'm* not going to wake him up,' Claire said. 'It'll just be more about how government regulation will be the death of civilization as we know it.' She tapped my arm. 'You do it.'

'OK, but you owe me,' I said.

I padded barefoot across the carpet and touched Daniel's shoulder. When I got no response, I shook it. 'Professor?'

Daniel slumped sideways, his head lolling. His glasses slipped from his face to the floor, making him look naked and vulnerable. His iPhone lay on the floor below his open hand, as if he'd been using it before he passed out.

'Professor?'

'He's out cold,' Claire said. 'Wine, edibles, vaping, Drambouie . . .'

Something wasn't right. I touched his cheek with the back of my hand. It was cold. I pressed my fingers against his neck, feeling for a pulse. There was none. I stared at his chest for a long minute, willing it to rise and fall, but it didn't.

I turned and looked at Claire. 'I think Daniel's dead!'

Claire started. 'He *can't* be! He was just telling me about . . .' Her voice trailed off, as if the seriousness of the situation had just sunk in. 'Do you know CPR?' she asked in a hushed voice.

'I do, but it won't do any good. He's ice cold, Claire. I'm guessing he's been dead for a while.'

'Oh, God!' she said. Then, 'Shit! What do we do now?'

I didn't answer her at first. I was staring too hard at Daniel's face, puzzling over it, trying to fit the pieces together. 'Claire, look!'

She backed away. 'I don't want to.'

'No, I'm serious. Look at him, Claire. Take away the glasses, add a beard and a little *Pirates of the Caribbean*-style mustache and what do you see?'

Claire screwed up her face and squinted. 'I don't . . .'

I elbowed her. 'The jerk on the plane!'

'No.'

'Yes,' I said. 'I'm sure of it.'

'I didn't get a good look at the guy, not like you did.'

'I didn't get a super close look on the plane, but I'd swear it's either him or his identical twin.'

'But, the beard . . .'

'Razors?'

'My God, Hannah. What does it mean?'

'I sure as hell don't know, but whoever this guy is, we can't leave him like this. Go wake up the Nortons. Meanwhile, I'll call nine-one-one.'

Eight

A girl student, still in her teens, told a reporter she had seen some of her friends under the influence and named a boy and a girl who lost their senses so completely after smoking marihuana that they eloped and were married.

St Louis Star-Times,
January 18, 1935.

While waiting for the EMTs to arrive, Claire and I sat side by side in our bathrobes on a loveseat, hands folded in our laps like patients in a clinic waiting our turn for mammograms. We talked in whispers so as not to disturb the other guests and complicate an already complicated situation.

Meanwhile, Desiree wore a path in the sitting-room carpet until Austin, his patience worn as thin as the Turkish kilim, dispatched her to the kitchen to fire up the high-tech coffee machine. He'd just turned on the porch lights and unlocked the front door when two uniformed EMTs, a man and a woman, clattered up the sidewalk, lugging hard-sided cases of emergency equipment.

'Hell of a way to start the day, huh, Austin?' the woman said as she and her partner trundled through the door.

83

'Shit, yeah.' Austin rubbed a hand over the stubble on this chin, then thumbed them in the direction of the solarium. 'He's in there.'

'Thanks,' she said, turning hard right.

'Coffee?' Austin asked as they passed by.

'You are reading my mind,' she tossed over her shoulder. 'But I'll have to take a raincheck. I'm on call.'

'So, how do you know those guys?' Claire asked as the two techs disappeared into the next room.

Austin flung himself into an armchair, leaned forward and rested his forearms on his knees. 'Started EMT training at Aurora with Gina there, but decided to drop out when Happy Daze took off.'

Through the half-open doorway, we watched Gina and her assistant officially determine what we already knew. Daniel Fischel was dead.

'Have you ever had a guest die before?' I asked to fill the silence that closed in deafeningly around us.

'Twice. One nutcase, dressed all in white, took an overdose of sleeping pills, lay down on the bed and died. She was gorgeous, I'll give her that. The maid found her clutching a red rose to her bosom like something out of a Victorian novel. And just as dead as Cathy in *Wuthering Heights*.'

'How sad,' I said.

'At least she wanted to die,' Austin continued. 'Not like the big wig from New Jersey last August who keeled over from a heart attack. Collapsed on his girlfriend like a house. Fortunately the guest in the next room heard her calling in this tiny little voice, "Help, help."' He mimicked a high falsetto. 'Otherwise, she might have suffocated before we got her out from under him.'

'How embarrassing,' Claire said.

'Yeah, both for her and for the guy's wife.' He stood up. 'I'd better go see what's taking Desiree so long with the coffee.'

'I feel sick,' Claire said after Austin left the room.

'Do you need to go to the bathroom? There's a powder room behind the staircase.'

'Not barfing kind of sick, Hannah, more like soul-sick.' Her arm rested against mine. I felt her shiver. 'I was the last person to see Daniel alive. If I had been awake, maybe I could have helped him.'

'You don't know that, Claire. You saw how peaceful he looked. He couldn't have been gasping and writhing in pain, calling out for help. It was probably something quick. A heart attack or a stroke. Nothing you or anyone else could have done.'

'*If* he was the same guy we saw on the plane . . .' Claire paused, then gave me a look, '. . . and that's a big if, why did he change his appearance?'

It seemed obvious to me. 'He didn't want to be recognized,' I suggested. 'Which could mean that he's famous.'

Claire stiffened. 'I'm sure *I've* never seen him before.'

'Me neither, but would we recognize, say, Lady Gaga if she walked in not wearing any makeup?'

85

'Good point.'

My eyes strayed to the solarium door. The EMTs seemed to be scrutinizing the arms of the chair Daniel's body was still sitting in. Fortunately, the dead man's face was turned away. If I didn't know better, I'd think Daniel was simply admiring the luscious pink gloxinia hanging in the window.

'Maybe he didn't want anyone to know he was here, like if a photo got leaked to the press or something,' Claire said after a moment or two had passed.

That was certainly true in Colin McDaniel's awkward situation, I reminded myself, but I couldn't see why it would matter to Daniel Fischel. 'Then answer me this, Claire. Why did Daniel hand Austin his cell phone when we took that group shot at the weedery yesterday?'

'I get you,' she said. 'Unlikely he simply wanted a souvenir.'

'Exactly,' I said. 'He doesn't seem like the souvenir type to me. The only thing that makes sense is that Daniel intended to take a picture of somebody else in our group.'

'Not me,' Claire said. 'Everyone knows where I stand on marijuana.'

Would my being caught in a weedery endanger Paul's job? Unlikely. If I'd believed that, I never would have come. He worked for the federal government, not me.

'Nor me,' I said.

I found Fischel's behavior over the previous two days distinctly odd, but then he had been stoned a good deal of the time, and I hadn't.

Suddenly something else struck me as odd.

86

Neither Austin nor Desiree seemed to have noticed anything strange about Claire that morning, but I had. If she had gone straight to the solarium after dinner and her bed had not been slept in . . .

'Why are you wearing a bathrobe?' I whispered into her ear.

'Oh!' She grabbed both ends of the terry cloth belt and cinched it tighter. 'I went upstairs not long after you did, Hannah, got ready for bed, then realized I'd left my stash in the solarium. It was probably perfectly safe there, but old habits die hard. I'm so used to hiding it. So, I came down to fetch it. Daniel was still in the solarium, Mark and Cindy, too. Then Colin came back from wherever and we got to talking. I smoked another joint. You know how it goes.'

After two days in the Mile High City, I was beginning to. 'What time was that?'

Claire shrugged. Clearly, she had no idea. 'After Mark went up to bed, Cindy hung around for a few minutes. Then Daniel and Colin got pretty chummy. They ended up singing old rugby songs, something about the sexual life of a camel. It was pretty funny.'

'I'm sure it was hysterical.'

'Then I must have dozed off,' Claire concluded.

Austin reappeared just then carrying a cup of cappuccino for each of us. I peered into my cup and in spite of (or perhaps because of) the seriousness of the situation, I failed to suppress a giggle. Floating cheerfully on top of the crema was the cinnamon outline of a marijuana leaf.

'Sorry,' Austin said as he sat back down in the

chair opposite us, 'but that's the way it comes out of the machine.'

I'd taken a careful sip of the hot liquid when Austin said, 'I wonder what's taking them so long?'

I considered him over the rim of the cup. 'You could ask.'

Austin played nervously with his fingers, as if counting them to make sure they were all there. 'Usually it's a quick in and out. Call the coroner and you're good to go.'

'Gosh, even deaths from natural causes?' Claire asked.

Austin nodded. 'Always if they're unattended.'

Claire shifted uncomfortably in her seat. 'Will there be an autopsy, Austin?'

'Probably,' Austin said. 'Unless Fischel's physician back home says he had a chronic heart condition or something.' He shrugged. 'That guest from New Jersey I told you about?'

Claire and I nodded.

'You know that Viagra ad: "Ask your doctor if your heart is healthy enough for sex?"'

We nodded again.

'Should have asked his doctor.'

Like Austin, I was growing impatient, too, and feeling a bit uncomfortable. I wasn't in the habit of sitting around having theoretical discussions with near strangers in my bathrobe. I was about to ask if we could go upstairs to dress when the EMT named Gina shouted, 'Austin!'

Behind her, the other EMT was scrutinizing a pillow, his blue rubber gloves standing out boldly against the bright yellow floral print.

Austin met Gina at the door.

Quiet words were exchanged.

Gina made a call on her handheld radio.

Her partner set the pillow down, presumably where he had found it, and started packing up.

Austin turned back to the sitting room, then steadied himself with a hand on the piano, his face ashen. 'It's going to be a long day, ladies.'

Using an elbow, Gina eased the doors to the solarium shut so we could no longer see what was going on.

'Did he have a heart attack?' Claire wanted to know, staring hard at the door as if she had X-ray vision. 'Or, maybe he overdosed on something?'

Austin smiled grimly. 'Nobody ever in the history of the world OD'd on marijuana. You can look it up.'

'Then what?' I asked.

'It won't be official until the medical examiner weighs in after the autopsy, but the EMTs suspect he may have been smothered.'

'Uh, oh,' I said, based on extensive experience watching late night reruns of *Law & Order*. 'Bloodshot eyes?'

Austin's nod confirmed it. 'Petechial hemorrhages. You can get bloodshot eyes from smoking dope, too, so we'll have to see. Crime-scene investigators are on the way. I'd scream, but I don't want to wake the whole house.'

'The cops will wake everyone up soon enough,' I said.

'I better warn Desiree.' Austin checked his watch. 'Nearly five. Marilyn won't like it, but I'll have to roust her out, too. Breakfast will be early, I think.'

Claire stood, straightening her bathrobe. 'In the meantime, can we get dressed?'

'I don't see any reason why not.'

I stood up, too. The last time I'd entertained police in my nightgown, I'd ended up spending the weekend in the company of US Marshals, an experience I didn't care to repeat.

I trailed Claire up the staircase. The sun wouldn't be up for another thirty minutes, but the cool gray of dawn was already limning the Tiffany-style stained-glass patterns in the windows.

I paused on the landing. 'Claire?' I hissed.

From three steps up the next half flight, she turned and looked down at me. 'What?'

'Do you know which room is Daniel's?'

'You wouldn't!' I couldn't see her face, but I imagined it wore a disapproving frown.

'It's probably locked anyway, but . . .' I let the thought die.

After a thoughtful silence, Claire said, 'He's one floor up, just over my room, I think.'

I passed her on the stairs and headed up. 'You coming?' I whispered.

While I waited for Claire to make up her mind, the antique case clock in the hallway loudly ticked off the seconds. 'OK,' she whispered.

Once on the third floor, we crept down the hallway like ninjas, although any ninja trying to be stealthy in a bright white bathrobe would be ceremoniously stripped of his nunchucks. Behind me, Claire whispered, 'It's that one.'

I paused in front of the door she had indicated, squinting at the handle in the semi-darkness. Not an antique brass knob, like ours on the floor below, but a modern, lever-style handle. Using my elbow, I pressed down on it.

To my astonishment, Daniel's door swung open.

'You're not actually going in, are you?' Claire whispered.

'Don't worry,' I whispered back. 'I won't touch anything.'

'You're crazy, Hannah. I'm staying out here.'

'Let me know if anyone comes along,' I said as I eased my way into Daniel's room.

At some time the previous evening, Daniel Fischel must have returned. The desk lamp was still on. A laptop computer sat open next to it, the screensaver active, playing a canned slide-show of what looked like world heritage sites. As I watched, photos of the Great Barrier Reef, the Taj Mahal, Angkor Wat, the Great Wall of China, Chartres Cathedral and the Grand Canyon slid on and off the screen in leisurely succession.

Why couldn't the man use family pictures like normal people? Daniel had been somebody's son, at the very least. Maybe a husband and father. A brother, a co-worker, a friend. Somebody would miss him.

The room had no closet, but an oak wardrobe dominated the far wall, its door slightly ajar. Keeping my hands well to myself, I peered in. After checking out the bathroom, I rejoined Claire in the hallway.

'Thanks for riding shotgun,' I said.

'What did you see?' she asked.

Using the tail of my terry cloth belt, I closed Daniel's door behind me. 'Let's get out of here first.'

I invited Claire back to my room, where we sat side by side in the striped armchairs.

'He's definitely the guy from the airplane,' I told Claire. 'The suit, shirt and tie he wore then are hanging in the wardrobe. I checked out the bathroom sink for signs that he'd shaved, bits of whiskers and so on, but nada. I'm guessing he shaved at the airport.'

Claire played nervously with her bathrobe belt, twisting it into figure eights. 'What does it mean, Hannah?'

'It might mean absolutely nothing. I simply assumed Daniel was a banker type because of the way he dressed.' I paused. 'And ditto because of his asshole behavior over the drinks. But college professors can dress up and act like Wall Street swells if they feel like it. There's no law against that. And he seemed to know a lot about agriculture.'

My iPhone was charging on the table between us. I picked it up and Googled 'Daniel Fischel.' There was an obituary for a Daniel Fischel, who died in 1952 in Lawrence, Kansas, survived by a loving wife named Louisa and ten children. I found a link to a hot-shot Chicago lawyer, and a guy who manufactured high-end, one-of-a-kind titanium bicycles. I clicked on their images, but neither of the men still living remotely resembled the guy lying dead in the solarium downstairs.

Did I want to search for Danielle Fisher? I told Google I did not.

My thumbs tapped out another search. 'Daniel told me he was working for Allen Peake, who is a genuine Georgia state representative, according to Google here, so that part of his story checks out.'

So, I reasoned, either our Daniel didn't have an Internet presence – hard to believe in this day and age – or Daniel Fischel wasn't his real name.

Claire was thinking along the same lines. 'But, if he's a real professor teaching at a real school, why doesn't his name show up on Google?'

'Good question. And it should also pop up on those professor rating sites like RateMy-Professors, MyEdu and Uloop, and it doesn't.'

'So, he's using an alias.'

'Apparently.'

'And felt it necessary to alter his appearance.'

'Obviously.'

'So, who is he, really?'

'We could ask Desiree,' I suggested. 'She checks in all the guests. He must have left an address when he registered, and he probably paid by credit card.'

Claire sprang to her feet. 'Good. Sounds like a plan. I like plans.'

For the first time in several hours, I grinned. 'So, let's get dressed, go downstairs and see what we can do to help Desiree with breakfast.'

Nine

*Dear Agent _____ Glad to hear
you are working hard to give effect to
my directive of October 24, 1947. We
will have a great national round-up
arrest of musicians in violation of the
marijuana laws all on a single day.
Don't worry, I will let you know
what day. Sincerely yours, H. J.
Anslinger, US Commissioner
of Narcotics.*

Henry J Anslinger, Form Letter,
US Treasury Department, Federal
Bureau of Narcotics, 1947–1948.

We found Desiree and Marilyn perched side by
side on kitchen bar stools. Desiree was warming
her hands around a mug of cappuccino, while
Marilyn nursed a cup of tea, the teabag tag hanging
forlornly over the rim. From the iridescent skim
on top, I guessed her tea had grown cold.

Marilyn wore a flowered kimono. Her eyes were
red-rimmed and swollen.

I laid a gentle hand on her shoulder. 'I'm so
sorry about Daniel, Marilyn. I know you two were
friendly.'

Marilyn sucked in her lower lip, fighting back
fresh tears.

'Claire and I just came down to see if we could help. Once the police get here and everyone wakes up, it's going to get complicated.'

'We're all in shock,' Desiree said, stating the obvious.

Marilyn plucked a fresh tissue out of the box that sat on the counter in front of her. She dabbed at her eyes. 'Just give me a minute. I'll be all right.'

While we waited for Marilyn to regain her composure, Desiree took us at our word about helping. She presented Claire with a serrated knife, shoved a basket of grapefruit in her direction and got her started on halving and sectioning the fruit. My job was to lay out slices of bacon in single layers on a cookie sheet. 'We bake it at four-fifty for twenty minutes,' Desiree explained. 'Eliminates the excitement of getting grease spit in your eye.'

In the meantime, Desiree filled a large crystal bowl with ice and began nestling cartons of Noosa Australian-style full-fat yogurt into it – strawberry-rhubarb, mango-peach and, incredibly, pineapple-jalapeno. Although locally sourced from Colorado cows, you knew the recipe came from Down Under because they spelled it 'yoghurt' on the label.

Eventually, Marilyn slid off the bar stool. Still wearing her kimono, she crossed over to the gas range and began stirring raw oatmeal into a pot of boiling water. I'd finished with the bacon by then, so I said, 'I'm sure you've got plenty to do. Why don't you let me stir that for you?'

Marilyn smiled gratefully and surrendered the

95

wooden spoon. Our eyes locked. The last time we'd been standing at the stove together, Daniel had been standing beside us. Thinking about the cannabutter, I said, 'Daniel seemed very sweet on you, Marilyn.'

Marilyn's face collapsed, tears coursed down her cheeks. 'Noooh!' she wailed, and fled.

Desiree threw down the dishtowel she'd been using to dry her hands and scowled. 'Thanks heaps, Hannah. After I just calmed her down. Do *you* want to cook breakfast for a dozen people?'

'I'm so sorry,' I said, wondering what on earth had set Marilyn off. She'd only recently met the man. 'Of course I'd like to help,' I said.

By the time Marilyn reappeared, dressed in black slacks and a crisp white blouse, Desiree, Claire and I had set out a simple breakfast buffet for the early birds in the dining room. Marilyn, her eyelids still puffy, tied on an apron, assured us in no uncertain terms that it was back to business as usual, and shoed us out of her kitchen.

Our exile lasted as far as the dining room, where Austin sat by himself at the head of the table, eating yogurt one thoughtful spoonful at a time.

'Might as well join me,' he said, waving his spoon. 'The police are here.'

I popped half an English muffin into the retro-style toaster and pushed the lever down. 'They'll want to talk to us, I suppose.'

'Is the Pope Catholic?' He snickered. 'Does a chicken use foul language? Does a bear . . .?'

Desiree cut him off in mid-meme with a friendly bop to the side of his head.

'Ouch!' he said, but he was smiling.

Claire helped herself to half a grapefruit, poured honey over the top and sat down. By the time my muffin popped up, brown and hot, she was sharing our concerns about Daniel with the Nortons.

'We don't think he was really a college professor,' Claire said.

'And his name might not even be Daniel Fischel,' I added as I joined them at the table.

'Many of our guests are looking for anonymity,' Desiree said. 'I'm sure you can appreciate that. Cannatourists tend to skew older. The average age is . . .' She turned to her husband. 'What would you say, Austin? Fifty to eighty?'

Austin grunted. I guessed that meant 'yes.'

'More conservative, certainly,' Desiree continued. 'Other states aren't as enlightened about marijuana as Colorado.'

'I hope to change that in Maryland,' Claire said.

Austin toasted her with his empty yogurt cup. 'Here's to Maryland, then.'

'When Daniel checked in, how did he pay?' I asked, thinking his real name would have been on the credit card.

Desiree shrugged and consulted her husband.

'Fischel paid in cash,' Austin informed us, 'so there's no credit-card information, if that's what you're thinking.'

'Dang,' I said. 'So you have no idea who he really is?'

'We take our guests at their word,' Desiree said.

97

'If what he wrote in the guest book is accurate, he's Daniel Fischel from Atlanta, Georgia.'

Claire rolled her eyes as if to say that's a helluva way to do business, but thankfully she kept her thoughts to herself.

'It's really not so unusual for a guest to pay in cash,' Austin explained. 'As long as marijuana remains against federal law, cannatourism will be largely an all-cash operation.'

'How about Colin McDaniel? Did he pay in cash, too?' I asked, fairly certain that I knew the answer.

'Yup,' Austin said. 'Not sure where that boy's from, but you just gotta look at him to know he's not a regular stoner.'

Thinking about the conservative Arkansas college where they both taught, I asked, 'And Josh and Lisa?'

Austin shook his head. 'Credit card.'

He checked his watch, threw his head back and blew air out through his lips in a long, slow stream. 'It's only seven o'clock, but, hell, it feels like noon.'

Austin pushed his chair away from the table, then fixed his eyes on Claire. 'If the police don't get in the way, are we still on for a chat at nine-thirty?'

Claire nodded. 'Where shall we meet?'

Austin waved toward the back of the house. 'My office. Know where that is?'

'I do,' I said. 'Marilyn pointed it out when she was showing me one of her cookbooks.'

'Great.' He stood, gave Desiree's shoulder an affectionate pat, then left us to finish eating.

I served myself a bowl of oatmeal, pressed a

pat of butter into the center with my thumb and topped it with brown sugar. I was pouring half and half into the bowl, making a creamy moat, when Hugh burst into the room, rubbing his hands together. 'Morning, morning, everyone! What's for breakfast today?'

Desiree waved an arm, indicating the buffet. 'Help yourself. I imagine Marilyn will be out in a minute or two if you want to place a special order.'

'Great, great, don't mind if I do,' he boomed. He grabbed a plate off the stack and began loading it up with bacon. Phyllis wandered in looking fresh and pretty in white jeans and a pale pink sweater. 'Hugh?' she said, tugging at his sleeve to get his attention. 'Hugh?'

'What is it, my dear?'

'There's a police car out front. And an ambulance.'

'I'd love an omelet.'

'Ambulance,' Phyllis repeated, raising her voice and standing on tiptoe to better reach his ear. 'And a police car.'

Hugh's plate tilted downward at a dangerous angle. 'Why? What's happened?'

Desiree gently explained the situation, carefully avoiding, for the moment, any suggestion that Daniel's death hadn't been from natural causes.

'Unbelievable,' Phyllis exclaimed. 'He seemed so jolly when we came in last night, talking, laughing, singing songs with that young man.'

'*Carpe diem*,' her husband said, and helped himself to more bacon.

Ten

*I am very glad to hear that the Gardener
has saved so much of the St foin seed, and
that of the India Hemp. Make the most you
can of both, by sowing them again in drills
. . . Let the ground be well prepared, and
the Seed (St foin) be sown in April. The
Hemp may be sown anywhere.*

George Washington to William Pearce,
24 February, 1794.

Although smoking pot was perfectly legal in
the city, after the police arrived at Bell House,
perhaps out of habit, most guests made themselves
scarce.

Some dawdled over breakfast in the dining
room, especially after Marilyn declared it a 'wake
and bake' morning and brought out the magic
muffins wearing their festive flowered skirts.
Others retreated to their rooms to read or watch
television, waiting to be called down for an interview. Others, perhaps in the grip of cabin fever,
eventually ventured outside to smoke on the
garden patio, a luxury not afforded to me or to
Claire, who had discovered Daniel's body and
were first on Detective Joseph Jacobs' hit list. I
didn't envy Jacobs the job, interviewing folks
who were either sleep-deprived, stoned or both.

Through Austin, we learned that the crime-scene technician had estimated the time of death at between one and two in the morning, subject to confirmation by the medical examiner. Armed with that knowledge, as folks appeared for breakfast and were informed of the unpleasant situation, we compared alibis.

Desiree alibied for Austin and Austin for Desiree. Both snored, apparently, turning their night into a jab-fest.

Lisa had been sleeping soundly, her husband claimed, while he FaceTimed a colleague in Hong Kong for an article they were writing on olfactory reception in *Drosophila melanogaster*, or the common fruit fly. That would be easy enough for the police to confirm, I figured. The FaceTime call, not the fruit fly's schnoz.

Mark claimed he had had a migraine. He'd dragged himself to the solarium where he'd self-medicated with a little Blue Dream before saying goodnight to Cindy and retreating to their room.

The Grahams had returned to Bell House around twelve-thirty, both agreed on that, stopping by the solarium to pick up more water before heading up to bed.

After his late night, Colin must have been sleeping it off because, magic muffins or not, he never appeared for breakfast.

And we all knew where Claire had passed the evening.

Claire was summoned from the dining room first. 'Break a leg,' I told her.

As she passed my chair, she grabbed my hand. 'You're coming with me.'

I swallowed hard. 'Is that allowed?'

'I don't care if it's allowed or not,' she said, tugging me to my feet. 'I'm a politician. I never talk to anyone without a witness.' Considering the fiasco that was Washington, DC at the moment, I could hardly blame her.

Jacobs stood when we entered the sitting room, every inch the seasoned professional from short-cropped brownish hair and loosely-knotted tie down to his brown cordovan shoes.

'Your name?' he asked Claire after we got settled.

'Claire Thompson. Thompson with a P.'

'And you are?' Serious blue eyes behind fashionable aviator frames bore into mine.

'Hannah Ives.'

His eyes narrowed. 'So, why are you two joined at the hip?'

Claire put on her politician's face, openly friendly but serious. 'We're part of a delegation.'

'A delegation?' He made a notation in a pocket-sized, spiral-top notebook.

'That's correct. From Maryland. I'm a state senator, and we're looking into the legalization of recreational pot.'

'Representative Mark King is part of our delegation, too,' I volunteered.

Jacobs' head popped up. 'The linebacker?'

'That's right,' I said.

'Ah. I read that he'd gone into politics. Always wondered what made him quit football when he was at the top of his game.'

'Injuries, I believe,' Claire said.

'A shame,' Jacobs said. 'I remember him in the playoffs. Oh, man!' He whistled. 'Recovered that

102

forced fumble and ran it ninety yards for the touchdown! Classic.'

Jacobs cleared his throat and studied me speculatively. 'So . . . your role is?'

That stumped me for a moment. What exactly *was* I doing there, other than taking notes and holding Claire Thompson's hand?

'Consultant,' I blurted, figuring it was as good a title as any. 'With legalization,' I babbled on, slipping seamlessly into my role as consultant, 'has Denver seen an increase in crime?'

'It's not my division,' Jacobs pointed out, not seeming to mind the interruption from the task at hand. 'But, from what I read, crime is actually down overall. Court dockets were crowded enough without overloading them with petty drug offenders. Leaves Narcotics time to go after the kingpins – the guys who traffic in the hard stuff.'

Being a professional and not easily sidetracked, Jacobs quickly switched gears. He walked Claire through her account of the previous evening, paying particular attention to the comings and goings of bud-and-breakfast guests to the solarium, although Claire, no surprise, was a little fuzzy on the timeline.

Me, not so much.

Those disconcerting blue eyes were staring at me again. 'So, Mrs Ives, you came downstairs at approximately three-oh-six, I understand?'

'Exactly three-oh-six,' I said.

He arched an eyebrow.

'Digital clock,' I explained.

'Ah. And you found Claire and Daniel alone in the solarium?'

'That's right.'

'Did you notice anything unusual?' Pen poised over the notebook, Jacobs was ready to write.

'Other than Fischel being dead, no.'

Jacob's head shot up. 'Fischel? Who's he?'

'The dead guy,' Claire squeaked. 'Professor Daniel Fischel. From Atlanta, Georgia.'

Jacobs' eyes ping-ponged from Claire to me and back again. 'That's not what his driver's license says.'

I felt like snapping my fingers and exclaiming, 'Ah ha! Just as I suspected!' but wisely thought better of it. 'It isn't?' I said, widening my eyes to appear as shocked as possible.

'And he's not from Atlanta, Georgia, either. According to the state of North Carolina, the victim's name is Daniel Morecroft-Hill. Does that name mean anything to you?'

'No,' I said, quite honestly. 'Ever heard of him, Claire?' My fingers itched to Google the name, but that would have to wait until after the interview was over and I could retrieve my cell phone from upstairs.

Jacobs turned his attention back to Claire. After ascertaining that Mr Morecroft-Hill was a stranger to her, too, he said, 'So, Miss Thompson, let's go over it again, please. Who was in the solarium when you, uh, dozed off?'

'Colin and Daniel. The Grahams came back from their dinner around midnight, as I said before, but stayed just long enough to pick up some bottled water and say hi.'

'So, Colin and Daniel.'

'That's right.'

'Does Colin have a last name?'

104

'Last name?' Claire started to snigger. Damn, was the woman stoned?

'Claire?' I said. 'Are you all right?'

Claire gave me the evil eye. 'Daniel and McDaniel. I never thought of that before. It just struck me as funny, is all.'

High-larious.

'When did Colin leave the solarium?' Jacobs wanted to know.

Claire shrugged. 'I have absolutely no idea.'

'Anyone else come in?'

'Could have, but I wouldn't have noticed.'

Jacobs looked up from his notes. 'Is Colin in the dining room?'

Once again, Claire and I exchanged glances.

I spoke for the two of us. 'He could be by now, I suppose, but we didn't see him at breakfast.'

Jacobs looked at me. 'I have a few more questions for Miss Thompson here, Mrs Ives, but I'd like to talk to this Colin . . .' He glanced at his notes. 'McDaniel. Can you track him down for me?'

I hesitated. If I agreed, Claire would be left without a witness.

She must have been reading my mind. 'It's OK, Hannah. I'll be fine.'

I got to my feet, then smiled at the man agreeably. 'Sure. If he's not in the dining room, I'll check his room.'

As I left the room in search of Colin, I heard Claire ask, 'Will we be able to leave as planned on Tuesday?'

Jacobs grunted. 'Don't worry about it, Miss Thompson. We'll know where to find you.'

Colin was not in the dining room. When I checked

the patio, I found Mark and Cindy stretched out in Adirondack chairs, smoking. When I asked if they'd seen Colin, Cindy gazed at me with languid eyes, took a moment to focus and said, 'Not since last night.'

So I trotted upstairs and knocked lightly on the young man's door.

There was no answer.

I pounded harder, calling out his name.

Colin was either not in his room, wasted or dead. Under the circumstances, I felt it wise to determine which, so I trotted back downstairs to find Desiree.

I interrupted our hostess in the middle of loading plates into a dishwasher the size of a golf cart; she didn't seem to mind. Together, we went up to Colin's room and tried knocking again.

'Maybe he's in the bathroom?' I suggested.

Desiree made a fist and pounded on the door. 'Colin McDaniel! Open up!'

When Colin still didn't answer, she got out her passkey and yelled, 'I'm coming in!'

Colin's bed was neatly made. Naval Academy discipline was strict – beds always had to pass inspection – but who makes their bed when there's a maid to do it? I figured Colin hadn't gone to bed at all. The wardrobe, when I inspected it, contained only empty hangers.

Desiree emerged from the bathroom, shaking her head. 'Gone. Poof!'

'I hope he paid in advance,' I said.

'His loss, our gain,' she said. 'But it is curious.'

'More suspicious than curious,' I said. 'The timing stinks.'

Desiree waited until I was out in the hall, then closed the door firmly behind us. 'Daniel gets murdered and Colin disappears, you mean? Coincidence? I think not.'

'I'm sure the police will look into it,' I said, thinking – no – praying that Colin had taken the advice I'd given him the day before and simply packed up his things and gone home.

At the bottom of the staircase, we ran into Austin. He'd showered – his ponytail dangled wet over one shoulder – and changed into a T-shirt from what I now gathered was an extensive collection. Borrowing a familiar meme, this one said, 'KEEP CALM, IT'S JUST A PLANT.'

'Colin McDaniel's skipped out,' Desiree informed her husband.

Austin bobbed his head toward the sitting room. 'Better tell Jacobs.'

'Tell Jacobs what?' someone growled.

The owner of the voice was Jacobs himself, just emerging from the powder room under the stairs, adjusting his belt. Apparently he had finished interviewing Claire.

Desiree flinched and pressed a hand flat against her chest. 'Gosh, you scared me to death.'

'Sorry, ma'am.' He turned to Austin. 'You were saying?'

'It may be a coincidence,' Austin told the detective, 'but one of our guests, Colin McDaniel, seems to have checked out prematurely.'

'I expect you have contact information for him.' Austin and Desiree exchanged glances.

'Uh . . .' Austin began.

Jacobs frowned. 'Don't tell me you don't.'

Desiree cut in. 'We have the address he wrote down when he checked in, but he paid for the weekend with cash, so I don't have any credit-card information.'

Jacobs clicked his tongue. 'Give me what you have, then.' After a moment, he added, 'I notice you have security cams. Are they in operation?'

Austin bristled. 'Of course. Twenty-four seven. With all that cash coming and going, we'd be crazy not to. There's one out front and two in the back.'

'We'll need the tapes.'

'No problem. My security people will see that you get them.'

'Who are your security people?' Jacobs wanted to know.

Austin named the company, then added, 'We have daily cash deliveries from the weedery, and weekly to the co-op, but the guards don't stay on the premises.'

'Are they here today?' Jacobs asked.

'It's Sunday,' Desiree pointed out.

'Yesterday,' Austin clarified. 'They brought the day's proceeds to the house in the late afternoon.'

Ah, Nick and Borys, the Pawlowski twins. I'd run into 'those boys' myself around five, as I recalled. 'I met them yesterday,' I said, sticking in my oar. 'If I had robbery in mind, I wouldn't want to tangle with either one of them.'

Austin formed his hand into a gun, then blew 'smoke' off his index finger. 'Ex-Army Rangers.'

'Austin, why do you keep all that money here on the property?' I asked.

Austin smiled indulgently, as if amused by my naivety. 'I'll explain it all shortly.'

'Nine-thirty, right?' I wanted to confirm that, in spite of all that had happened, his meeting with Claire and me was still on.

'In my office.' He checked his watch. 'Ten minutes.'

Detective Jacobs made a hurry-up motion with his hand. 'If you all don't mind, I'd like to speak to the Grahams next.' He paused. 'And Mr Norton? I'll take that information on McDaniel whenever you have a minute.'

'Desiree will make sure you get it,' Austin said, glancing quickly at his wife, who nodded. 'Anything else I can do for you, Detective?'

I'd obviously been dismissed, so I hurried off to locate Claire.

Eleven

XI. Concerning Gnats. If you also lay a sprig of green hemp in blossom near you, when you are going to sleep, gnats will not touch you.

The Geoponica: Agricultural Pursuits. Translated from the Greek by Rev. T. Owen, London, 1805.

It's a good thing I had convinced Claire to pass on the magic muffins. Keeping up with Austin's discussion on the financial aspects of running a successful weedery required our undivided attention. No way one could do it stoned.

The Pawlowski brothers were fresh on my mind, so as we settled into chairs in Austin's office – a spacious, dark-paneled room with track lighting and library shelving that extended to the ceiling, I asked, 'So, how come you risk bringing the money here? From what we saw yesterday, the weedery could withstand a nuclear attack. Surely money's safer there than here.'

'Convenience, really, as you shall see,' he explained. 'We require security at the weedery as well, of course. We have bags of pot, bags of cash. It's a disaster waiting to happen. Once or twice we got followed home.' He leaned back in his chair, propped his feet up on the antique desk and grinned good-naturedly. 'But nobody messes with the Pawlowskis, as you wisely noted, Hannah.'

'So it's cash – all cash?' Claire said.

'Yup.'

'Can buyers use credit cards?'

'Nope. We've got two ATMs at the weedery for the convenience of our customers, but that's as close as we're allowed to get to a regular bank.'

'How astonishing,' I said.

'Because growing and selling marijuana is still a federal crime,' Austin continued, 'no federally-insured bank is going to touch pot money. If they do, they risk being charged with drug racketeering.'

'Sounds like a catch-22,' I said.

'You bet. And here's another catch. I have to

pay taxes on that income. By doing so, I admit that I'm violating federal law. How do you spell self-incrimination?' He snorted. 'Can't even plead the Fifth. But if I don't report the income, they can send me to jail for tax evasion. That's how the feds got Al Capone.'

'He didn't fare well in prison, as I recall,' Claire said.

Austin snorted. 'Cocaine will do that to you. Look,' he continued, putting his feet down and leaning forward over the pale gray desk blotter, 'marijuana growers like me have to pay their bills and meet payroll, just the same as any other business. In the beginning, some smaller banks were willing to handle financial services for pot shops if we didn't talk about it too much. They didn't want to be brought up on money laundering charges. Then the feds started rattling sabers – busted some totally legit medical grows out in California – and the banks started getting cold feet and pulling out. It wasn't until 2014 when Colorado passed the Marijuana Financial Services Cooperatives Act that we got some relief.'

'Co-ops?' I asked. 'How does that work?'

'They're more like credit unions than banks. But, according to the law, they can't *call* themselves a bank or a credit union. Yet they have to have access to the Federal Reserve System in order to be licensed. Go figure.'

'Do you belong to a co-op?'

Austin nodded. 'Happy Daze and eleven other growers. It's working fine so far. But you want to know another dumb-ass thing?'

I'd been scribbling furiously, but I looked up

at that point. Dumb-ass things were always fascinating.

Austin aimed the eraser end of a pencil at the blotter and brought it down hard, emphasizing each of his points. 'The co-op has to disclose that it's subject to federal seizure, that the money is not federally insured and that Colorado will not defend the co-op if its assets do get seized.'

'What a deal,' Claire commented dryly. 'I'm wondering how we can avoid that in Maryland.'

'Until the feds loosen up, it's going to stay a game of clever workarounds for everyone.' He flipped the pencil into a beer stein, where it rattled around and settled down with half-a-dozen others. 'I'll give you an example. IRS Code 280E.'

Claire raised a finger to interrupt. 'It's on the tip of my tongue, but . . .?'

Austin laughed. '280E covers expenditures in connection with the illegal sale of drugs. They actually have a rule for it! Anyway,' he continued, 'according to 280E, I can't deduct the cost of rent, advertising or payroll like any other business can, but I *can* deduct the cost of growing marijuana under the category Cost of Goods Sold. How crazy is *that*?'

Claire and I agreed that it was nutty.

'But you wanna know a good thing? We don't fuss about it too much because all these silly rules are keeping Big Tobacco, Big Alcohol and Big Pharma out of the competition. At least for now.'

'That brings us back around to why you're keeping the cash here,' I said.

'As I mentioned earlier – convenience. The co-op is in the city. I'll be making the deposit on Monday, escorted by security.'

I must have looked skeptical.

'You think I stuff cash under a mattress, Hannah? Keep it in the deep freeze?' He laughed. 'We've got a safe. Let me show you.'

Austin rose to his feet and walked around the desk, pausing in front of a curtained alcove. He grabbed the curtain, a lush red velvet fabric that hung from a brass rod on brass rings, and pulled it aside. *'Voila!'*

Nestled in the alcove behind the curtain, half-hidden in the dark, was an antique safe about thirty inches high and twenty inches wide, the size of a small refrigerator. 'It's original to the house,' Austin told us. 'Fannie's husband was a jeweler. Kept lots of gems on hand.'

Austin reached up and flipped a switch, bathing the safe in warm, museum-style light.

'It's a beauty,' I said truthfully.

Austin's safe was painted fire-engine red. Raised gold lettering announced that it had been manufactured by the Tucker Safe & Lock Company in Cincinnati, Ohio in the year 1892. A painting of a sailboat decorated the door; seashells adorned each corner.

'Nobody's going to crack this baby!' Austin declared, patting the top of his safe like a proud father. 'No electronics. Sometimes you can get too fancy, you know.'

I had to agree. My sister's washing machine had more buttons than the Starship Enterprise. She could steam her cottons, sanitize her towels.

Mine had just three settings: wash, rinse and spin. Less to go wrong that way.

As Austin extolled the virtues of nineteenth-century safe technology, I had visions of bad guys dressed in black, stethoscopes hanging from their ears, squatting in front of that little beauty, spinning the dial, listening to the tumblers click into place.

'Couldn't someone just pick it up and haul it away?' Claire wondered.

'No way.' Austin snorted. 'It's lined with concrete. Must weigh a thousand pounds. One of the reasons we kept it, actually. Couldn't move it if we tried.' He stamped his foot on the carpet. 'It sits on a metal plate over a reinforced floor.

'I had it completely restored,' he continued. 'Cost me a bundle.'

'On the inside as well?' I asked.

'Inside, outside, top and bottom. Would you like to see?'

We said we would.

Austin stooped. His back blocked our view as he twisted the numbered brass dial – right, left and right again – and pulled down on the brass handle.

The door swung wide.

I leaned forward for a better view.

The top half of the safe had three drawers – for Fannie's hatpins, brooches, necklaces, bracelets, rings and tiaras, I imagined – and the bottom consisted of two shelves lined with green felt.

Austin fell to his knees, stuck his hand inside the safe, pulled out a packet of documents tied up in string and threw it aside. 'Damn!'

He thrust both hands into the safe, pawing

114

through the remaining contents: a red rope expanding folder, a military medal in a clear plastic case and a yellow tobacco tin with a cupid on the front joined the pile growing next to him on the carpet. 'Damn, damn, damn!'

'What's wrong?' Claire asked, and then stated the obvious. 'Something's missing.'

'It's impossible!' Austin said, head down, his voice muffled.

He sat back on his heels and turned a worried face in our direction. 'The money's gone.'

'All of it?' I asked.

He nodded forlornly. 'The whole damn satchel.'

'How much was in it?' Claire asked.

'Nearly two hundred thousand.'

'Good Lord!' Claire said. 'What will you do?'

Austin leaned back against the open safe, closed his eyes and massaged his temples with his fingers. 'How the hell will I make payroll?'

'The security guards came in with a satchel around half past five last night,' I offered. 'Was that the satchel you're talking about?'

'You bet.'

'Who did they give the satchel to?' I asked.

'Me, of course. They call when they get to the house and I meet them in my office.'

'Do the security guards have the combination?'

Austin looked at me like I'd lost my marbles. 'Good Lord, no. Not even Desiree knows the combination.'

'But what if something happens to you?' Claire asked reasonably.

He shrugged. 'She'll have to hire a professional safecracker, I guess.'

Austin stood up and wiped his hands nervously on his jeans. When he reached for his phone, I sidled in for a closer look at the safe. There seemed to be no obvious signs of tampering. Either somebody was a clever safecracker indeed or they had known the combination.

We watched silently as Austin punched numbers into his phone. 'Who are you calling?' Claire asked.

'The goddam security company. They need to get their asses over here PDQ.' He covered the microphone with his hand. 'One of you go see if Detective Jacobs is still here. If this doesn't have something to do with Fischel's murder, I'll eat my hat, leather tie, fishing lures and all.'

Twelve

At El Paso, a peon came across the International Bridge firing a rifle at all and sundry. Much talk against the Americans and a dose of Marahuana had decided him to invade the United States by himself. The bridge-keeper quickly put a bullet into the poor wretch.

Emily F. Murphy, 'Janey Canuck',
The Black Candle, Toronto,
Thomas Allen, 1922, p.333.

Detective Jacobs, Desiree, Claire and I observed in respectful silence as the man we knew as Daniel

116

Fischel left the building, feet first, via the front door. I held my tongue as his covered body was slotted into the rear of a bright white ambulance and spirited away, presumably to the medical examiner's office in downtown Denver.

Jacobs moved toward the open door and appeared about to head out after the ambulance, so I opened my mouth and brought him up short. 'There's been a robbery,' I announced matter-of-factly.

'What?' Desiree's shriek split the air.

Jacobs' blue-gray eyes remained steady. While Desiree seemed to be coming to pieces, he regarded me calmly.

'The Happy Daze payroll,' I said, gesturing toward the kitchen. 'Austin sent us to find you.'

Desiree took off like a sprinter.

'It's quite a lot of money, I'm afraid,' Claire said, eyeing our departing hostess. 'But, if you don't mind, I have some calls I need to make.' She took two steps back and bowed slightly, clearing a path for the officer. 'I'll be in my room, Hannah.'

At his request, I escorted Jacobs into the kitchen, where Marilyn stood at a counter deftly slicing cucumbers. She looked up, knife poised over the cutting board. 'Can I help . . .?' Then, after a moment, perhaps in response to our grim faces: 'Why, what's happened now?'

I held up a finger in an I'll-tell-you-in-a-minute kind of way and, leaving her puzzled face in my rearview mirror, pushed through the door that led into the back hallway with Jacobs hard on my heels.

117

Austin sat where we'd left him, elbows on the desk, forehead propped on an open palm as if deep in thought. Desiree stood quietly behind him, a hand resting on her husband's shoulder. The safe still yawned open.

'Norton?' Jacobs said.

Austin seemed to shake himself awake, shivering like a wet dog. A vape pen now lay on the blotter. My bet? He'd been sucking on it to ease the tension. 'Can the day get any worse?' he said.

'Tell me about it,' Jacobs replied with a pointed look at me. It telegraphed plain as day: *Thanks, Hannah, you can go now.*

Reluctantly, I took the hint. 'I'll leave you to it, then. If you need me, I'll be up in my room.'

After Jacobs closed the office door behind me, I briefly considered lurking around outside, spying in the old-fashioned way with a drinking glass pressed between my ear and the door. But I was eager to log on to my laptop and see what I could find out about Daniel Fischel, aka Daniel Morecroft-Hill. If the Bell House crime wave continued at the current rate, I'd discover the man's true identity before Detective Joseph Jacobs did, unless he already had his people working on it.

On the way to my room, I stopped in the kitchen to bring Marilyn up to date, as promised. She had finished with the cucumbers and was using an old-fashioned peeler to convert a carrot into a pile of decorative curls. I pulled out a stool and cozied up to her at the counter. Before saying anything, I snitched a carrot curl and popped it into my mouth. 'May I?'

'You already did.' She considered me for a moment, then added, 'So, what's going on in there?'

'The safe's been robbed.'

Marilyn dropped the peeler. It seemed to leap from her hand to skid away, spinning, clattering, across the spotless tile floor. 'What? But that's impossible.'

'Impossible or not,' I said, 'it happened. Maybe there's a Houdini among the guests.'

'Not funny, Hannah.'

'I'm sorry. That was insensitive of me.'

Marilyn stared at me for so long without saying anything that I grew uncomfortable. I wished I could read her mind. 'This looks really good,' I said in an attempt to crack the ice. 'Is it lunch?'

That elicited a smile – lackluster, but I'd take it. 'Yes,' she said. 'Once I've added tomatoes, it'll be finished with a lightly infused basil pesto dressing, to accompany the broccoli-and-cannabis quiche.'

'Sounds delicious,' I said, helping myself to another plain, unenhanced carrot curl. 'Is there anything for the guests who don't do edibles?'

'Of course,' Marilyn said with measured patience, as if she'd answered the question a hundred times, which she probably had. 'I always try to accommodate the dietary needs of our guests, no matter how peculiar. Vegan, vegetarian, lactose-free, gluten-free, peanut allergies . . .' She sighed wearily. 'Everybody's got some sort of restriction these days. Had a couple last month that ate only raw foods.' Marilyn bent down to retrieve her runaway peeler. When she straightened up, she said, 'Answer me this: are olives raw food?'

I pondered the question for a moment. 'Only if they're not canned?'

She rinsed the peeler under the hot-water tap and shook it dry. 'A point scored for you, Hannah Ives.

'But, you were asking me about edibles,' she continued. 'I always prepare cannabis-free versions of the dishes. I need to eat, and so does the housekeeper. It may surprise you to know that I don't partake of my own infusions.'

Actually, that didn't surprise me. As chef, she had a job to do. I suppressed a grin, imagining a stoned chef careening around the kitchen, brandishing an oversized carving knife and toodleing 'Save the liver!' like a *Saturday Night Live* television skit. 'That's probably just as well,' I said, returning to the kitchen at hand. 'You wouldn't want to mistake the salt for the sugar.'

'There really isn't any danger of overdosing, you know,' Marilyn said with Martha Stewart-like cool. 'The infusions are, as I said, light, and the dinner meal is spread out over a considerable period of time. The worst that will happen is a pleasant buzz. You know what I like about it?' she added after a thoughtful pause. 'There's something for everybody. Mark King doesn't drink, you may have noticed, but his wife, Cindy, does. So by coming here, they can both enjoy themselves.'

'Maybe you've talked me into it,' I said cautiously.

'After all that's happened today, I could totally use the full Happy Daze Experience.'

Marilyn beamed. 'You won't be sorry.' After a moment, she added in a more serious tone, 'Do you think that Daniel's death and this robbery are connected?'

'It seems a highly unlikely coincidence.'

She shook her head. 'It's just so hard to take in.'

'Other than Austin,' I said, quickly moving past the tear-inducing potential of Daniel Fischel, 'who do you think might have the combination to the safe?'

'Gosh, no one. Austin guards it like it's the Hope Diamond or something.'

'Not even the security people?'

'*Especially* the security people.' She began to decorate the rim of the platter with carrot curls. 'Everybody thinks just because Austin dresses like a hippie and grows weed that he has to be laid-back and chill. He is, about most things, but he's positively obsessed with that safe. Not even Desiree knows the combination.'

'That's what Austin told me, but I didn't really believe him.'

'Oh, it's true all right.' Wielding the peeler, she attacked another carrot. 'And he changes the combination every week or so. Makes a big production out of it.'

'Really? You can do that? That safe is over one hundred years old.'

'Oh, absolutely you can. It never would have worked for old Fannie Bell, the original owner, otherwise.' She paused, mid-curl. 'She outlived three husbands, Hannah, and it was all her money, not theirs. No way she was going to give them access to it.'

'So, how do you do it?' I asked, genuinely curious. 'Change the combination, that is?'

Marilyn shrugged. 'Dunno. But Austin does it for sure. Shuts everyone out of his office. Takes a bit of time, too. You'll have to ask him.'

I said I would.

'She lived to be ninety-eight,' Marilyn said dreamily.

'Who? Fannie?'

A sly grin crept over the chef's face. 'Fortunately, while on her deathbed, Fannie gave her grand-daughter the combination. The woman had been hovering around for days, fetching and toting, sucking up to Fannie. She expected jewels, I think, or piles of cash, but when she opened the safe she was sorely disappointed.'

Finished with the carrots, Marilyn selected a plump, ripe tomato from a bowl, steadied it on the cutting board and began slicing it thinly.

'So what was in Fannie's safe?' I asked. 'It's cruel to keep me in suspense!'

Marilyn kept slicing. 'All she found were love letters, tied up in bundles. Greedy bitch was fifty years old, waiting all that time for Granny to die, and all she got was a bunch of old letters.' After a moment, she added, 'She got Bell House, though. Then Desiree's dad bought it from her.'

I flashed back to a horrific train wreck in Washington, DC and to a box of love letters that had accidentally fallen into my hands, changing my life and the lives of several other people forever. 'What happened to the letters, Marilyn?'

'I heard they went to the Denver Public Library's western history archives,' she said. 'But that was a long time ago.'

Marilyn had finished with the tomatoes. She tipped the knife and the cutting board into the sink, then headed for the refrigerator. As she rummaged around the top shelf, muttering to herself and looking for something, I took the time to read the day's menu written on the chalkboard. The quiche and veggies lunch was purposely light, I figured, because of the no-holds-barred, five-course gourmet dinner scheduled for that evening as part of our package. *Arnold Palmers*, I read, followed by *Spinach/Strawberry Salad* and *Rib-Eye with Chile Relleno*. 'Is dinner still on?' I wondered aloud as my eyes skimmed to the bottom of the list: *Dark Chocolate Ganache Torte*. My stomach rumbled.

'Of course,' Marilyn said, emerging triumphant from the bowels of the refrigerator holding a jar of what looked like capers. 'All bought and paid for. We've never had to cancel a dinner, not even when the power went out during the blizzard last March.' After several unsuccessful attempts to unscrew the lid, she handed it to me. 'We had almost twenty inches of snow. In March!'

I wrapped my hand around the stubborn lid and gave it several savage twists. 'I was just wondering, because of Daniel . . .'

Marilyn's eyes glistened. She blinked rapidly. 'I'm sure he didn't suffer, Marilyn.'

She started to say something but a timer buzzed, making us both jump. 'The soup!' she exclaimed.

'We're having soup, too?' I asked, giving the caper jar another go. This time the lid turned easily.

'Cream of celery,' Marilyn called over her shoulder as she raced to the stove and twisted a knob. 'You'll try this, surely. Only ten milligrams of TCH in a serving. You'll hardly notice.'

I laughed. 'I think I need to keep my wits about me. Work to do, sadly.'

'A little pot can unlock your creativity,' Marilyn said, stirring the mixture slowly.

'It'd put me straight to sleep, Marilyn. I've been up since three.'

'Nothing a bit of *indica* couldn't cure. Ask Austin for some Grandaddy Purple. It'll help you rest.'

'I'll consider it,' I said, feeling my reserve weakening.

'And you wouldn't *dare* refuse my brownies.' She covered the soup with a lid and moved the stock pot to one side.

My experience with pot brownies was limited to the dry, crumbly version whipped up in Oberlin's Keep Cottage Co-op by my then boyfriend, Ron. They tasted like chocolate-covered grass clippings. As if reading my mind, Marilyn said, 'Mine are nothing like the Alice B. Toklas brownies of the sixties, Hannah. They're moist and fudgy. Contain actual chocolate, which Alice's definitely did not.' Her face flushed, either from modesty or the heat of the stove. 'They won first place at last year's Canna-Gro Expo.'

'Every cannabis chef needs a signature pot brownie, right?' I teased.

'Yes, indeed,' she agreed. 'Before Keebler gets his elves working on it.'

* * *

124

Up in my room, I could hear Claire talking on the phone. From the occasional word that drifted through the connecting bathroom doors, I gathered she was letting her administrative assistant know what had happened, coaching the woman in preparation of an official response should Daniel's death and Claire's connection to it hit the Baltimore–Washington local media.

I stuck my head through her bedroom door, waved to catch her eye and let her know I'd returned, then sat down at my desk and powered up my laptop.

With a double-barreled name like Daniel Morecroft-Hill, I figured the guy would be easy to find. I Googled his name inside quotation marks but came up empty. Searching without quotes provided some links, but all to some fictional characters in a cast list for an episode of *Midsomer Murders*.

A William Esselmont had married a woman named Mary Ann Morecroft Hill back in 1879, but clearly there was no connection to the late Daniel. I sat back. How could anybody in this day and age not have an Internet presence? My grandkids even showed up on the Internet thanks to their youth league soccer expertise. Either I was losing my touch, or Daniel Morecroft-Hill wasn't the man's real name, either.

While I was feeling disgusted with myself, Claire materialized behind me. 'All set,' she said. 'And I called my attorney, too.'

'A good plan,' I said, turning to study her over the tops of my reading glasses, a favorite pair of bright red Harry Potter circles. 'You look exhausted. Have a seat.'

Claire fell back wearily into the armchair.

'Are you OK?' I asked.

She flapped a hand. 'I'll live. What are you up to?'

I outlined my search strategy and reported on my lack of results.

'How's it spelled?' she asked.

I told her.

'Are you sure you're spelling Daniel's last name correctly?' she asked reasonably. 'Detective Jacobs didn't exactly write it down for you.'

'No, he didn't.'

'Then maybe it's Moorcroft with three Os. Or Moore, with an e.'

'Good idea!' I said, but the alternate spellings didn't pan out either.

I thought for a moment and said, 'Do you think it could be Morecraft, with an a?' My fingers flew over the keyboard as I spoke.

Daniel Morecraft-Hill didn't have a Wikipedia entry. He hadn't signed up for Facebook or LinkedIn or any other social media platform. And as far as I could tell, he didn't Tweet. But three screens in, the name Daniel Morecraft-Hill cropped up with a link to a document in the *Congressional Record*. I clicked on the PDF, drumming my fingers impatiently while it downloaded, glacier-like, over the laptop's cranky wireless connection. I swiveled in my chair to complain about sulky bandwidth to Claire, but she had dozed off.

When the document finally materialized, I drilled down, refining my search and scanning page after page of monotonous testimony until I found the reference.

126

I sat back, stunned. 'Holy cow!'

Behind me, Claire snorted and jolted awake. 'What?'

'Claire! Daniel's the enemy!'

Claire uncoiled and sprang from her chair like a cat. She leaned over my shoulder for a closer look.

'He's the enemy, Claire,' I said, tapping the entry. 'He's Mr Big Tobacco. This is the *Congressional Record* for last March. Daniel testified before Congress on the Ending Federal Marijuana Prohibition Act, a bipartisan bill introduced by a half-dozen Congressmen that would remove marijuana from the 1970 Controlled Substances Act.'

'Why does that make him the enemy?'

'His credentials. Check this out. Daniel Morecraft-Hill heads up – and I quote – research and development for Churchill-Mills Tobacco Company, a wholly-owned subsidiary of a multinational conglomerate called the Nepenthe Group.'

Thirteen

I dreamed about a reefer five feet long
Mighty Mizz but not too strong
You'll be high but not for long
If you a viper.

Leroy 'Stuff' Smith, 1937.

'What does it mean?' Claire asked me about half an hour later. Bell House was crawling with cops, so we'd retreated to the patio carrying bottles of juice that I hoped would hold us until lunchtime.

Jacobs had been joined by a colleague from the Robbery Unit of the Major Crimes Division. Both men were holed up with Austin and Desiree while their evidence technicians flitted around taking photos and dusting for prints everywhere except the insides of the toilet tanks. There, too, for all I knew.

What Claire and I had learned about Daniel from the Internet was that he oversaw a division of Churchill-Mills that had to do with 'New Tobacco Growth Platforms.' His people dealt with scientists and academic collaborators as well as contract farmers. Plant breeders worked for this man, and were expected to develop proprietary breeding lines and hybrids with commercial potential. They also contributed to the tobacco germplasm, which I gathered was some sort of tobacco seed bank maintained by the US Department of Agriculture somewhere in North Carolina. And he had a PhD in cell and molecular biology from Boston University. No wonder he looked like a professor.

I stretched out my legs, using a blue ceramic planter as a footstool. 'It means, my dear Claire, that Daniel Fischel was working undercover. He was a spy.'

'But what did he hope to learn?'

I studied the label on my juice bottle – Wacky Apple! Gluten free! – while I considered Claire's question. 'Trade secrets?' I suggested. 'When the federal government lifts the ban on marijuana, tobacco companies will want to hit the ground running. With a head start, Big Tobacco could easily force independent growers like Austin out of business.'

'I still don't understand why he used a fake name.'

'It is a puzzlement,' I said. 'Especially considering the difficulty I had finding information about him on the Internet.'

Claire took a sip of her cranberry juice. 'If he's so all-fired important, you'd think his name would be listed on the Churchill-Mills corporate webpage, wouldn't you?'

I had to agree. Surprisingly, the only names we found listed on the webpage were those of the company's CEO and Board of Directors. Except for the signatories, no names were mentioned in their annual reports either. Daniel had kept a low profile. If he hadn't provided his CV to Congress, we'd still be in the dark about his identity.

'So, are we working on the theory that someone at Bell House found out who he really was and killed him for it?' Claire asked.

While I considered her question, I drank slowly, savoring my organic ginger-apple juice. 'Can you think of a better explanation?'

'Nope.'

'It wouldn't trouble *me* to have a tobacco scientist tagging along on the tour,' I said.

'Me neither, Hannah. Frankly, I applaud his efforts to amend the Controlled Substances Act. Had I but known, I would have thumped the man on the back and bought him a drink.'

We sat in silence for a while, listening to a mourning dove's sweet song of lament. 'I don't know enough about the other guests to form an opinion,' I said, 'but in the motive department, it doesn't look good for Austin and Desiree Norton.'

'Are you going to tell Detective Jacobs that we figured out who the guy is?'

'I'm sure he already knows, Claire. He has Daniel's wallet with his driver's license and credit cards. He's got the guy's cell phone. I'm sure his people are way ahead of us on that.'

I'd finished my juice by then, so I crumpled the plastic bottle and screwed the cap back on, ready for recycling. 'They must be busy notifying his next of kin.'

'Ugh. I'd hate that.' After a moment, she said, 'Once a conglomerate like Churchill-Mills moves into the local market, all the little people will be forced out of business.'

'I'm not so sure about that,' I said. 'Using the tobacco industry business model, it's more likely that local growers would end up working for Churchill-Mills.'

'Maybe that's not part of Austin and Desiree's game plan. Maybe they won't want to work for The Man.'

'No matter how it shakes out after legalization,' I said, 'I think there'll always be a market for boutique companies like Happy Daze. Can you imagine Churchill-Mills hosting a weekend like this one?'

'It's certainly high-end,' she said, 'except for the murder, of course.'

'Mrs Ives?'

As if he'd been waiting in the wings, listening for his cue, Detective Jacobs' entrance made me jump. He'd arrived on the patio via a side gate, presumably coming directly from the tradesmen's entrance off the kitchen. 'I wonder if I might have a word.'

'Uh oh,' Claire murmured.

'Behave,' I whispered back. I composed my face into a mask of calm, then turned to answer him. 'Of course, Detective.'

Jacobs' khaki suit needed pressing, there was a mustard stain on his shirt, and if he was going for the designer stubble look, he was certainly succeeding. I gestured toward a nearby lounger. 'Would you be more comfortable sitting down?'

He ignored my invitation. 'I understand you spent some time talking to young McDaniel before dinner last night.'

'A few minutes, yes.'

'What can you tell me about that conversation?'

'Not much,' I said struggling to keep my gaze steady. I took a deep breath, stalling for time. 'Why do you ask?'

'The address McDaniel left with the B and B turns out to be bogus. Seems he used a fake ID.'

Instantly, I was back in the sitting room, standing in front of the fireplace, promising a distraught young midshipman: *If someone at the academy finds out you were doing dope in Denver, it will not be from me.*

Colin's disappearance so soon after Daniel's murder needed to be investigated, of course it did.

But getting involved with the police, even if Colin were innocent, would not be career-enhancing for him. I weighed how much I should tell the detective.

Above all, I mustn't lie.

'This and that,' I said at last. 'Colin was pretty psyched about being in a place where he could smoke pot and not get busted.' As I talked, I watched Jacobs' face, wondering if he could tell that I was holding something back.

'He said he came from Beaufort, South Carolina,' I added. 'Does that help?'

Jacob glanced from me to Claire and back again. 'Can you tell me what he looked like?'

Claire jumped in. 'He's about five-ten, buzz cut . . .' She stopped and raised her eyebrows as if a light bulb had gone off over her head. 'He'll show up on the security cams, of course, but we can do better than that! Austin took a photograph of our group, yesterday, before we toured the weedery. Colin will be the one standing next to me, wearing the droopy captain's hat.'

I held up a hand. 'You know what, Claire? I bet Detective Jacobs already has a picture of Colin.' I twisted in my chair, looked up and faced the detective squarely. 'It's probably in a plastic evidence bag, on Daniel's cell phone. Daniel wanted a picture of the group, too.'

'Ah,' Jacobs said. 'My technicians tell me the phone is password protected.'

'It's an iPhone Six. It uses fingerprint ID,' I said, feeling a chill scamper along my spine. 'All you need to unlock it is Daniel's thumb.'

Fourteen

All the bodily fatigue of the day,
all the preoccupation of mind which the
events of the evening had brought on,
disappeared as they do at the first
approach of sleep, when we are still
sufficiently conscious to be aware of
the coming of slumber. His body
seemed to acquire an airy lightness,
his perception brightened in a
remarkable manner, his senses seemed
to redouble their power, the horizon
continued to expand.

Alexandre Dumas, *The Count of Monte Cristo*, London, Chapman and Hall, 1846, v.1, p.235.

Alone at last in the solitude of my room, I settled into a chair, rested my hands on my knees and closed my eyes. I'd planned to meditate like my sister, Ruth, had taught me, but after several minutes of reciting my mantra, peace failed to come.

What had I just done? Obstructed justice for a kid I barely knew? What was I thinking?

And yet . . .

The Naval Academy holds midshipmen to high standards. They pledge allegiance to country and to an honor code that states, first and foremost, that 'Midshipmen are persons of integrity: they stand for that which is right. They tell the truth and ensure that the truth is known. They do not lie.'

Colin had made that pledge and, although I didn't know him well, I'd befriended a number of my husband's students over the years and I trusted them – and him – to do the right thing. I needed to get in touch with him, however. But how?

If school had been in session and I knew his room number – which I didn't – I could simply have dialed his room. Since the brigade had dispersed for the summer, I decided to call the main office in Bancroft Hall, the academy's only dormitory, an eight-winged, double-H-shaped building that housed all four-thousand-plus midshipmen during the academic year. Perhaps they could get a message to him.

When the midshipman officer of the day answered my call, I decided to play dumb.

'Oh, hi,' I began. 'I'm trying to reach Midshipman Colin McDaniel.'

I held my breath for a moment while he checked his records. After what Jacobs had told us about Colin's fake ID, I had the sudden, wild thought that the midshipman would say, 'I'm sorry, we have no Midshipman McDaniel listed,' but after a bit he came back on the line and told me that Midshipman McDaniel was on leave.

'Oh, dear,' I said, working a bit of a quaver into my voice. 'This is his Aunt Hannah. Colin's grandfather is gravely ill and I really need to contact him. Colin gave me his cell phone number at Christmas, but I'm afraid I lost the piece of paper I wrote it down on.'

'I'm sorry, ma'am,' he said, 'but I'm not allowed to give out phone numbers or email addresses without permission of the midshipman.'

'I quite understand, young man, I really do. But if I gave you *my* telephone number, would you pass it along to Colin and ask him to call *me*?'

'Yes, ma'am, I could do that.'

I gave him my number, spelled my name for him twice, thanked him and hung up.

Lunch would be in ten minutes, so I slipped into the bathroom to wash my hands. I was drying them on a towel when Colin called me back.

'Aunt Hannah?' he began. 'That gave me a good laugh. What's up?'

I didn't beat around the bush. 'Daniel Fischel died last night.'

'Oh, shit!'

'The police think he may have been murdered.'

'Man,' Colin said. 'That's bad.'

I took a deep breath and dived in. 'Did you kill him, Colin?'

'Me? No way.' His voice cracked. 'We were having a hell of a good time, Daniel and me, telling jokes, singing old rugby songs. For a professor, he was pretty cool.'

'Turns out, he's not a professor.'

'Get out!'

'He's a scientist, Colin. He does R and D for Churchill-Mills, a big tobacco company.'

'Damn.'

'Needless to say, the police are here right now

135

and they are treating your sudden disappearance as suspicious.'

He took a long, shuddering breath. 'If the guy's dead, I'm sure sorry, but I didn't have a thing to do with it, Mrs Ives. You gotta believe me.'

'Can you tell me what happened last night, after the rugby songs and stuff?'

'Yeah, sure. Daniel kinda dozed off, so I went up to my room. I took a long shower and gave what you told me a lot of thought. Decided to take your advice and clear out.'

'What time was that?'

'Gee, I don't know,' he said, panic in his voice. 'Wait a minute! I called an Uber, and they took me to the car rental place at the airport. Hold on.'

The phone went silent. I was beginning to worry that I'd lost the connection when Colin came back on the line. 'I just checked the Uber app. The guy picked me up at two-fifteen.'

'He can vouch for you, then,' I said reassuringly, but depending upon Daniel's actual time of death, it might not prove much in the way of an alibi.

'After I got the rental, I drove to—'

'Don't tell me!' I interrupted. 'It's best I don't know.'

'But . . .'

'Don't argue with me, Colin, just listen. The police will need to talk to you. Even if you didn't kill Daniel, you might have witnessed something, or noticed something that would point the finger in the direction of his killer.'

'I *swear* he was alive when I left him.'

'Was anyone else still in the room?'

'Just Senator Thompson, but she was asleep.

136

Mark and Cindy might have come in a bit earlier.' He paused. 'Crap, I don't know anything for sure. I was pretty wasted, knowing it was my last shot at pot for, like, years.'

'You need to come back, Colin.'

His voice grew suddenly wary. 'What did you tell them?'

'Nothing. When I make a promise, I keep it. But it puts me in an awkward situation. I can't lie to the police.'

'Jeesh, I don't know, Mrs Ives. If they rat me out to the academy . . .'

'Maybe they will and maybe they won't, but you are honor-bound to face up to your responsibility here.' I decided to twist the screws a little tighter. 'They have your photograph, Colin. Do you want to come back to Denver on your own terms, or wait until your picture gets plastered all over the Internet and there's an ABP out for your arrest?'

'Shit.'

'As someone once said, it's all messy. The hair, the bed, the heart . . . and life.'

Fifteen

The addict has delusions of persecution or of measureless grandeur. Speaking of the latter delusion, Dr Palmer writes that in India, under its influence, your servant is apt to make you a grand

137

salaam instead of a sandwich, and offer
you an houri when you merely
demanded a red herring.

Emily F. Murphy,
'Janey Canuck', *The Black Candle*,
Toronto, Thomas Allen, 1922, p.334.

'Everything in moderation,' my late mother used to say, 'including moderation.' I keenly missed Mom's unflappable good humor as I waited in line behind Claire for my turn at the luncheon buffet Marilyn had prepared for the Bell House guests.

Neatly printed tent cards identified each item, both high test and regular, and the infused items – soup, salad, quiche and brownies – were further labeled with their THC content per serving. When Claire moved past it to the quiche, I picked up a soup bowl and the ladle. I bent over the tureen and inhaled, delighting in the aroma. Only ten milligrams of THC per bowl. What harm could that do?

With Daniel dead, Colin on the lam and Hugh and Phyllis downtown attending their friend's wedding, our numbers were so reduced that Austin had taken a leaf out of the table so we wouldn't have to use megaphones to converse with one another. Carrying soup in one hand and a plate of un-infused veggies in the other, I chose a seat opposite Claire and sat down. After a few minutes, Cindy and Mark joined us, followed by Josh. Like good hosts, Austin and Desiree had not joined the queue, choosing to wait until all of their guests had been served. 'Is Lisa coming?' Desiree asked when she noticed Josh was alone.

'Here I am!' Lisa breezed in, her ankle-length, lace-trimmed denim skirt flapping. She made a beeline for the buffet, where she trailed behind her husband, hovering over each offering like a timid helicopter. Desiree waited by her place at the head of the table, observing Lisa's hesitancy with a look of quiet exasperation until Austin, picking up on his wife's sour humor, sidled up next to Lisa and cajoled her along.

Once we were all seated, I dug in. The celery soup went down easily, smooth and creamy, with a hint of lemon. I may have closed my eyes and moaned with pleasure.

'Jah Kush,' Austin explained, swallowing a spoonful of soup himself. 'I like the woodsy overtones.'

I took another spoonful and rolled it around on my tongue. 'A hint of floral, too. Delicious.'

Austin nodded. 'Jah Kush is a hybrid, but leans toward sativa, so you'll find it relaxing as well as curiously energizing. Perfect for lightweights like yourself, Hannah.' He observed me for a moment, then added, 'There's plenty more soup. Help yourself.'

I waved the offer away. Remembering my mind-blowing experience with the space cake in Amsterdam, I said with a grin, 'Thanks, but it's been a while. I should take it easy until I know how one serving will affect me.'

From across the table, Josh said, 'You know those Sleep Number beds?'

'The ones where you dial in your comfort level?'

I asked, wondering where on earth the conversation was going.

'Yup.'

'I've seen the ads,' I admitted.

'Well, I've got a number like that for weed. For general relaxing, I'm a fifty milligrams kind of dude. For pain relief, I go for seventy-five. If I want to sleep, I'll up it to a hundred.' He leaned back in his chair. 'Different strains have different effects, of course, depending on their balance between TCH and CBD.'

'Spoken like a true cannasseur,' Desiree said with a grin. 'Austin, we should give the man a job.'

Austin opened his mouth to say something, but Josh laughed off Desiree's suggestion. 'I already have a job, thank you.'

Cindy regarded Josh over the rim of her wine glass. 'I'm surprised you have that much opportunity to experiment in Podunk or wherever.'

'Sulphur Rock,' Josh corrected.

'That, too,' Cindy said. 'You grow weed on the farm or something?'

'I wish,' Josh said. 'They're so conservative at Stafford that they conduct staff meetings in Aramaic.' The dining room grew suddenly silent. 'Joke,' he added.

'Not like Boston,' Lisa said wistfully.

'That's where you're from?' I asked. 'Boston?'

Lisa nodded. 'Josh went to school there.'

A fire alarm began clanging in my head. I took aim and shot, directly from the hip. 'Boston University has a great school of public health, doesn't it?'

And scored a bull's eye.

'Super good, but Josh was over at the medical school, doing graduate research on antibiotic drug resistance under a National Science Foundation grant.' Lisa turned her head to beam proudly at her husband, who stared modestly at his plate.

I took a bite of my stuffed celery and chewed thoughtfully.

Confirmed.

Both Daniel Morecraft-Hill and Josh Barton had attended the same university. But so had thirty-five thousand other students spread across multiple campuses.

Both had degrees in biology.

There had to be at least a twenty-year difference in their ages, though. What were the odds the two men had overlapped?

And then I recalled the previous day's 'discussion' I'd observed among the three of them at the weedery. A little too intense, I'd thought at the time, for folks who had just met. If they had known one another in a previous life, though, why not say so? I recalled my conversation with Lisa in the ladies' room, where she'd remained tight-lipped. There had to be a reason. After lunch was over, I'd corner Lisa and press her about it.

Thinking about the research paper Josh claimed to have been writing, I asked, 'Is that why you're studying fruit flies, Josh?'

'Flies? Ugh,' Cindy said. 'I saw that movie. The one with Jeff Goldblum? Gross.'

Josh frowned across the table. 'When we finally cure Alzheimer's, Cindy, you'll probably have a fruit fly to thank.'

'Why flies?' asked Mark. As a former college

141

gridiron star, I suspected that biology wasn't his forte.

Josh smiled. 'They're ideal for research,' he explained, warming to his subject. 'They're smaller than mice, they eat less, they reach sexual maturity in around eight days and the anti-vivisectionists won't be picketing your lab when you have to euthanize them.'

'Poor flies,' Claire said, then excused herself to revisit the buffet.

I was considering going for seconds myself when Detective Jacobs shambled into the dining room. The man popped up so frequently that I suspected he'd pitched a tent somewhere on the premises.

Desiree frowned, laid her fork down on her plate, crossed her knife over it then leaned back in her chair. 'How can we help you, Detective?'

Jacobs' gaze swept the room, considering each of us in turn.

I felt my face flush. I was still conflicted about Colin, but had resolved that if he hadn't shown up by tomorrow morning, I'd pass his cell phone number – now safely saved in my own phone's incoming calls directory – along to the police. I'd given the kid a chance to do the right thing. If he blew it – well, he deserved to be tracked down.

As luck would have it, Jacobs settled on me. 'You mentioned that Daniel took a picture of the group with his cell phone?'

Tongue-tied, I began to panic. Had I imagined it? Then Lisa, bless her heart, chimed in. 'Yeah, he took one. My hair looked a mess.'

'Forensics has checked the victim's iPhone. It's not there now.'

Austin waved for attention. 'Actually, Detective, to be perfectly accurate, Daniel handed the phone to me and I took the picture. Several of them, in fact. I held my finger on the shutter so long it went into burst mode.'

Jacobs wagged his head slowly. 'We got photos of the weedery off his phone, but nothing that could be described as a group shot.'

'What?' I said.

'Maybe they were erased?' the detective drawled.

'What does it matter?' Austin said. 'I took photos of the group with my Nikon. I'll be happy to download them for you.'

'Maybe Daniel didn't like the way he looked?' Lisa cut in. 'He had a paunch on him. Maybe his eyes were shut or something. He could've erased the photos himself.'

'Not unless he did it after he was dead,' Jacobs said dryly. His remark settled over the room like a shroud.

Cindy was the first to break the silence. 'Ohmahgawd,' she breathed.

I stared at Jacobs. Something wasn't right. I'd owned an iPhone ever since June of 2007. With hundreds of other maniacs, I'd waited in a long, hot line at the Apple store for five hours in order to buy the first one. Apple probably wouldn't hire me to staff the Genius Bar, but I did know a few things about how iPhones like Daniel's worked. 'Detective?'

His eyes swiveled in my direction.

'If the photos were erased,' I asked, 'how could you tell when they were taken?'

A slow grin spread over his face. He tapped his nose. 'A gold star for you, Mrs Ives.'

Desiree shot daggers in his direction. 'We have enough on our minds right now, Detective Jacobs. And we don't appreciate being jerked around.'

Jacobs held up a hand and bobbed his head apologetically. 'I didn't mean to mislead you.'

Of course he did. He'd had his antennae up, his eyes on scan the whole time.

Jacobs didn't rush to explain, so I jumped in. 'When you delete a photo from an iPhone, it doesn't exactly go away, Desiree. It sits in an album called Recently Deleted for about thirty days. You just go to the album, select it and tap Recover.'

'So, iPhone photos are time-stamped?' Desiree mused. 'Who knew?'

'It's stored in the EXIF data,' her husband explained, rising from his chair. He faced Jacobs and added, 'The photo I have is digital, too, of course. I'll be happy to put it on a flash drive for you.'

Jacobs nodded, then flapped a hand to wave him away on the errand.

'Is there anything else, Detective?' Desiree asked, each word a shard of ice.

'Now that we have the security tapes, no. Thank you, Mrs Norton.' Jacobs smiled, but made no move to go. The awkward silence was gradually broken by the clink of silverware against china as first Mark and then Josh resumed eating lunch.

'Well, that was special,' Lisa announced. She popped up from her chair and headed for the buffet.

'Who's up for dessert?' Claire asked, leaving the table to follow Lisa.

A minute later, Austin eased into the dining room from the kitchen, followed by the scream and hiss of the coffee machine. 'Here you go,' he said, and handed Jacobs a purple-and-white flash drive.

Jacobs tucked the drive into his breast pocket, thanked him and finally, to everyone's apparent relief, wandered away.

Claire returned from the buffet just then balancing a dessert plate in one hand and a cup of coffee – infused! – in the other. She passed behind my chair, then leaned in between Desiree and me. 'Brownie?' she said, thrusting the plate in front of me. I counted four dark, moist brownie squares on it. 'Only five milligrams each.'

After saying yes to the soup, my canna-number stood at ten. Could I afford to up it to fifteen? I decided I could and took a brownie, setting it down on the rim of my salad plate.

Claire sat down in her chair and tucked in. She devoured one brownie, then started on a second.

'Hang on, Claire,' I said. 'One piece is enough, don't you think?'

She made a Hollywood production out of rolling her eyes. 'But they're *so* good!'

'If someone offered you a single shot of expensive whisky, would you drink the whole bottle?'

She set the second brownie down and pushed the plate toward the center of the table. 'Sorry, you're right. I'm just a teeny bit high.'

'That's what you get with edibles,' Austin said, reaching for the plate from his seat at the head of the table. 'You hear about the comedian who tweeted about the five stages of edibles?'

I said I hadn't.

'Something like not high, not high, still not high, not high, then please get me to the emergency room.'

'You got that wrong, dude,' Josh said. 'They don't sell weed in the emergency room.'

We shared a long laugh after that. We needed it.

Sixteen

The auditory sense is particularly distorted, which accounts for the not infrequent use of marihuana by members of 'hot' orchestras.

Frederick T. Merrill, *American Journal of Nursing*, August, 1938.

Catching up with Josh and Lisa after lunch turned out to be easier than I had expected.

It was a warm, sunny afternoon and the patio beckoned. Claire had gone up to her room for a nap. With a canna-number of over sixty by my unofficial count, I wasn't surprised.

I found Josh and Lisa lounging side by side in teak deck chairs, taking turns with a glass-pipe bubbler. 'May I join you?' I asked.

Lisa chuckled. 'If you don't mind our cooties.'

I laughed, too, and sat down in a chair facing them. 'I didn't mean the pipe, Lisa.'

'Totally OK if you did,' she drawled. 'We're doing a bit of Grape Ape. Super relaxing.'

Josh exhaled a thin stream of smoke. 'Tastes like grapes.'

With her eyes at half mast, Lisa disagreed. 'More like gummy bears.'

Soft jazz wafted in over the outdoor speakers. The sun warmed the back of my head. I relaxed into my chair, seduced by the easy sax of John Coltrane flirting with Thelonious Monk on piano. Whatever I'd come out on the patio to do could wait.

'On KUSA just now?' a woman shrieked, totally harshing on my mellow.

I opened my eyes to see who it was: Cindy. Mark stood directly behind her, looking helpless, like he wished he had a leash to rein her in. 'Cin just saw it on TV. She says the M.E. ruled Daniel's death a homicide,' he added matter-of-factly.

'Well, duh,' Josh said. 'Everybody knows he was suffocated.'

Cindy babbled on, 'And did you hear that Daniel Fischel isn't his real name? Ohmahgawd. My mind is totally blown.'

Under the fabric of his polo shirt, Mark's massive shoulders heaved. 'Not his real name? Cindy, you're shitting me.' His eyes scanned our little group. 'Pardon my French, ladies.'

'Nobody had any idea he wasn't who he said he was,' I said. 'Not even Austin and Desiree.'

147

Cindy waved my comment away. 'I call bullshit on that, Hannah. They must have seen his credit card.'

'Desiree told the detective Daniel paid cash,' I explained.

'*We* know who he really was,' Lisa volunteered.

'Shut up, Lisa!' Josh warned.

Lisa turned to face him. 'No, I won't shut up! He was a horrible man and I'm glad he's dead!'

'I noticed the three of you arguing yesterday at the weedery,' I said. 'A few minutes before I ran into Lisa in the ladies' room.'

'It wasn't an argument, exactly,' Josh clarified, laying the glass pipe down on the table between them. 'It was a Mexican standoff.'

'Do you want to tell us about it?' I asked.

'Not really,' Josh said in a none-of-your-business tone of voice. 'We were upfront with the police about it, so that's all that matters.'

'I didn't recognize him at first,' Lisa said, ignoring her husband. 'When we knew him at BU, he was a lot skinner. He had a shaggy beard and wore dorky wire-rim glasses, too. But, the minute I heard him laugh, oh, I knew then – I knew.'

Josh reached out and laid a silencing hand on her knee, but she batted it away and barreled on. 'Josh was Daniel's research assistant. They were working together on something to do with bacteriophages and multi-drug resistance to antibiotics – I couldn't begin to explain it to you – but the bottom line is that Daniel stole Josh's research paper. He stole it outright and published it as his own. Josh was lead author on the paper, and he didn't even get a co-author listing.'

Josh sagged, as if he were somehow to blame for Daniel's treachery. 'You have to understand. Daniel was my thesis advisor. If I tried to go over his head, he could have screwed up my PhD big-time.'

'We were popping champagne all over the place when Daniel left BU for a position at UNC,' Lisa said. 'Good riddance to bad rubbish.' Her face grew serious. 'I never thought we'd see him again.'

'You can imagine what we thought when he showed up here using a fake name,' Josh said.

'I was all "I know who you are and I know what you did,"' Lisa intoned. 'I really wanted to blow the whistle on the sonofabitch. But Daniel said that if we told you guys who he really was, he'd make sure that Stafford U found out what two of their prize professors were doing while on vacation.'

'We'd be fired.' Josh snapped his fingers. 'Quick as that.'

'Drug fiends, that's us,' Lisa added.

'For sure,' Josh said. 'And he had a photograph to prove it.'

Looking confused, Mark made a timeout gesture with his hands. 'So, who *is* he then? Nobody's saying.'

I told him. 'His real name is Daniel Morecraft-Hill.'

Mark shrugged. Clearly the name meant nothing to him.

'We'd heard that he's some big muckety-muck at Churchill-Mills Tobacco Company,' Lisa added.

'Churchill-Mills!' Mark exploded. 'Damn them to hell!'

Cindy grabbed his arms with both hands and tugged. 'Sit down! Mark! Mark!'

He shook her off. 'I will *not*!'

Mark began pacing the flagstones, muttering almost to himself, seemingly oblivious to us. 'Sneaky bastard. I *knew* Churchill-Mills was up to no good. When they bought out Matthews, it was the beginning of the end. I told Matthews! I warned Cantwell!'

'Who are Matthews and Cantwell?' I asked Cindy, raising my voice so I could be heard over Mark's raving.

'I don't *know*,' she wailed.

Mark ranted on. 'When they bought the Cantwell Place, I should have put a stop to it then. I had Matthews look it up. Sotweed Factor Group, LLC.' He paused, then, 'Ha! Who the hell knew where the money was coming from?'

'What's an LLC?' Lisa asked, keeping her voice low.

'A limited liability corporation,' I explained. 'A shell corporation. Useful if you're the kind of person who wants to hide money from the IRS.'

Josh knew all about LLCs. 'You can create an anonymous shell corporation in one country that controls an anonymous trust in a completely different country and it, in turn, controls a bank account in a third country. Once you've got it up and running, you can use your shell company to stash any spare millions you happen to have lying around and nobody will know you're doing it.'

Cindy finally persuaded Mark to sit down, but sitting did little to check the torrent of words. From his lounge chair, Mark kept hammering away. 'Matthews hired an attorney who did a good bit of digging. Hard to prove, but he thinks he traced the Sotweed Factor Group back to a subsidiary of Churchill-Mills.'

He paused to draw breath, so I jumped in.

'Hold on, Mark. Are you telling us that Churchill-Mills is secretly buying up land? In Dorchester County?'

Mark took a deep breath and let it out slowly. 'Not Dorchester yet, as far as I know. Southern Maryland. Calvert County. They've been growing type thirty-one burley down there, but since the state started paying farmers not to grow tobacco about fifteen years ago, the market for burley's dried up. Matthews had switched to soybeans, but wasn't turning much of a profit.' He raked a hand over what little remained of his light brown hair. 'Here's the deal. The Sotweed Factor Group is one of the twenty-three companies licensed to grow and process marijuana in Maryland. When Matthews sold out to them, too, they'd amassed over three hundred acres. And in March, Maryland gave the Sotweed Group the go-ahead. They'll have weed ready for market by this fall. They're killing the competition.'

We all sat quietly for a moment, letting the significance of this sink in.

Josh was the first to speak. 'When Lisa recognized Daniel, we knew right away he was up to no good.' Josh leaned forward. 'If he works for

Churchill-Mills, it's the clearest case of industrial espionage I've ever seen.'

I didn't get it. 'But we *all* went on the tour, Josh. What kind of trade secrets could Daniel get away with? Austin and Desiree were totally open about their business.'

Mark answered first. 'It's the principle of the thing, Hannah. If Big Tobacco is sneaking into the marijuana biz via a back door, that's a grave cause for concern among independent growers.'

'But can you *prove* it?' I asked.

Mark's face sagged. 'Not yet. Daniel What's-his-name showing up here is a big red flag, though.' He sprang from his chair. 'I've got to make a few phone calls.'

Cindy flounced after him, but paused at the patio doors. 'Mark was hoping to get one of the grow licenses for our land in Dorchester County, so this really hits home.' And then she was gone.

'Did Austin and Desiree know about Daniel?' I asked Josh.

'No,' he said.

Lisa flushed a bright red that had nothing to do with the sun. 'I didn't tell them. Not exactly.'

Josh exploded. 'Lisa!'

Lisa folded her hands in her lap, stiff and prim. 'I took Desiree aside after the tour and told her to watch out for Daniel, that's all.'

Her husband hissed air out through his teeth. 'Jeesh.'

'I knew he had to be up to no good, coming to Denver using a fake name and all. I couldn't let him get away with screwing over the Nortons the way he did Josh,' Lisa said, keeping her voice low. 'Not again.'

Thinking about Daniel's attempt to derail Josh's career, I said, 'It seems like you both landed on your feet at Stafford. Have you been there long?'

'Six years,' he said. 'And we're both in tenure-track positions.'

'Josh is up for tenure next year,' Lisa said. 'That's why he's working so hard on getting his fruit fly research published.'

Josh managed a grin. 'You know what they say about academia? "Publish or perish."' Josh's ice-blue eyes met mine. 'And in Daniel's case? Two out of two. Not bad.'

Seventeen

Then follow errors of sense, false convictions and the predominance of extravagant ideas where all sense of value seems to disappear. The deleterious, even vicious, qualities of the drug render it highly dangerous to the mind and body upon which it operates to destroy the will, cause one to lose the power of connected thought, producing imaginary delectable situations and gradually weakening

*the physical powers. Its use frequently
leads to insanity.*

H. J. Anslinger, Commissioner of Narcotics.
The Marihuana Tax Act
of 1937, Transcripts of Congressional
Hearings, Additional Statement.

The door on Claire's side of the bathroom was closed, but as I stood at the sink washing my hands, I could hear the furious *click-click-click* of her laptop keyboard. When the clicking let up for a moment, I tapped lightly on the door.

'Hannah?'

'Who else?'

'Might as well come in,' she said, sounding tired. Perhaps she hadn't gotten a nap in after all.

I found my friend, fingers still poised over the keyboard, sitting at a desk made out of an antique suitcase supported on trestle legs. 'Catching up on emails,' she explained.

'Story of my life,' I said. I pulled a straight-back chair out from the wall and sat down. While she regarded me steadily, I told her about Mark King's meltdown on the patio.

'I'm totally pissed off at Mark,' Claire said after I'd finished. 'Until this trip, I hadn't seen him since the session ended. He volunteered to come, so I agreed. I *knew* I should have asked Craig Waller.'

'Who's Craig Waller?'

'An oncologist. Retired now. He's a delegate for Baltimore County.' She paused for a moment as if weighing up how much to tell me. 'I should

154

have paid more attention to the signs. I thought it was a one-off at first, last January, when Mark blew up at a witness who was testifying on behalf of the Chesapeake Bay Foundation about phosphorous management. Manure, chicken shit mostly,' she clarified, before I could ask. 'Another time, I watched him argue over something stupid – Mac versus PC – with a delegate over lunch at Harry Brown's. He squirted catsup on the guy's cheesecake and stalked out.' She sighed. 'Now this! I'm afraid Mark's got a problem with impulse control.'

'Is that why Cindy came along? As wrangler?'

Claire hooted. 'That's hilarious, Hannah.'

I smiled back. 'Just saying.'

The silence between us grew, filled only with the pulsing drone of a riding mower somewhere in the neighborhood. 'I was surprised to hear that Mark was applying for one of Maryland's marijuana grow licenses,' I said. 'Isn't that a conflict of interest, Mark being a state delegate and all?'

Claire's face clouded. She picked up a glass paperweight and turned it over and over in her hands, like a worry bead on steroids. 'In this political climate, traditional ethics seem almost quaint.' She set the paperweight down on the desk and gestured at her laptop. 'It's all moot, in any case. I'm just responding to Michael Busch.'

'The Maryland Speaker of the House? That Michael Busch?'

'One and the same.'

'What's up? A little too late to call off this trip, I should think.'

155

'I'm simply furious!' she said, punctuating the remark by slapping the lid of her laptop shut. She faced me, leaning forward, with her forearms resting on her knees. 'Mark's resigned his seat in the House of Delegates. He sent a formal letter to Busch late yesterday but didn't even bother to cc me on it.'

'That's rude,' I said. 'Why is he resigning – did he say?'

'The letter cited personal reasons, but I just got the scoop from Michael. Remember that football scandal at Maryland State?'

I nodded. It had been front-page news for months, then splashed all over national television in a segment of *60 Minutes*. Four female students claimed they'd been drugged and abducted by members of the football team. As too frequently happens, heavy drinking and gang rape ensued. Maryland State authorities either ignored or mishandled the investigation. When the truth came to light, several members of the school's senior administration were fired, along with the coach of the football team, who'd tried to cover it all up.

'So the head coach was given the boot. Zero tolerance and all that.' Claire paused. 'Eventually.' She leaned back in her chair and took a deep breath. 'Long story short, they've offered the head coach position to Mark and he's accepted.'

'Get out!'

'He'll be moving to Hagerstown for the job, so he'll be out of Baltimore and couldn't represent the city anyway, but what really fries my grits is this deal has to have been in the works for *ages* and I'm just now finding out about it.'

'To be fair,' I offered, 'maybe Mark simply wanted to make sure it was a done deal before telling anyone.'

Claire snorted. 'Bull. I know why. If he'd told me before, I'd have scrubbed him from this trip. He can live in Hagerstown or New York City or effing Timbuktu, but he'll still own that farm in Dorchester County, and he'll still have aspirations to be The Maryland Baron of Pot.'

It struck me that 'Head Football Coach' and 'Baron of Pot' were mutually exclusive job titles, especially in a state where recreational pot was not yet legal.

'It's curious,' I said. 'If Mark was angling for that job at Maryland State, why was he so hot to come along on the trip? He approached *you* about it, right, not the other way around?'

'Right.' She reached for her Juju vape pen and fired it up. 'Sorry,' she said after taking a toke. 'I'm super stressed just now.' She offered the pen to me, but I smiled and waved it away. I was feeling mellow enough from the celery soup at lunch.

'With the coaching job not yet nailed down, you'd think it would actually be risky for him to come,' I said. 'But suppose Mark already *knew* Daniel Morecraft-Hill?'

'If he did,' Claire mused, 'he'd have to know about the man's connection to Big Tobacco.'

'Exactly. So, maybe Mark wanted to come along precisely because he knew Daniel would be here?'

157

'To what end?' Claire took another toke and considered me through half-closed eyes.

I described in some detail Mark's recent outburst on the patio.

'I see what you mean,' she said. 'With property changing hands at such a rapid rate, perhaps Mark wanted in on the ground floor. With a new job on the horizon, maybe he hoped to unload his farm. What if he tried to cut a deal with Daniel and Daniel refused?'

I nodded. 'And you said Mark had anger control issues.'

'Damn,' Claire said.

'What did he do before?' I asked. 'After retiring from football, I mean. The forty-eight thou he gets from the state of Maryland couldn't have gone very far.'

'Former NFL players aren't exactly paupers,' she said. 'I'm assuming he's well-invested. And Cindy doesn't strike me as the kind of gal who'd let him fritter a fortune away on Dom Perignon, private jets, luxury condos in Cannes and fleets of antique cars.'

Realizing that I'd be joining Mark and Cindy for dinner in a couple of hours, I asked, 'Am I supposed to know about this head coaching thing?'

Claire shrugged. 'Hell if I care. Honestly, Hannah, I could just kill him!' She flapped a hand, waving the thought away. 'Sorry. Don't quote me on that.'

She looked so panicked that I had to laugh. 'You're the ringmaster of this circus. Why don't you simply tear up his return ticket and let him pedal back to Annapolis on a bicycle?'

That elicited a grin. 'You're a mean girl, Hannah Ives.' She reached out and patted my knee. 'But I like the way you think.'

Eighteen

It is now much too late to debate the issue: Marijuana versus no marijuana. Marijuana is here to stay. No conceivable law enforcement effort can curb its availability.

Marijuana Decriminalization:
Hearing Before the Subcommittee to
Investigate Juvenile Delinquency.
US Congress. Senate. Committee on
the Judiciary, May 14, 1975, p.73.

I peered into the vintage oak armoire that dominated my room, considering my options. Although I'd hung my clothes up on arrival, none of the tops I'd brought seemed ready for prime time. 'In my next life, I'll learn to pack like a pro,' I called out to Claire through the connecting door. 'This shirt looks like I slept in it.'

I'd seen the YouTube videos. Smiling millennials folding their garments into neat little origami packages, demonstrating how you can fit the entire contents of your closet into a single carry-on. 'What are you wearing to dinner, Claire?'

'Navy blue slacks and a colorful top,' she called back. 'It's not exactly the White House, you know.'

I extracted a long-sleeved tie-dyed tunic from the wardrobe, the least wrinkled of my three choices, and carried it next door for consultation. 'What do you think?'

Claire grinned. 'If pleats were in, you'd be good to go.'

'That's what I was afraid of,' I said. 'Are there irons in the rooms?'

'Not that I've noticed,' she said. 'Not that I'd recognize one anyway. I haven't ironed anything since . . .' she paused to think, '. . . 1992.'

'What happened in '92?'

'Had the iron set to "Cotton." Melted a favorite polyester blouse.' She pressed a hand to her chest and rolled her eyes dramatically toward the ceiling. 'It was traumatic, Hannah. I still have nightmares.'

I laughed out loud. 'Something that has always puzzled me . . .' I said, catching her eye. 'Why is there a permanent press setting on my iron?'

'I rest my case,' she said. 'Do you have something else you can wear?'

I shook my head. 'Everything's pretty fragrant, except what I wore on the flight coming over, which I hope will work its magic again on our way back.'

'I'll bet there's an iron down in the laundry room,' Claire suggested. 'Ask Desiree.'

* * *

160

I found Desiree easily. She was busy in the kitchen helping Marilyn prepare dinner.

I offered up my tunic, draped despondently over its hanger, as an illustration. 'Do you have an iron I can use?'

Desiree was up to both elbows in dough. Flour dusted her cheeks. She didn't stop kneading, simply jerked her head toward the back hallway and said, 'In the laundry room. Help yourself.'

'Thanks,' I said, stepping up to the counter for a closer look. 'What are you making?'

Desiree smiled. 'Angel biscuits so light and fluffy you'll swear you've died and gone to heaven.'

Marilyn stood at the stove, sautéing something that smelled heavily of garlic. She called over her shoulder, 'With infused honey. Worth dying for.'

'I'll remember that,' I said.

'The iron's probably still hot,' Marilyn added. 'I just finished pressing a tablecloth.'

'Thanks,' I said, moving toward the service door, thinking how delightful it would be to dine at a table where the hostess cared enough to press the tablecloth. 'I'll be sure to turn it off when I finish.'

To reach the laundry room, I had to pass Austin's office. His door stood ajar, so I couldn't resist peeking in.

If Edward Hopper had painted the picture, he'd have titled it *Desolation*.

Wearing a cherry-red T-shirt that said THE BIG BONG THEORY, Austin squatted on the oriental carpet, staring morosely into his empty safe.

'Any news on the robbery?' I called out.

'Afraid not,' he said, without bothering to look my way.

'Are you changing the combination?' I asked.

Austin struggled to his feet. 'About to. Why?'

I shrugged. 'Just curious. I'd like to see how it's done.'

Austin studied my face, serious as a judge. 'You planning to make off with the payroll, too?'

'I'd be a pretty lame thief if I waited to crack the safe until *after* the money was gone.'

Austin laughed out loud and motioned me in. 'What harm could it do, then?'

I hooked the hanger holding my tunic over the cut-glass doorknob and stepped into the office.

'You need two things,' Austin began. 'The current combination and . . .' He paused dramatically, reached into the pocket of his jeans and drew out a metal rod about the size of a ballpoint pen refill. '*Tah-dah!* The change key.'

I leaned in for a better look.

'This is an old-style change key. It has a fully-rounded shaft with notches that engage with each wheel,' he said, touching each of the notches for emphasis.

I counted three notches. 'So, there are three wheels?' I asked.

He nodded. 'Three wheels, three numbers.'

Austin invited me over to the safe. As I observed over his shoulder, he inserted the change key into the back of the lock and turned it a quarter turn clockwise. 'Give me three numbers,' he said.

'Thirty-six, twenty-four, thirty-six?' I suggested, trying to keep the mood light.

'Very funny,' he said. 'Seriously, now.'

I picked my birthday – nine and seventeen – and the last two digits of the year I was born.

'Got it,' he said. Austin turned the dial several times around, stopped, reversed direction, stopped and repeated the process until all three of my chosen numbers had been registered. Then he twisted the change key back to its original position and removed it from the lock. '*Voila!*' he said. 'Now, we test the combination. Check the heck out of it while the door's still open.' He extended his hand, palm up. 'Be my guest.'

I knelt, and with Austin watching over me like a proud teacher, I used the combination I'd given him to successfully open the lock. 'Again,' he said.

I obeyed.

I'd just finished testing the new combination for the third time when the telephone began to ring.

At first, Austin ignored it. 'Desiree will pick it up.' With a hand on my arm, he eased me gently to one side, then crouched and inserted the change key into the lock again. 'Gotta switch it back before you start getting ideas.' He winked and made a shooing motion with his hand.

'You change the combination every month?' I asked, heading toward the door, intent on retrieving my rumpled tunic.

'That's right,' he said. His eyes drifted to the right. Had someone passed by in the hallway?

'I don't know how you remember all those combinations,' I said, glancing over my shoulder but not seeing anyone. 'After you run out of birthdays and anniversaries . . .' I shrugged.

Austin's gaze flicked from my face to something behind me, but just as quickly came back, accompanied by a grin. 'One number at a time, Hannah, one at a time.'

'Thanks for the lesson,' I said, and prepared to go.

But the phone hadn't given up. On the fifth ring, Austin looked up from his task and said, sounding exasperated, 'Why doesn't the machine kick in? Get that for me, will you, Hannah?'

'Sure. No problem.'

I crossed to the desk, picked up the receiver and answered the phone the way all Navy juniors are taught. 'Bell House, this is Hannah speaking.'

The voice on the other end sounded young, female and equally polite. 'Hannah, thanks. Could you connect me with Hugh or Phyllis Graham, please?'

'They're not here right now,' I said. 'They're still at the wedding.'

There was a long pause, followed by, 'What wedding?'

'Somebody named Marjorie Ann, as I recall.' When the woman didn't say anything, I added, 'Can't you reach them on their cell?'

'I would if they *had* a cell phone. I've been after them like forever, but Hugh doesn't hear all that well and Phyllis, well, she says she doesn't need to be available twenty-four seven. I pointed out all the cool features of an iPhone,' the woman nattered on, 'like GPS directions and news updates, but Phyllis says getting lost while following written directions is part of the adventure, and she can watch the news on TV at eleven, thank you very much.'

'I'll be happy to take a message,' I said as I eased around the desk and sat down in Austin's chair. While looking for something to write on, I moved several pieces of correspondence aside. Tucked under a letter from Great Western Bank, I uncovered a notepad bearing the Bell House logo that Austin apparently kept on his desk for just such note-taking purposes. A dark green 'Wake & Bake' mug held an assortment of pens. I reached for one, clicked it open and told the caller, 'Go ahead.'

'Thanks. This is their daughter-in-law, Cybele. I'm housesitting while they're away. Will you let them know that a pipe burst in the kitchen but it's all under control? I turned off the water and the plumber is on his way. A few tiles will need to be replaced, but nothing major.'

'OK,' I said, scribbling as fast as I could. 'I'll leave the message in their room.'

'I appreciate it.'

'Is there anything else?'

'No, no,' Cybele said, sounding distracted. 'A wedding, you said?'

'Uh huh. Phyllis is matron of honor.'

'I thought . . .' Cybele paused. 'Well, never mind.'

After Cybele ended the call, I remained at the desk, fingering the note I had written for her in-laws and thinking. So what if the daughter-in-law didn't know about Marjorie Ann's wedding? I didn't tell *my* father everything I was up to. I didn't even mention I was going on this trip.

I ripped the note off the pad and tucked it into my pocket.

'Grateful for the help,' Austin said as I passed him by.

'Consider it payment for the lesson,' I said, snagging my clothes hanger and heading out the door. 'See you at dinner.'

Nineteen

An ordinary man or woman becomes in the eyes of the Marijuana addict, beautiful beyond compare. Marijuana, grown by trusties on prison farms unknown to prison officials, has been taken to the inmates. Under its influence the prisoners fall desperately in love with each other; as they would with members of the opposite sex outside prison walls. One can understand the debaucheries that take place.

Robert James Devine, *The Moloch of Marijuana*. Findlay OH, Fundamental Truth Publishers, 193[4].

It's the little things that sneak up on you, catch you unaware. I ironed the collar first, the way my mother had taught me, then the sleeves. The clean smell of hot cotton brought Mom instantly to mind. A crystal-clear image, sitting on the screen porch in her favorite chair, wearing a crisp, white shirt with the collar turned up and a lipstick-red cardigan that didn't clash in the least with her apricot-colored hair.

Damn, I missed her.

Behind me, two heavy-duty washing machines droned and churned as I put the final touches on the tunic, carefully arranging the pleat in back and pressing it into place. Perfect! At least until I sat down in a chair and leaned back while wearing it, that is.

My late mother had had a sense of adventure, almost a pre-requisite in a Navy wife, it seemed to me. She would have accompanied me to Bell House in an instant, experimented with weed in the same devil-may-care way she approached everything, even tripping across the vine bridges in Iya Valley, Japan, where I had cowered behind her, paralyzed with terror.

'So, Mom,' I said aloud. 'Why would *you* go off to Denver and not tell me the reason why? Was it simply an oversight, or did you have something to hide?'

Mother wasn't saying.

I draped the now-wrinkle-free tunic over the hanger, unplugged the iron and headed back down the hallway. The door to Austin's office stood ajar, so I stuck my head inside. 'Austin?'

The safe was safely curtained and Austin had gone.

Austin claimed that he changed the combination every month or so. Prudent, for sure, but that would drive me insane. I maintained a list of accounts, user IDs and passwords that was three pages long, single-spaced. No way could I remember them all, and I wasn't high fifty percent of the time. How could he? Unless he had a photographic memory, I figured he must write the latest combination down somewhere close at hand.

Once again, I hooked my tunic over the doorknob, wandered over to the desk and sat down in Austin's chair. If I were a combination, where would I hide?

The correspondence I'd noticed earlier was still strewn over Austin's desktop. At home, I often jotted things down on whatever was at hand. Perhaps Austin did, too. Quickly, I pawed through his papers: a supplemental bill for the renovations going on upstairs, a notice from Xcel Energy about a planned outage, an inquiry about availability and group rates for a senior citizens' club from Fort Worth, Texas and the letter from Great Western Bank I remembered seeing before.

I stared at the letter, hard.

Five years before, Austin had taken out a mortgage to renovate Bell House and convert it to a B&B. Perhaps to keep his monthly payments low while building up his business, he'd agreed to a balloon loan. I held the amortization schedule in my hand. If Austin didn't refinance or come up with the final payment – a whopping two hundred thousand dollars – by a week from Friday, he risked foreclosure.

From all the Happy Daze propaganda, the business seemed to be growing like gangbusters. Yet, thinking about Austin's ambitious expansion plans for the weedery, I wondered if he'd spread himself too thin?

Math had never been my strong point, but I knew enough about balloon loans to understand that if interest rates rose, or the value of your property dropped over the course of the loan, you could be screwed when the final payment came due.

Had Austin robbed *himself* to pay off the mortgage?

I slipped the letter to the bottom of the pile, feeling ashamed at the thought. Austin's distress over the robbery seemed genuine. If he'd managed to pull off the ultimate inside job, the man deserved a best actor Academy Award.

Was I barking up the wrong tree?

Had someone else discovered the combination, but how and where?

The blotter pad? Austin had doodled extra-terrestrials, a cat and a reminder about getting the furnace serviced for winter, and circled it with curly-cues. Nothing remotely resembled a combination, not even disguised as a phone number for the nearest pizza delivery joint. While holding on to the correspondence, I eased a corner of the pad out of the blotter and peeked underneath. As unblemished as wind-driven snow. Nothing under the blotter itself, either.

Austin's desk, an antique like almost everything else in Bell House, had a pull-out shelf on the left, just above the top drawer. My grandfather's desk had just such a shelf, designed to support a manual typewriter. Granddad kept a list of World War Two-era telephone numbers taped to his shelf – MA3-7032, TU9-1997 – but when I grabbed the knob and slid the shelf on Austin's desk out, there was nothing but clean, polished oak staring up at me.

I thrust my hand under the center drawer, feeling around blindly for a Post-it. Stuck my head into the kneehole and took a closer look. Nada.

Did I dare open the drawers?

After checking to see if anyone was coming, I dared, but when I tugged on each drawer in turn, they were locked. Not a total surprise. A sniff test indicated the drawers probably contained marijuana, except for the one on the bottom right, which was unlocked and held a pair of ratty jogging shoes, a battery testing gizmo and a bottle of Knob Creek Kentucky straight bourbon whisky, half-full.

A man of fine taste, our Austin.

Modern cell phone technology had made printed calendars practically obsolete, except for decorative purposes such as frolicking kittens, wonders of our national parks, family photos and the like, but I wandered around the office looking for one anyway.

I struck out.

Austin most likely kept his appointments – and his passwords and combinations – safely locked away in his cell phone, password-protected itself.

And yet . . . somebody had obviously found it.

I pulled aside the velvet curtain and stared at the safe. I flashed back to Austin crouching there, discussing how he reset the combination. His eyes had kept darting to something over my shoulder. I didn't think much of it at the time, but now? I turned around to consider the door. What had he been looking at?

I pushed the office door half closed, but nothing was behind it except a bouquet of peacock feathers in a Tiffany-style vase standing proud and tall on a plant stand. To the left – required by law, I presumed – a fire extinguisher was attached to the wall. The bright red paint didn't exactly complement the decor – my grandmother would have sewn a slipcover for it – but what can you do? An inspection tag dangled from the device.

On one side of the tag, P.A.S.S. instructions were printed:

Pull pin

Aim at base of fire

Squeeze handle

Sweep side to side

Good to know.

I turned the tag over. Printed on the reverse side were numbers. Dates, to be precise. A record – or so it first appeared – of when the extinguisher had last been inspected.

There was a row for each month, January through December, and a column for each of the next four years, '2017' through to '2020.' This year, January's inspection had been on the twelfth, February's on the ninth. More recently, the inspector had signed off on June twenty-third. What if . . .?

17 – 1 – 12 . . . 17 – 2 – 9.

If my theory was right and Austin's worried

glances had been aimed at the fire extinguisher, the most recent combination would be: 17 – 6 – 23.

It couldn't possibly be that easy, could it? Only one way to find out.

I pushed the office door closed until the latch clicked. Once again, I pulled the curtain aside, knelt in front of the safe and dialed in the combination. I yanked down on the handle and the door opened.

I was so shocked, I fell back on my heels.

Quickly, I scrambled to my feet, grabbed a pen and the notepad off the desk and scribbled a note: *Austin: If I can figure out where you keep the combination, anybody can! Hannah*

I put the note into the safe, closed the door and spun the dial.

Two seconds later, I was standing in the hallway holding my tunic, taking deep breaths and thanking my lucky stars I hadn't been caught, when movement caught my eye. Marilyn emerged from the laundry room carrying a stack of folded napkins. 'Can I help you, Hannah?'

'I was just . . .' I began, and held up my tunic.

Her eyes narrowed. 'I thought I saw you coming out of Austin's office.'

No use denying it. 'I had a question about checkout time, but he doesn't seem to be in.'

'He's driven out to the weedery,' she said, 'but he'll be back in time for dinner.'

'Well, I can ask him about it then, can't I?' I flashed my sincerest, most innocent smile.

She wasn't buying it. 'What were you *really* doing in Austin's office, Hannah?'

'I, um, I was just . . .' I stammered.

Marilyn's hands were full, but she stared pointedly at my unwrinkled, beautifully pressed tunic. 'The iron is cold.'

Busted.

Before I could lie again, she said, 'Did *you* rob the safe?'

The question so surprised me that I nearly dropped the hanger. 'Of course not!'

'You must have been in there a long time.'

I took time to gather my thoughts and appeal to reason. 'Look, Marilyn, if I had robbed the safe yesterday, why would I go back in there today?'

She stared at me silently, still clearly suspicious.

'And why would I stick around Bell House just waiting to be arrested?' I hastened to add.

Marilyn stood between me and the back door, frowning, as solid and immovable as a tree.

I decided to come clean. 'Look, whoever robbed the safe was in possession of the combination. After I talked to Austin earlier, I thought I could figure out what the combination was, and I did.' I jerked my head toward Austin's office door. 'So, I opened the safe and left a note inside to prove it.'

I was expecting her to ask me how I'd done it, but she simply stared.

'Oh,' Marilyn said after a moment. 'I was hoping . . .' Her voice trailed off.

'Hoping what?'

Her face flushed. 'Do you have time to talk?'

'Of course!' Apparently I was no longer a robbery suspect.

Marilyn invited me into her apartment, where

173

she set the napkins down on a table, then offered me a chair. She sat at the foot of her bed, a vintage iron single with what looked like a hand-quilted coverlet.

'Daniel seemed like such a nice guy, you remember? That time in the kitchen?'

I paused to think. 'When you showed him how to make cannabutter?'

She nodded and took a deep, ragged breath. 'Saturday night, after dinner, he came looking for me.' With a quavering voice, she continued, 'He said he wanted my recipe for magic muffins. I was reluctant at first and offered to give him a copy of my cookbook instead – the one I gave you – but he was so charming, I gave in.'

She flushed, and her eyes glistened with tears. 'I told him to wait while I came back here to my apartment to print the recipe out for him, but he followed me. I thought he was waiting in the hallway by my door, but then I heard the door close and I turned around. Suddenly his hands were all over me! He grabbed my shoulders and backed me up against the table. Then he started kissing me.' She wiped her lips with the back of her hand.

'Marilyn! How awful!' I reached out and touched her arm. 'Tell me this story gets better.'

She managed a wan grin. 'I kneed him good and hard, Hannah. Then I split for the door, but he caught up with me in the hallway. Grabbed me by the arm, spun me around and pushed me up hard against the wall.' She trembled, tears now flowing freely. 'I can still feel the cold tiles against my back as he flattened his nasty self against me.'

No wonder Marilyn had teared up every time Daniel's name had been mentioned.

'Marilyn, have you told anyone else about this?'

'Desiree knows,' she sniffed.

'How about the police?'

She shook her head. 'What does it matter? The man's dead now.' After a moment, she added, 'Besides, Borys came along just in the nick of time.'

'Borys?' I began, and then I remembered. 'One of the security guards.'

'Yes. The boys are usually long gone by then, but Borys said he'd forgotten his cell phone, so he came back for it.' Incredibly, a sly smile crept over her face. 'Borys grabbed Daniel by his silly bow tie, hoisted him up against the wall and got right in his face. "If you ever try that again, mister, I will personally hunt you down and gut you like a fish!" He held Daniel up in the air for the longest time, letting the threat sink in.'

I'd met both men, so I could picture the scene. I shuddered. 'What happened then?'

'I didn't stick around to see. I ran back here and locked the door. But Borys must have let Daniel go, because a few minutes later Borys tapped on my door and asked if I was all right. I told him I was a little shook up, but I'd be fine.' She stared at me for a long moment, tight-jawed and grim. 'Clearly, I'm not.'

'What time did all this happen, Marilyn?'

'Around ten o'clock. Why?'

'Just curious.' I had been in bed by then, but Claire and some of the others had retreated to the solarium to smoke and sip cognac, schnapps, madeira and Grand Marnier. My liver quivered just thinking about it. Daniel had certainly joined them at some point after ten. Following his encounter with Borys, he probably needed a calming slug or two.

Marilyn reached for a tissue. 'You won't say anything, will you?' she said, using the tissue to wipe tears from her cheeks.

'About Borys?' I figured she didn't give two hoots about Daniel.

She nodded vigorously. 'The cell phone was just an excuse, Hannah. Borys had no legitimate reason to be here then. I'm grateful that he was, but . . .'

Suddenly, I knew what was worrying her. 'You think Borys robbed the safe, don't you?'

She nodded miserably.

'And that Daniel, had he lived, would have put two and two together the following day and ratted Borys out.'

The tears began again. 'Something like that,' she sniffed.

I got up from my chair, sat down on the bed next to Marilyn, put my arm around her and drew her close. 'If I were Daniel, facing a charge of attempted rape, I would have kept my mouth shut about Borys.'

'But that's just it!' Marilyn sobbed into my shoulder. 'I'm afraid Borys decided to shut the professor up permanently!'

Twenty

*Penalties against possession of a drug
should not be more damaging to an
individual than the use of the drug
itself; and where they are, they should
be changed. Nowhere is this more clear
than in the laws against possession of
marijuana in private for personal
use . . . Therefore, I support legislation
amending Federal law to eliminate
all Federal criminal penalties
for the possession of up to one ounce
[28g] of marijuana.*

Jimmy Carter, President of the US,
1977–1981. Drug Abuse Message to the
Congress, August 2, 1977.

On the way back to my room, I stopped outside
the Grahams' door to tuck the message from their
daughter-in-law into a wicker basket marked
'MAIL' that hung from a decorative hook on the
wall nearby. A note from Desiree was already in
the basket, inviting the Grahams to join our party
for dinner if they were available. I peeked at it,
I admit. The note was unsealed.

As I hung my freshly ironed tunic in the
armoire, I could tell that Claire was awake, her
spirits noticeably boosted. She was singing in

the bath, in any case, in a strong, seductive alto along to the Beatles.

I tapped on the bathroom door, cutting her off in mid-*nah, nah, nah, nah-nah-nah, nah* . . .

'Yes?' she said dreamily.

'Are you decent, Claire?'

'Not really, but you're welcome to come in.'

'You sure?'

'I played field hockey in college, Hannah. I've been in women's locker rooms before. Nakedness doesn't bother me.'

I turned the knob and pushed the door open.

Claire lay in the tub, her disembodied head floating above a sea of bubbles. Damp tendrils framed her rosy-red face. 'Golly! How much bubble bath did you use?' I asked.

The bubbles shrugged. 'Rosemary, lavender, cedar wood and THC. My lady parts are in a happy place. Plenty more in the canister over there. You should try it.'

'Maybe I will,' I said as 'Hey Jude' segued into 'Penny Lane.'

'Turn off my iPod, will you?' Claire asked. 'My hands are wet.'

'If I can remember how, Miss Troglodyte,' I teased, reaching for the device. 'I haven't seen an iPod for years.'

I held down the play/pause button until the iPod went dark, then moved a terry cloth robe aside and sat down on a narrow wicker bench. I decided not to mention the balloon loan until I'd had an opportunity to talk to Austin about it. It was all speculation on my part. Starting an unsubstantiated rumor wouldn't be fair.

I moved on to explore the second surprise of my day. 'Claire, do you remember where Hugh and Phyllis said they were going for their friend's wedding?'

Claire thought for a moment. 'Brown Palace Hotel?'

'Ah, right. The posh one.'

'Mmmm,' Claire agreed.

'I just took a call from their daughter-in-law. She doesn't know anything about a wedding.'

Another shrug from Claire. Bubbles slid down her wet shoulders. 'Should be easy enough to find out. Call the hotel.'

'Hold that thought,' I said. 'I'll be right back.'

'Mmmm,' she said, and sank deeper into the tub.

I found my cell phone on the bedside table where I'd left it charging, unplugged it and Googled the Brown Palace. When the website came up, I tapped the phone number and waited to be connected.

'I'm trying to get a message to some friends who are attending a wedding at your hotel today,' I explained to the hotel operator. 'I don't know the groom's name, but the bride is named Marjorie Ann.'

The operator put me through to the concierge. 'Let me check for you, ma'am,' the young man said after I had repeated my question. I listened to his keyboard click. 'We have three weddings today. Tuckerman-Dutton, Chase-Fosher and Job-Purdy.'

'Are any of the brides named Marjorie Ann?'

'Checking. Please hold.' After a moment, he

told me, 'We have an Elizabeth, a Carol and a Samantha. Is it one of those?'

'No, I'm afraid not,' I said.

'Possibly you have the wrong hotel?' he suggested. 'The Ritz-Carlton is the most likely alternative. If that isn't it, you could try the Grand Hyatt.'

I thanked him and asked to be put through to the Ritz, but struck out there, too. Ditto the Grand Hyatt. I called the high-end Hilton Garden Inn and the Courtyard by Marriott, but met a blank wall. Based on what Phyllis had said about Marjorie Ann's taste for luxury, I figured the Holiday Inn, Days Inn and Ramada were out of the running, but I tried them anyway, and a handful of bargain-rate hotels further out of the city center, with similar lack of success.

Clearly, I was wasting my time. Marjorie Ann may have been real, but her wedding today in Denver was almost certainly a figment of some-body's active imagination. What were Phyllis and Hugh Graham *really* doing in Denver?

Back in the bathroom a few minutes later, I asked Claire the same question. Hot water was trickling noisily into the tub, so she turned off the tap with her foot.

'You remember the movie, *Dirty Dancing*?'

I patted my chest rapidly. 'Patrick Swayze, oh em gee. Be still my heart.'

'Tell me about it,' Claire said. 'The dancing in that movie is so sexy that I find it hard to breathe.'

'Every girl dreams of losing her virginity to Johnny Castle,' I said, enjoying the conversation but wondering what on earth it had to do with my question about the Grahams.

'Remember that simply darling older couple, the Schumachers?'

Now I knew exactly where Claire was going. Sidney and Sylvia Schumacher were the old dears who wandered around the periphery of the Kellerman Resort picking pockets, but they were so charming nobody suspected them until the end of the movie. 'I remember,' I said. 'Mrs Schumacher stole Moe's wallet and Johnny got blamed for it.'

'Hard to picture Phyllis and Hugh as murderers, I admit,' Claire said. 'But they're obviously not what they seem. Can we pin the robbery on them?'

I thought about that for a moment, then said, 'It's possible, but I have a better suspect for the robbery, and maybe for Daniel's murder, too.' I confessed to Claire about how I'd discovered the combination to the safe, how Marilyn had caught me red-handed coming out of Austin's office and about the heart-to-heart I'd had with her afterward.

'Good lord,' Claire said. 'I understand how she might feel conflicted about reporting the attack, but she really must tell the police about it.'

'I strongly encouraged her to do so,' I said. 'I reminded her that it was quite possible that Borys didn't rob the safe or murder Daniel to cover it up, but if it turns out he did, and she knew about it, she could charged as an accessory after the fact.'

'Could she?'

I shrugged. 'I don't know, but they say that all the time on TV.'

'The robbery and the murder could well be connected,' Claire pointed out reasonably.

'True. Two unrelated crimes happening in the same house within hours of one another would be a stunning coincidence.'

Claire nodded in agreement.

'So, let's take it one step at a time,' I said. 'Daniel. Who wants him dead, and why?'

'We can eliminate me,' she said. 'It gives me the creeps to think that I was asleep in the room when it happened, but I didn't do it, Hannah, and I have no idea who did.'

'I was out cold, too,' I said, 'so let's eliminate me.'

In spite of the seriousness of the discussion, she grinned. 'See? We're making progress already.'

'If we assume that Daniel was murdered because he knew who robbed the safe,' I continued, 'Borys Pawlowski jumps to the top of the list.'

And maybe Austin wasn't far off the top, too, I mused. If Daniel had wandered into Austin's office and seen the same bank papers I had . . .

'It could have been Marilyn,' Claire said, interrupting my train of thought. 'It wouldn't have taken a great deal of strength to hold a pillow over someone's face, especially if that someone were drunk or stoned. Marilyn might have done it to punish Daniel for what he tried to do to her.'

'And don't forget the mysterious Grahams,' I added. 'They came home last night in time to observe Colin and Daniel singing. She said as much at breakfast, you may recall.'

We sat in silence for a moment, mulling it all over. In the high humidity of the bathroom, sweat beaded on my brow. I grabbed a washcloth off the towel rack and dabbed it away. 'I think it's far more likely that whoever killed Daniel knew exactly who he really was.'

'Josh and Lisa, obviously,' Claire said.

'I'd agree, except that Lisa was surprisingly straightforward about it. She actually volunteered the information when we were talking out on the patio. She didn't need to do that.'

'Deflection?' Claire suggested.

'I don't think they're that devious.' I paused. 'However, Lisa also told me she warned Desiree to watch out for Daniel, but according to Lisa, she didn't tell Desiree the reason why.'

Claire moaned. 'Vaguebooking! It's one of the many things that soured me on Facebook.' Her hands emerged from the sea of bubbles long enough to draw quote marks in the air. 'Well, there go my dreams!' She turned her head to look directly at me. 'Do I look like I give a damn about your dreams?'

I laughed. 'For me, it's the humble brag, like, "Having big boobs makes shopping for bikinis sooo hard!"'

Claire winced. 'Ouch!'

'So,' I said, getting back to the subject at hand, 'it's possible that Desiree was curious enough about Lisa's warning to investigate Daniel, but since he was using a fake name, I can't imagine she'd have been successful. Even when we learned his *real* name, it was difficult to track the man down.'

183

'Have you given any thought to who might have tried to erase the photographs from Daniel's iPhone?' Claire asked.

'Josh would be my guess.'

Or, I thought to myself, perhaps it was Colin McDaniel in his last act before fleeing the scene of the crime. I pictured him picking up the phone and pressing Daniel's lifeless thumb to the home button. I shuddered.

'I don't get how the photo is linked to Daniel's death,' Claire said. 'Austin took a group photograph, too, and he's still among the living.'

'Yes,' I agreed, 'but I'm betting that Austin wasn't threatening to send that photo to anybody. Lisa and Josh had a lot to lose if a photograph of them touring a Colorado weedery fell into the hands of the president of Stafford U.'

The same would apply to Colin, I reminded myself. In spades. The Commandant of Midshipmen would ship Colin out of the academy with a rocket tied to his tail.

Claire's hand emerged again from the sea of bubbles. She examined it closely. 'I'm getting prune-y. Hand me the towel, will you?'

She stepped out of the bath. Bubbles slid off her body, puddling on the bathmat at her feet. A shiny, puckered scar marched horizontally across her chest, marking the place where her left breast used to be. She accepted the towel from my outstretched hand and began to rub herself briskly, starting with her hair. 'I'm considering reconstructive surgery,' she said, knowing that I could not have missed seeing her scar. 'But I thought I'd wait until I'm done with chemo.'

'I had mine after the fact, too, Claire. A TRAM flap.'

'I considered that, but I'll probably get an implant,' she said. 'Less recovery time, they say.' She wrapped the towel, a generous-sized bath sheet, twice around her body and wandered into her room, indicating with a twitch of her head that I should follow.

While Claire dressed, I sat in a chair by the fireplace staring at the blue flames that licked the ceramic logs. 'How about Mark King?' I suggested. 'What you said about Mark's anger management issues caught my attention, and he was far from cool-headed when I saw him on the patio. He could have lost his temper with Daniel, picked up a nearby pillow . . .' I let the thought die. 'Mark seemed genuinely surprised to learn that Daniel was visiting Denver under a false flag, but it's possible he already knew all about Daniel's connection to Churchill-Mills. Maybe his spontaneous temper tantrum was just an act.'

Claire eased into her bra, hooked it in front and adjusted her prosthesis. 'I wouldn't count Cindy out, either,' she said. 'She's super protective of her husband, although it's hard for me to picture her killing for him.'

I threw up my hands. 'It's like *Murder on the Orient Express*. Everybody killed Daniel.'

'Maybe we need to gather all the guests together in the conservatory . . .' she suggested, her voice muffled by speaking directly into the wardrobe.

'We should all be at dinner tonight,' I said. 'And unless the Grahams are there, too, I'll be the only tee-totally-straight person in the bunch.

185

I can ask questions. Maybe everyone will be so blissed out they'll let something slip.'

Claire stepped into her slacks. 'Aren't you forgetting somebody, Hannah?'

'Who?'

'The out-of-sight but not so out-of-mind Colin McDaniel? For all we know, he murdered Daniel, cleaned out the safe and is sunning himself on a beach in Playa del Carmen, surrounded by swim-suit models.'

'I don't know where he is,' I said truthfully. 'But once he hears about Daniel's murder, I'm hoping he'll do the honorable thing and come back to face the music.'

Twenty-One

*The musician who uses 'reefers' finds that
the musical beat seemingly comes to
him quite slowly, thus allowing him
to interpolate any number of improvised
notes with comparative ease. While
under the influence of marijuana, he
does not realize that he is tapping
the keys, with a furious speed
impossible for one in a normal state of
mind; marijuana has stretched out the
time of the music until a dozen notes
may be crowded into the space
normally occupied by one.*

Harry J. Anslinger, 'Marijuana, Assassin of Youth,' in *Marijuana Decriminalization: Hearing Before the Subcommittee to Investigate Juvenile Delinquency of the Committee on the Judiciary*, US Senate, May 14, 1975, p.622.

Dinner at Bell House. A Cannabis Tasting Experience. 7:30 for 8:00 p.m., the invitation read, in a distinctly British way. Even the font – something swirly and Edwardian – screamed formal: *In the Garden.*

At seven twenty-two, dressed as formally as possible considering the contents of my suitcase, I presented myself to Claire for inspection. 'Sadly, I seem to have left my tiara at home.'

Claire grinned and held out a necklace made of Venetian glass beads. 'Help me with this, will you?'

I fastened the necklace around her neck from behind. 'This is beautiful,' I said.

'A gift from me to me,' Claire said, patting the beads. 'A souvenir from Murano. Hugely expensive but what the hell. I'm worth it.'

I had to agree.

Five minutes later, at seven-thirty on the dot, Claire and I were passing through the solarium, stepping out into a warm, summer evening without a hint of chill. A bar had been set up at the far end of the patio, strategically positioned to draw guests into the formal garden, beyond where they could carry their drinks and wander along stone paths bordered with lavender phlox and blue sage, stroll among the raised beds of bleeding heart and columbine, or sit on Chippendale-style benches surrounded by roses – floribundas and hybrid teas.

'They've added staff for the party,' I commented to Claire as we closed in on the bar that was being tended by a Nordic blonde with a buzz cut, a guy I guessed to be in his mid-thirties. A plastic nametag read: Kai. Another guy, dark-haired and roughly the same age as Kai, circulated among the guests, carrying a silver tray loaded with *hors d'oeuvres*. The young men were dressed identically in black chinos, crisp white shirts and black shoes so shiny a girl could use them as a mirror.

'What's your pleasure?' Kai asked. 'We have wine – both kinds,' he added with an exaggerated wink, 'and the drink of the day is an Arnold Palmer.' The bartender indicated a tray of tall, frosty glasses sitting at the end of the bar, each glass filled with ice cubes and an amber liquid. 'Half iced tea, half lemonade,' he explained, in case we didn't know. 'Infused or plain.'

'Arnold Palmer for me,' I said, sidling down the bar. Six glasses were arranged on the tray, each with a thin wedge of lemon straddling the rim. Green straws were stuck in four of them, clear straws in the other two. As my hand hovered over the tray, the bartender said, 'The ones with the green straws have five miligrams of THC.'

'Thanks,' I said, selecting a glass with a clear straw. I took a refreshing sip.

Claire, meanwhile, had decided on wine – a Cabernet Sauvignon rosé. 'An excellent choice,' the bartender commented as he poured her a glass. 'Aromas of orange and cherry with a black-currant finish. And may I suggest,' he added, reaching under the bar and pulling out a tray of perfectly rolled joints, 'a pairing with Bubba Kush.' He indicated a joint in the top row. 'Fruity and earthy, a most attractive combo.'

Apparently Kai did double duty as budtender, too.

'Thanks,' Claire said, accepting the joint.

Kai produced a butane lighter. 'He who rolls it, sparks it,' he said, setting the joint on fire. He waited quietly as she inhaled, held the smoke in her lungs for several seconds, then slowly exhaled.

Claire took a sip of wine, then rolled it around on her tongue. 'Ah.' She sighed. 'Kai, you are my new best friend.'

Having been summarily demoted to second best friend, I bid Claire a good-natured see-you-later, leaving her to discuss with Kai what best to pair with Mirassou pinot noir – White Widow, a hybrid weed, as it turns out – and wandered off in search of an *hors d'oeuvres*.

I found Desiree first, dressed like a gypsy in a full, patchwork skirt and a white, off-the-shoulder peasant blouse. She'd coaxed her abundant hair into a twist and secured it with a comb carved from an abalone shell. She was sipping an Arnold Palmer – green straw! – holding forth as Hostess with the Mostest with Cindy King, whose generous curves were encased in a puff-sleeved sheath as orange as a highway traffic cone. Mark stood nearby, head thrown back, oblivious to the two women and apparently fascinated by the antics of a pair of finches setting up housekeeping in a birdhouse. In Finch World, homes designed like Swiss chalets must be all the rage.

'Hi, Mark,' I said.

He gestured at the birdhouse with his drink, a virgin Arnold Palmer with a clear straw, just like mine. 'That's the male,' he said. 'Note the red head and chest.'

'I didn't know you were a birdwatcher.'

He shrugged. 'I'm not, not really. But don't you think it's interesting that the male of the species usually gets the fancy plumage? With humans, just the opposite.'

I smiled, assuming he was referring to Desiree and Cindy. Before I could further explore Mark's philosophy of avian evolution, the second server materialized at my elbow, proffering a tray of cheesy mushroom caps. 'Two miligrams,' the server – whose nametag read Miguel – informed us. Three-quarters of the broiled mushrooms were skewered with green toothpicks, the others with plain white. My hand hovered over one of the plain toothpicks. 'Do I detect a theme here?'

Miguel nodded. 'The green ones indicate infused.'

'Two milligrams, you said?' Mark asked. When the server nodded, Mark selected a green tooth-pick, pinched the mushroom off and slid it between his lips.

I chose a plain mushroom cap and popped it into my mouth whole, then bit down gently until it exploded with juice, richly flavored. I heard a moan of pleasure. I think it was coming from me.

'Damn, that's good!' Mark said, echoing my thoughts exactly. Still chewing, I simply nodded.

'Hannah?'

I turned.

Lean and long-limbed, Austin approached from the solarium, carrying a glass of red wine in one hand and a large bowl of popcorn in the other. Tonight he was dressed formally, at least for Austin, in black slacks and a black T-shirt. Over the shirt he wore an elegant vest made of silk, the design an intricate jungle of marijuana fronds rendered in green, violet and silver. Enameled buttons completed the look.

As he passed the bar, he dropped off the popcorn, then closed the distance between us. Austin acknowledged Mark with a nod, then turned to me. 'Can we talk for a minute?'

'Sure,' I said, knowing almost for certain what the topic of conversation would be. 'Mark, will you excuse us, please?'

Guiding me gently by the elbow, Austin led me to the far side of the garden, near the ornamental gate that led to the driveway, where we sat down on a bench tucked into an alcove in the manicured boxwood hedge.

Austin set his wine glass to one side on the flagstones. 'You must think I'm pretty dumb.'

'I wouldn't say that. Not exactly.' I paused. 'I gather you found my note in the safe.'

'Marilyn told me.' He pressed his hands together between his knees and leaned forward, addressing his purple Reeboks. 'Was all that interest in my safe yesterday morning simply a sham? Are you some sort of professional safecracker?'

'I had a college roommate who kept accidently locking me out of our room, so I'm pretty good at picking your regular, garden variety door lock, but I don't have a clue about how to crack a safe.'

He glanced up at me sideways through pale, almost invisible eyelashes. 'Then how . . .?'

'You have a "tell," Austin. When we were talking about setting the combination, your eyes kept darting sideways, then down, then behind me. At first, I thought someone had walked by in the hallway outside your office, but then you did it again. After you left, I started looking. And found the fire extinguisher.'

'Shit!'

'We know that whoever stole the money had the combination to the safe. They must also have had access to your office, and a bit of leisure time to look around. As I said in my note, if I could find that inspection tag so easily, anyone could.'

Austin retrieved his wine, sipped thoughtfully, then set the glass back down. 'A somewhat limited pool of suspects, then. I'd hate to think . . .' His voice trailed off.

'How well do you know Nick and Borys Pawlowski?' I asked, picking up where Austin left off.

'They've been providing our security for over a year,' he said. 'The company they work for comes with a sterling reputation, and they're bonded.'

'Marilyn certainly thinks highly of them,' I said with a smile.

Austin snorted. 'And vice versa. They're crazy about her cooking, for one thing. A substitute for the mother they send money to back in Slovenia.'

Using the straw, I swirled the ice cubes around in my Arnold Palmer. 'The Pawlowskis are in and out of your office all the time, Austin. They had all the time in the world to stumble over the combination to the safe.'

'They're big, sure, but I don't think they're that smart,' Austin said.

'*Somebody* was,' I said.

'I just can't believe . . .' he began.

I suspected he was underestimating the brothers, and told him so. 'Did Desiree tell you what happened to Marilyn on Saturday night?'

'That scumbag, Daniel, you mean? Desiree didn't tell me – Detective Jacobs did. I'm surprised you know about it.'

Holding my drink in both hands, I turned to face him. 'The important question is what was Borys doing in the hallway outside your office so long after hours?'

Austin's face flushed. 'The police asked me about that, too, after they finished scolding me for being so careless with the combination.' After a few seconds, he added, 'I gotta write the number down *somewhere*, Hannah. The security company forces me to change the damn combination every month. I ran out of birthday and anniversary dates a long time ago.'

'I don't have a safe at home, but I have the same problem with my passwords. Drives me crazy when I'm forced to change one.' I sucked tea up through my straw, enjoying the perfect blend of sweet versus tart. 'For passwords, I usually think up a simple sentence, like 'Christopher Columbus discovered America in 1492.' The password is the first letter of each word, plus the number, in this case Ccdai1492.'

Austin nodded. 'Clever, but that won't work on the safe. Three numbers, remember.'

'True. After you change the numbers, though, couldn't you store the combination in a protected file in the Cloud?' I added. 'A file you can access from your iPhone?'

'I figured that could be hacked.'

'Anything can be hacked,' I said. 'But storing the combination in a protected file would be a lot more secure than on a tag hanging in plain sight on a wall. You could give the file an innocuous filename like Goodwill_Donations or Meditation_On_Psalm23.'

That made him laugh, and I joined in. 'But, nothing is foolproof.'

'A fool. That's me.'

'I know you're madly in love with that old safe, Austin. I'm crazy about my grandmother's 1934 Magic Chef, too, but I don't cook on it. I use it as a plant stand. I have a suggestion for you,' I continued. 'Keep your cash out at the weedery. You can always lock your pot up in the safe.'

He smiled. 'I usually do.'

'Marilyn gave me a crash course in the history of the house and told me about Fannie Bell. Fannie'd be having fits of the vapors at the very idea.'

'She might have been totally cool with it.' Austin chuckled. 'There's a picture of Miss Fannie somewhere, dressed in full flapper regalia, a Martini glass in one hand and a jewel-encrusted cigarette holder in the other.'

As guests went to and fro around us, nodding in greeting from time to time but keeping a respectful distance, we sat quietly sipping our drinks. I was trying to think of a tactful way to bring the conversation around to Austin's letter from the Great Western Bank when Austin opened his mouth and unlocked that door himself. 'Detective Jacobs thinks *I* did it,' he blurted.

I feigned surprise. 'No way!' After a moment, I pinned him to the bench with my eyes and asked, 'Well, *did* you?'

Austin snorted wine out his nose, apologized and then dabbed it away with the back of his hand. 'Stealing from myself, Hannah? I'd have to be nuts. Desiree got all spun up about the robbery,' he confided. 'Blabbed to Jacobs that we needed the money in a lump sum to pay off a mortgage.'

I decided to come clean. 'When I sat down at your desk . . . I couldn't help noticing the letter from your bank.'

He shrugged. 'I've got nothing to hide.'

'I know a little about balloon loans,' I said. 'Don't they usually come with a reset option? Can't you refinance the loan at current market rates?'

Austin sighed. 'If I convince Great Western that the business is sound, that those two slightly late payments are a thing of the past.'

'Ouch,' I said. 'How's the Denver housing market? Robust?'

Austin rocked his hand back and forth. 'Basically flat, but nothing to worry about. We've got plenty of equity in Bell House, if that's what you're wondering.'

As if on cue, Desiree hove into view, carrying a glass of wine and waving a vape pen, bangle bracelets jangling. 'There you are, Austin!' Her eyes narrowed, shooting daggers. 'I've been looking for you everywhere.'

Austin scooped up his wine glass and sprang to his feet. 'I'm being summoned.'

I shooed him away with my hand. 'We'll catch up later.'

He raised his glass. 'Innocent until proven guilty,' he whispered.

Somehow, I didn't find that reassuring.

Twenty-Two

Nearly all medicines have toxic, potentially lethal effect. But, marijuana is not such a substance. There is no record in the extensive medical literature describing a proven, documented cannabis-induced fatality. The record on marijuana encompasses 5,000 years of human experience . . . Yet, despite the long history of use and the extraordinarily high number of social smokers, there are simply no credible medical reports to suggest that consuming marijuana has caused a single death. By contrast, aspirin, a commonly used over the counter medicine, causes hundreds of deaths each year.

Francis L. Young. 'Opinion and Recommended Ruling, Findings of Fact, Conclusion of Law and Decision of Administrative Law Judge in the Matter of Marijuana Rescheduling Petition,' Docket No. 86–22, US Department of Justice, Drug Enforcement Administration (1988), pp.56–7.

After the Nortons left, I sat by myself for a few minutes, sipping my tea and thinking that there was no way I could host a dinner party if I started the evening with an infused Arnold Palmer followed by a glass of wine and a toke. But then, I was in training and Desiree was a pro.

I caught up with Austin again a few minutes later over a platter of crab rangoons. 'The duck sauce is spiked,' he told me, proffering the platter. 'The plum sauce not.'

I dredged my cheesy wonton through the plum sauce and took a bite just as Josh breezed into the garden with Lisa. Both were dressed for the evening like country and western singers, she in a short denim jacket over a pink, spaghetti-strap maxi dress, he in a red plaid shirt belted into a pair of slim jeans. Both wore boots.

'I like the look,' Austin said, taking it in. 'All you need is a black hat, Josh.'

Josh laughed. 'Left my guitar at home, too.'

'Seriously?' I said.

'Josh plays really well.' Lisa nibbled on a wing of her wonton. 'I always hoped he'd get an assistant professorship at Vanderbilt so he could take advantage of the music scene in Nashville.'

'Do you play, Lisa?'

'Does tambourine count?' She grinned hugely to show she was kidding.

'Lisa's being modest. She's got a lovely voice.'

'And Josh is just being sweet because he doesn't want to sleep on the sofa tonight.' Her lips brushed his cheek. 'I'm afraid the Dixie Chicks aren't going to be calling me in to sub any time soon.' She cocked her head, then listened for a moment. 'What's that playing?'

In contrast to the soft, moody blues that usually wafted out of the speakers in the solarium, keeping everyone mellow, tonight's background music evoked a twenties speakeasy. If Miss Fannie Bell had flounced in dripping with beads and waving a glass of champagne, I wouldn't have been the least surprised. A sassy clarinet and vibraphone number ended, giving way to dueling brass, a bouncy piano and a frisky feline vocalist covering Ella Fitzgerald's classic, 'When I Get Lo, I Get High.'

'It's my hot jazz mix tape,' Austin said. 'The Hot Sardines. Heard them at the Lawn Party on Governor's Island a couple of years ago and they blew me away. The Swamp Donkeys and the Grand Street Stompers and a couple of other groups are on there, too.' He stared at Lisa for so long that she probably thought she had lipstick on her teeth. 'Your tambourine?' he said at last.

'Don't knock it. Miz Elizabeth plays a washboard sometimes. A Dubl Handi. She bought it at Ace Hardware.'

Lisa snickered, Josh snorted, Austin hooted. Long after my ladylike tee-hee-hees had been exhausted, their mirth rolled on until Lisa, limp with laughter, held up a hand. 'Stop! You're killing me!'

Miguel saved me by appearing with a tray of crusty bruschetta. Already tuned in to my preferences, he advised me to avoid the ones topped with fresh basil leaves. I left those for The Three Amigos to enjoy and excused myself, claiming I needed to catch up with Claire.

I found her at the bar, getting a refill on her rosé. I exchanged the dregs of my Arnold Palmer for a glass of Sauvignon blanc and drew her aside into a clump of rhododendron forming a semi-circle around a birdbath. With all the excitement over the robbery and Daniel's murder, I'd clean forgotten the primary reason Claire had invited me along on this boondoggle. I patted the woven handbag that dangled from my shoulder by a crocheted strap. It contained essentials such as lipstick, a hairbrush, my iPhone and – ever since I'd hooked up with Claire – a notebook and pen. 'Am I supposed to be taking notes?'

Claire laughed out loud. 'The state of Maryland hasn't the slightest interest in what we eat for dinner.'

'Maybe, or maybe not,' I said, 'but they are paying for it.'

'Forget about the notebook, Hannah,' she drawled. 'And for heaven's sake, lighten up a little!'

'I'm doing it the traditional way.' I raised my wine glass.

She poked my shoulder with an extended forefinger. 'Don't be such a party pooper.'

I wasn't raining on anyone's parade by abstaining from weed, it seemed to me, and I told her so.

Her face clouded. 'I don't need a babysitter, Hannah.'

'I'm not . . .' I began, but I was talking to her back. Claire had executed a neat about-face and sashayed away.

Swell.

I remained in the rhodos for a while, sipping wine, observing from a distance as the party unfolded on the patio before me, hosts, guests and staff moving about and interacting like characters in a Noël Coward play. Was I really such a fuddy-duddy, a stick-in-the-mud? I was tempted, sorely tempted, to charge in from the wings shouting 'Oh, what the hell!' and snarf down a handful of Marilyn's high-octane canapés.

And then Hugh and Phyllis joined the cast, strolling in from stage right. They were holding hands.

I pounced upon the new arrivals. 'So glad you could make it,' I said. 'I was feeling a bit like an undertaker at an Irish wake.'

Phyllis was dressed in a navy-blue pants suit, Hugh in a forest-green, logo-less polo shirt and chinos. 'It was lovely of Desiree to include us,' Phyllis said. 'Hugh and I were planning on pizza at that *taverna* down the street, but I'm just as happy to stay in. It's been a long day.'

'We're just the B-list,' Hugh harrumphed. 'A

couple of warm bodies to fill up the chairs left vacant by others.'

Phyllis extracted her hand and confronted her husband. 'Hugh!'

He took her rebuke like a soldier, then muttered under his breath, 'Well, it's the truth. Can't have opinions about it.'

'Behave, for heaven's sake,' she said. 'Go find yourself a drink. And get one for me, too.'

'Arnold Palmers are the special,' I offered helpfully. 'Both regular and high-test.'

'I'm on it,' Hugh said, saluting as he about-faced and stepped away.

'Don't you *dare* go off the deep end, Hugh!' Phyllis called out to his departing back.

He turned, then cocked his head. 'Whatever do you mean, my love? I'm the poster child for moderation.'

After Hugh left on his mission, Phyllis rolled her eyes and said, 'I love the man to bits, but what'cha gonna do?'

I smiled back, wondering when would be a good time to bring up Marjorie Ann's supposed wedding. With Hugh at the bar, it was just one-on-one, so I decided to dive right in. 'Your daughter-in-law called. I took the message.'

'I got it, thanks,' she said. 'Why is it everything decides to break the minute you leave home?'

'Sod's law,' I said. 'One winter my husband and I took a cruise. While we were away, mice got into the pantry and ate their way through a bag of rice and two pounds of demerara sugar. Must have been on a sugar high when they partied down and chucked flour all over my kitchen.'

Phyllis chuckled, then raised an apologetic hand. 'Sorry. It probably wasn't funny at the time.'

'Mouse poop is particularly unamusing when you stagger in from the airport at eleven at night.'

Hugh was still busy at the bar, so I said, 'I hope I didn't cause any trouble for you at home when I spoke to your daughter-in-law.'

An eyebrow shot up. 'What do you mean?'

I shifted uncomfortably from one foot to the other, stalling for time, trying to choose my words carefully. 'When Cybele asked for you, I said you were at a wedding. She seemed surprised to hear that.'

'I see,' Phyllis said.

Should I admit that I called every hotel in Denver checking out the Grahams' alibi? I decided to cut to the chase. 'I know there wasn't a wedding,' I said. 'And I'm fairly certain the police know that, too.'

'We would never lie to the police.' Phyllis paused to let the significance of her statement sink in. In the background, a hot piano and a clarinet wailed away on 'My Blue Heaven.'

'Perhaps I'm inhaling too much secondhand smoke here, but are you saying that you told the police where you've *really* been this weekend?'

Instead of answering my question, she posed one of her own. 'How do you know there wasn't a wedding?'

I felt my face flush. 'I thought it was strange that your daughter-in-law seemed confused about it, so I made some calls. My friends will tell you that I'm nosy that way. I grab at threads and keep pulling.'

Her eyes locked with mine. 'Did you think we came here to murder Daniel? Maybe rob the safe?'

'No,' I began, then managed a sheepish grin. 'Well, yes. Not the murder, but I might have had you pegged for the robbery.'

Incredibly, Phyllis laughed. 'As if!'

'What's so funny?' Hugh wanted to know. I'd been so involved in conversation with Phyllis that I'd failed to notice he'd returned. He handed a weed-free Arnold Palmer to his wife, then toasted us with the beer he had chosen for himself, a local brew called Sweaty Betty Blonde. 'I don't usually drink beer,' he said after taking a long, appreciative swig from the bottle. 'But with a name like that, how could I resist?'

'I'm afraid I've been sticking my nose in where it doesn't belong,' I confessed, then gave Hugh a recap of my conversation with his wife. As I spoke, I watched his face morph from puzzlement to shock and, finally, to amusement.

'I'd just gotten up to the part where I ask what you were really doing this weekend,' I concluded.

Phyllis and Hugh exchanged baleful glances.

'Might as well tell her,' Hugh said.

Phyllis stared silently into her drink, stirring it with the straw.

'We were house-hunting,' Hugh prompted.

'You're going to move here?' I asked.

'More than likely. Phyllis is an expert COBOL programmer,' Hugh said, as if that explained everything.

Phyllis laid a hand on her husband's arm. 'Hugh. Enough.'

'It's not like it's top secret or anything, Phyl – not if NPR was reporting on the issue.'

Phyllis turned to me. 'There are several government agencies co-located at Buckley Air Force Base,' she explained. 'One of them deals with reconnaissance satellites but, incredibly, they're doing it with museum-ready computer systems operating on nineteen-seventies IBM platforms.'

Hugh leaned in. 'They're storing data on eight-inch floppies, can you believe it?'

My mind wandered for a moment. In the Internet Age, anything could be hacked. Maybe storing data on floppies wasn't such a bad idea. Or voting on paper ballots.

'COBOL was all the rage in the late fifties, early sixties,' Phyllis continued. 'There aren't many of us programmers left.'

'Phyl has been recruited to help with the conversion,' Hugh said. 'It might take as long as two years.'

'I can't tell you which agency, or exactly what I'll be doing,' Phyllis said, smiling modestly. 'But Hugh is correct. Uncle Sam wants me, it seems.'

'That's wonderful,' I said. 'But why did you make up that story about the wedding? Up until Friday, nobody at Bell House knew you. It's not like we were going to Facebook your friends back in Massachusetts and tell them you were out here being briefed about a job.'

'What I was afraid would happen, happened, Hannah. My daughter-in-law called, you took the call and you told her what we were doing, or what you *thought* we were doing. I have seven children and more grandkids and great-grandkids than I can count. They are definitely not going to be in favor of us moving more than halfway across the country.'

Hugh wrapped an arm around his wife, then drew her close. 'The children think we should be enjoying our golden years, playing shuffleboard and mah jong in a retirement community in Worcester.' Behind his glasses, his eyes twinkled. 'Now Phyllis has accepted the job, we'll move to Idaho Springs where I, for one, am looking forward to grabbing my skis and getting back on the slopes.' He smiled fondly at his wife. 'Assisted living can wait.'

'So, what about your girlfriend, Marjorie Ann?' I asked Phyllis.

Phyllis blushed. 'She *is* getting married again, Hannah, just like I said, but it's next month. In Philadelphia. It wasn't a very good cover story, but when you asked, Hugh said the first thing that popped into his head, and I . . .' She paused and winked up at her husband. 'Well, we know each other so well that I simply played along.'

Twenty-Three

I drew on the reefer and held tight,
while the smoke scratched my lungs
like tiny, scampering feet. Then, I felt
the lightness and the strident chords
from the band suddenly become like the
golden tones from a singing harp!

'I Was a Musician's Girl,'
Sweethearts, #122 [22], March, 1954.

The dining room glowed with understated elegance. The chandelier, shaped like a Victorian birdcage and dripping with crystals, shimmered and winked, shedding prisms onto the crisp white tablecloth. A pair of candelabra that might have been snitched from the top of Liberace's Steinway grand sat at each end of the long table, and the elaborate centerpiece was back, filled with floating lilies.

Guests wandered in and circled the room, looking for a place card with their name on it. As they had at lunch, Austin and Desiree sat at each end like Mom and Pop, but the rest of us had been shuffled to accommodate the Grahams. My place was on Austin's right, between Phyllis and Mark and directly across from Josh. I looped my handbag over the chair and sat down.

'Jiminy Christmas.' Mark studied his place setting with a look of dismay. 'You'd think the Queen of England was coming to dinner.'

True.

If she had walked through the door just then, Elizabeth the Second would have felt perfectly at home. Three forks ranged out to the left of our dinner plates and two knives to the right, while several spoons lay in the twelve o'clock position in the space above the plate – it was a how-to-set-the-table illustration straight out of Emily Post. Three crystal glasses of varying shapes and sizes added to the confusion. No fish knife or ice-cream fork, thank goodness, or even I might have thrown in the towel.

'The silverware and china belonged to Fannie Bell,' Desiree explained as she pulled out her chair and took her seat. 'The silver is Strasbourg by Gorham. It's so gorgeous, how could we not use it? And the china is Spode.' She slipped her napkin out of its ring, snapped it open and spread it across her lap. 'We're not sure about the crystal. It's kind of a mixed bag, but we love it.'

I loved it all, too. At home, my 'crystal' came from Target, my silverware from Bed, Bath and Beyond and my dinnerware – plain white with a thin blue rim and missing three cups – from a rummage sale at St Catherine's Episcopal Church. I was familiar with Spode's classic Indian Tree pattern, but Fannie's rusty-orange version was a stunner.

Mark raised both hands in a gesture of surrender. 'I'll need a playbook to get through this dinner.'

'Watch me,' I said, remembering an *aide-memoire* I'd learned from my grandmother. I made circles with each thumb and forefinger, like a pair of eyeglasses, holding my remaining fingers straight up. 'Left hand forms a "B." That's your bread and butter plate on the left. Right hand makes a "D" – stands for drinks – so those are your glasses.' I put my hands down. 'As for the silverware, simply start on the outside and work your way in.'

Mark laughed. 'Thanks, Hannah. Frankly, though, I'd have been fine with a spork.'

With Marilyn presumably slaving away in the kitchen, our budtender, Kai, made the rounds, pouring wine – a crisp Italian Pinot Grigio – to accompany the first course. When everyone's glass was full, Austin stood. 'Welcome to Bell House!' he said, raising his glass in a toast. 'Bong appetite!'

'Bong appetite,' we all said.

Austin sat down and Desiree became mistress of ceremonies. 'First, for your dining pleasure, we have a medicated *amuse bouche*. For those of you keeping count, it's five milligrams.'

As if by magic, Miguel appeared at Desiree's left elbow, proffering a tray of rye bagel crostini topped with a swirl of goat cheese mousse, garnished with dill. A sliver of pimento marked the crostini teetotalers could eat.

Mark reached to his right and grabbed Cindy's napkin. She swatted his hand away. 'Other side,' she hissed.

I scooted Mark's napkin toward him as unobtrusively as possible. He took it and flashed me a sly smile as he reached for a crostini.

Miguel served me next, and then Phyllis. As Miguel moved around the table to Austin's left, Phyllis said, raising her voice slightly, 'Hugh and I talked about whether we should come to dinner or not.'

From across the table, Hugh grunted.

'We're not baby boomers like you,' Phyllis said. Her glance swept the table. 'We grew up in the days of pot paranoia. Remember *Reefer Madness*?'

By the time I enrolled in college, that thirties-era anti-marijuana propaganda film had already become a cult classic. 'Worst movie of all time,'

I said. 'Even worse than *Plan Nine from Outer Space*, and that's setting a pretty low bar.'

'It is high-larious,' Lisa said. She leaned across her plate. 'There's a young couple living together, selling marijuana. And they aren't even *married*!'

'Shocking!' Josh said.

'Ironically, the first time I saw *Reefer Madness*, I was stoned,' Austin said.

'I saw it only once, years ago,' Phyllis recalled rather wistfully, 'but I remember everyone being young, dazed and confused – easy prey for the evil drug-pushers. Hit-and-runs, suicides, insanity . . .' Her voice trailed off. 'It's kind of hard for older folks to overcome those ingrown stereotypes.'

Hugh polished off his crostini. I was too far away to notice whether it had been garnished with dill or pimento. 'Are you suggesting we have some sort of expiration date, Phyllis? I don't think you're ever too old for pot.'

Phyllis aimed a long, neatly manicured finger in her husband's direction. 'Well, I don't want any unexpected trips to the emergency room, thank you very much.'

'No one ever overdosed on marijuana,' Austin said, repeating what he'd told us earlier. 'But if you're new to it, we advise being cautious with edibles. They can sneak up on you.'

'That's why we treasure Marilyn,' Desiree said, picking up a small silver bell and giving it a jingle. 'She's a genius with dosage in the edibles.'

In response to the bell, Marilyn appeared, an immaculate white apron wrapped around her petite frame. Manuel stood behind her, balancing a full-loaded tray.

'For the first course,' Marilyn announced, 'we offer a spinach-strawberry salad with THC-infused coconut poppyseed dressing. Sour Diesel, five milligrams, unless you go easy on the dressing.'

The salad Manuel placed before me was beautiful, like Christmas – deep green and bright red, with a dusting of feta snow. The dressing was served on the side in a little cup. Phyllis, Hugh and I had white cups – everyone else's were green.

Lisa leaned forward so she could address Hugh, who was sitting on her side of the table but at the opposite end. 'If you decide to experiment with pot, Hugh, you won't have to worry about being arrested. Recreational marijuana is legal in Massachusetts now, I understand. Well, sort of. You can grow it for personal use or to give away, but you can't buy or sell it.'

'It's the same in DC,' Claire pointed out. 'Luckily, there's a group of deaf artists who'll help with that. They'll sell you a wildlife painting for fifty-five dollars and throw in a bag of marijuana absolutely free. Credit cards accepted, and they deliver. I have DC friends who have wallpapered their condos with truly gawd-awful art.'

Phyllis chuckled. 'We could put a few plants in the garden, Hugh, along with the tomatoes. Then I can take up painting.'

'With two people in the house, you're allowed up twelve plants,' Lisa offered helpfully.

Hugh's eyes grew wide behind his glasses. 'You're not serious, are you, Phyllis?'

Next to me, Phyllis shrugged. 'You never know. It might be good for your arthritis.'

Cindy dumped dressing over her salad. Still holding the empty cup, she said, 'I vape occasionally for recreation, but Mark's dealing with chronic pain from a spinal-cord injury. One of the legacies of his gridiron career, I'm afraid.'

'Spinal injuries like mine are a big worry,' Mark said. 'And I watch these kids play ball, see their heads bang together, think how your brain floats around untethered in a pool of cerebrospinal fluid, and it's like Jell-O, your brain, crashing against a bony skull.' He made his right hand into a fist and pounded it repeatedly into his left palm.

Cindy's hand closed over his, stilling it.

'Ah, fall,' Austin drawled. 'The season of tailgates, touchdowns and traumatic brain injuries.'

As I've often said, the scientific instrument has not yet been invented that can measure how little I care about football. 'Football is one of the sacrifices I make for my marriage,' I said.

'Really? How so?' Mark seemed genuinely curious.

'One Army-Navy game, I don't remember which one, but it was long before Tivo was invented, anyway, Paul had to be in England. He asked me to tape the game for him. Like a good wife, I got my knitting, grabbed the remote and plopped down in front of the VHS. I thought I'd do Paul a big favor and cut out all the ads and time-outs, so I sat through the whole damn game, clicking the recorder off and on, off and on.' I paused to take sip of wine. Nobody jumped in to interrupt or to fill the silence, which I took as a sign to carry on. 'A week later, Paul got home, popped some corn, grabbed a beer and sat down to watch the tape. First, the Naval Academy Glee Club sang the national anthem, then Army streamed onto the field, followed by an ad for a snow tire, wild cheering in the Army stands, then a time-out and another ad and another ad . . .'

The laughter began with Claire and rolled around the table like a wave.

I grinned and speared a forkful of salad. 'Obviously, at some point early on, I'd gotten out of synch. It took a lot of steak dinners to get back into Paul's good graces after that. What a goof! And I wasn't even stoned.'

I turned to Mark. 'Do you smoke pot every day?'

'Mark didn't smoke when he was playing football,' Cindy said, not directly answering my question. 'You can't, if you're going to pass the NFL drug tests. They're damn serious about it, too. After you get the notice, you have four hours to report in, even if you're out of the country, like on vacation. If you don't show up, or if your pee is diluted, it's the same as testing positive.'

Leaning forward to speak around me, Phyllis said to Mark, 'Well, it's a good thing you got out of the sport before you got that brain disease you get from concussions.' She turned to her husband. 'Hugh, who was that football player who just hung himself in prison, the one who shot the boyfriend of his fiancée's sister?'

'Aaron Hernandez,' Hugh supplied. 'Played for the Patriots. He was acquitted of killing two other guys in a drive-by shooting, but they nailed him for murdering Odin Lloyd.' Hugh brandished his fork. 'Here's a crime tip for you, friends. If you want to get away with murder, don't intentionally destroy your home security system or smash your cell phone to smithereens. It might arouse suspicion.'

'Not funny, Hugh.' Phyllis scowled. 'Hernandez was only twenty-seven years old. I read that the family donated his brain to the brain bank in Boston, to test it for CTE.'

'CTE? What's that?' Desiree asked.

'Chronic traumatic encephalopathy,' Josh supplied. 'A kind of dementia. Like early-onset Alzheimer's. Frank Gifford famously died from it. So did Gale Sayers. The brain bank has hundreds of brains on deposit, but they singled out those of NFL players for special study. The *New York Times* reported just the other day that of one hundred and eleven brains, one hundred and ten showed signs of advanced CTE.'

Josh's arm snaked around Lisa's shoulders and drew her close for a moment. 'That's conclusive enough for me. If Lisa and I are lucky enough to have children, none of them will be playing football, I can promise you that.'

Lisa smiled and nodded. 'I agree. Totally.'

'To be fair, there are new rules for high-school players,' Mark pointed out. 'No headbutting allowed, for example, and if they do get clobbered they get sidelined, with minimum return-to-play guidelines.' He crossed his knife over his fork on his plate. 'The NCAA is getting serious about it, too. They've moved kickoffs to the forty-yard line instead of the thirty-five, and touchbacks are now marked at the twenty.'

I had no idea how messing around with yard lines could effectively prevent athletic injuries in a game whose main objective seemed to be crashing repeatedly into one another like randy buckhorn sheep. But, hey, the money was good.

Hugh seemed to share my view. 'College football, what a crock. You recruit kids who can't cut it academically, then you involve them in a sport that makes them stupider.'

'Hugh!'

'Well, it's true, and I'm not going to apologize for saying it. All these new rules? It's prevention after the fact. Any plan that depends on athletes to self-report how they feel after getting bonked on the head is destined to fail. It wouldn't be manly not to soldier on.'

'Can't they test for CTE?' Phyllis wanted to know.

'Scientists at BU are working on ways to diagnose and treat CTE in living patients, but right now?' Josh shrugged. 'The only way to know for sure is to examine a player's brain after death.'

'Eeeuw,' Lisa said.

'It's football,' Mark commented with a dismissive shrug. 'Goes with the territory. Until I retired and got into politics, football was my life. And now . . .' He paused, then glanced sideways at Cindy as if asking her permission to continue.

Claire pounced. 'Mark has a new job,' she announced, her voice dripping acid. 'He'll be leaving the State House to coach football at Maryland State.'

Lisa bounced in her chair. 'Mark! That's super. You must be thrilled.'

'I am,' he said. 'It's a big responsibility, pulling the program out of the gutter. The team was on suspension last year and it's time for a fresh start. I'll be getting to work right after July the fourth.'

'What about the Dorchester County farm?' I asked.

'Completely up to Cindy,' Mark said. 'I won't have time to worry about it.'

Cindy beamed. 'We're going ahead with the grow application, of course, but Mark has already started the process of divesting himself from it.'

How one could completely divest oneself of something owned by one's wife was beyond me, but that was Mark's ethical problem, not mine.

The main course arrived – grilled ribeye steak with a golden, deep-fried *chile relleno* on the side, oozing *asiago*. Before we were allowed to dig in, Kai appeared, cradling a bottle of red wine. He made a ceremony of offering it to Austin for inspection.

'A Malbec 2013,' Austin announced. 'Pairs beautifully with Gorilla Glue, a rather potent hybrid, though, so we go easy on it.'

'I could mention my vast experience in the late eighties pairing Mateus Rose with moldy Mexican brick weed,' Claire said as she leaned to one side so Kai could fill her wine glass, 'but I wouldn't want to brag.'

'When I'm stoned,' Josh offered, 'pickles and peanut butter are a great combo.'

'I love Cheetos and Pop-Tarts,' Lisa added.

'No, no, no. We're all curated now,' Desiree scolded, emphasizing the word *curated*.

'Well, OK,' Lisa drawled, 'although you have to agree that for the casual stoner, Cheetos and Pop-Tarts are much more accessible than, say, garlic edamame or *escargots de Bourgogne*.'

'*Coquilles Saint-Jacques!*' Claire crowed, igniting a free-for-all.

'*Foie de veau!*'

'*Calamari fritti!*'

'*Nam tok moo!*'

'*Hachis parmentier!*' was my contribution to the fantasy banquet.

Eventually our empty plates where whisked away and an intermezzo appeared: lemon lollypops – ten milligrams – with frozen grapes as a chaser. The grapes were plump, seedless and deliciously cold. I popped one into my mouth and bit down. The crisp skin burst, giving way to the inside – lush, creamy and sweet, like sherbet. Heavenly. I reached for another grape, then another. My body was slowly letting go of the stress of the past few days. I felt calm and deeply relaxed, as if discovering a gear I'd never used before.

'Ah, chocolate and weed,' Josh was saying when I tuned in again. 'Total proof that God loves us.'

I had no idea how it had gotten there, but on the placemat before me sat dessert – a dark chocolate ganache torte with raspberries perched in perfect symmetry on top.

'Don't eat it yet!' Austin warned. 'Kai has a surprise for you.'

As Austin spoke, Kai was making the rounds, handing each of us a neatly rolled joint.

'I don't think . . .' Phyllis began, holding the joint gingerly between thumb and forefinger.

Austin raised both hands, palms out, silencing her. 'Once everyone has a joint, I don't want you to light it. I want you to take a pull on the unlit joint so that you can experience the essential oils in the herb – a terpene pull, if you will.'

'The herb,' Claire repeated, pronouncing the 'h' just as Austin had. 'What exactly *is* the herb, if we may inquire?'

'Girl Scout Cookies,' he said. 'It will launch you to euphoria's top floor.'

A terpene pull never hurt anyone, I reasoned as I followed the example of everyone else at the table: I put the joint to my lips and sucked in. The herb tasted earthy and sweet, like brown sugar with overtones of nutmeg.

'It's a hybrid of Durban Poison and OG Kush,' Austin explained. 'Good for stress, migraines and depression. And you can simply wave insomnia goodbye!'

'The first time I smoked OG Kush, I thought it tasted like Mexican food,' Josh commented. 'This hybrid is surprisingly different.'

While Josh and Austin lit up, I abstained. I exchanged the joint for a fork and used it to attack my dessert, counting on the phenethyl-amines in chocolate to launch me to euphoria's top floor.

'Hannah tells me you knew Daniel Morecraft-Hill at Boston U,' Claire said, addressing Josh.

'Almost a decade ago,' Josh said, exhaling a thin stream of smoke. 'Small world, huh? He was my thesis advisor.'

'Poor, poor man. Did he have any family?' Phyllis asked.

'Not that I know of. He mentioned a brother once, but other than that . . .' Josh shrugged. 'He pretty much lived in the lab.'

'He sometimes heated up soup in a beaker,' Lisa said. 'Disgusting. You'd think he'd never heard of microwaves.'

My body went squiggly. My head swam. Boston University. The brain bank. CTE. Football. I turned to look at Mark, the former linebacker, who, like me, was chewing his torte appreciatively. A handsome profile, I thought, not at all spoiled by traces of a frequently broken nose. Mark was all angles. You could draw his portrait with a ruler.

'Was Daniel involved with the brain bank at BU, Josh?' I asked.

'Could have been, I suppose. It dates back to 1996 or thereabouts. But, frankly, what with his schedule, I wouldn't have thought he had the time. And it wasn't exactly his area of expertise.'

'I had a chemistry teacher who used to toast marshmallows over a Bunsen burner,' Phyllis said. 'I kept thinking the chemistry department was playing a joke on us, that they'd show up any minute and say "Gotcha!" but it never happened.'

'I had a professor once . . .' Lisa was saying, when I noticed that my wine glass was empty.

I nudged Mark with my elbow. 'My glass seems to have a hole in it,' I joked. 'I wonder how that happened?'

I raised the glass to catch Kai's attention. He was at my side in a moment with a generous refill.

'I love the idea of pairings,' I said, taking a sip. 'It's just like in wine country, isn't it? My husband and I took a wine train in Napa, or was it Sonoma? Maybe Mendocino?' Holding the wine glass by the stem, I swirled the wine, smelled it and took another sip, letting it spread over my tongue – front to back and side to side – the way the sommelier had taught us then. 'See, swirl, sniff, sip and savor,' I muttered to nobody in particular.

In mid-savor, I caught Mark looking at me curiously.

'What was I saying? Sorry. Lost my train of thought. There's a point here somewhere. We took a wine train, or trolley, or maybe a limo. Somebody's limo, anyway.'

While I was trying to sort it out, Desiree pushed back her chair and stood. '*Digestifs* will be served in the solarium,' she announced grandly. 'Amaretto, cognac, schnapps, galliano, grappa, ouzo . . . you name it, we got it.'

Just what I need, I thought as I struggled to my feet, holding on to the table for support. A *digestif* would be *le denier coup*.

I was feeling weightless, relaxed and a bit giddy, like I'd taken too much Motrin.

As Claire passed by, I looped onto her arm and mumbled, 'Stick with me, girlfriend.'

Claire's face wore that puzzled look where her eyebrows almost met. 'Hannah?' she began, then she smiled indulgently and patted my hand where it rested on her arm. 'The blind leading the blind,' she murmured.

Twenty-Four

Medical cannabis, stop eating, let go.
Eat more you will see white ghosts
walking around and eat long enough,
you will know how to talk to the Gods.

Pen Ts'ao [The Herbal],
1234 A.D. edition.

Jefferson Airplane. An album from my college days, taking me back and back and back.

What did the dormouse say? I struggled to remember. *Did Alice even know?*

'Don't do Northern Lights,' Austin warned someone. 'It's a heavy hitter. You'll get couch lock.'

Couch! I heard myself laughing. *This is a chair. Comfortable, though. The same chair that . . .? No, Desiree had taken that one away.*

'Off to bed for me. Early flight.' It sounded like Lisa. I cracked an eyelid. Josh was sprawled in the chair opposite me, one leg draped over the arm. Lisa bent down, brushed her lips against his cheek. 'Don't be too long.'

He grabbed Lisa's hand and pulled her into his lap so he could deliver a proper kiss. Feeling like a voyeur, I closed my eyes, withdrawing.

Grace Slick's voice, husky, drenched with echo, reached out with seductive arms, sucking me in.

Down and down and down, crawling into a tunnel, following the White Rabbit.

The Red Queen something something something. I tried to sing along, but Grace was moving too fast for me.

A hand on my shoulder, a gentle shake. 'Hannah? Are you all right?'

I opened my eyes and took a moment to focus. Claire.

'You're stoned!' she said. 'What happened?'

'Buh . . .' My lips weren't working. Were they still there? I reached up and located them with my fingers. Pinched. Exercised my tongue. Tried again. 'Fine, just fine.'

'I'm getting you some orange juice,' Claire said from somewhere far away.

Stoned. Yeah, how did that happen? Somebody . . . who?

I opened my eyes. Josh had gone. His chair was empty.

'I thought she didn't consume,' Mark said.

I turned my whole body in his direction, feeling like a bobblehead doll. Mark was looking at me but speaking to his wife.

'Hell if I know,' Cindy said. 'Must be some sort of mixup.'

Mixup. Swell.

Claire suddenly filled the frame, her hand extended. 'Here, drink this.'

I accepted the bottle, gulped from it greedily and handed it back. 'I'm hungry.'

'She's got the munchies,' somebody whispered. 'Classic.'

'Shut up, Mark.' Claire handed me a cookie.

221

I studied it for a while, admiring the chocolate chips, dark and glossy, peaked caps standing proud and tall. One, two, three . . . but it was too hard. They were moving around, refusing to be counted. I ate them.

After minutes, maybe hours, Claire said, 'Feeling better?'

I started to laugh, couldn't make myself stop. 'Haven't felt so good since Amsterdam,' I said between hiccups. 'Another cookie would be nice.'

Claire patted my leg. 'Good. I think you'll live.'

'Where's everyone?' I asked, glancing around the solarium.

'Everyone's gone to bed except Mark, Cindy and me,' Claire said. 'It's after one o'clock.'

I ate the second cookie slowly, turning it clockwise, nibbling the edges until it was the size of a quarter, then finished it off.

'Come up to bed, Hannah.'

Jefferson Airplane had moved on to 'Plastic Fantastic Lover.' I shook my head no. 'I love this album, Claire. Let it finish.' Conducting with my hand, I sang along, pleased that I remembered every word of a song I hadn't sung since, like, forever. When it ended, I smiled up at Claire and said, 'People think the song's about a dildo, but it's not. It's about Marty Balin's new stereo system.'

Claire laughed. Apparently, I'd convinced her I was sobering up. 'Well, if you can rap along with Marty Balin, you're going to be fine.'

'I'll stay with her, Claire,' Cindy volunteered.

'I don't need a babysitter,' I said, waggling my fingers. 'Buh-bye.'

Still laughing, Claire left.

Cindy gave Mark a gentle shove. 'You go on up, too. I won't be long.'

'What if . . .?' Mark asked, keeping his voice so low I could barely hear it over the throb of Paul Kantner's acoustic guitar.

'How many men on a football team?' Cindy whispered.

'Eleven.'

'Room eleven,' she repeated softly. 'Say it.'

'Eleven.'

'The number's on the door, sweetheart.'

Still, he hesitated.

'Go to bed, Mark.'

I listened hazily while Grace Slick moved on. 'Somebody to Love' sucked me in, as it always did, Slick's rich vibrato pulsing with natural reverb as she sang about finding the truth . . .

Truth. A sobering knot twisted my gut. Mark's headaches, his faulty memory, the unexplained anger.

My eyes flew open. Mark had disappeared. Gone up to bed, as instructed. Cindy stood by the casement windows, staring into the dark. We were alone.

'Mark has it, doesn't he, Cindy? CTE?'

Cindy turned to face me, arms crossed over her chest like a petulant child. She scowled silently, her face immobile yet easily read.

'I'm so sorry,' I said. 'Mark's a super guy. He doesn't deserve that. Nobody does.'

Cindy didn't budge.

'Sit down, Cindy. Please. Talk to me.'

223

After a long moment, during which she was apparently considering my invitation, she crossed the room and plopped down in a chair directly opposite mine.

'How long has it been going on?' I asked her.

She sidestepped the question. 'We don't *know* that he has it, not for certain. Mark's forgetful, sure, but so am I.' She managed a wan smile. 'I need one of those GPS tags to keep track of my car keys.'

'Me, too,' I said, trying to keep the conversation light but moving along. 'I walk into the kitchen, open the fridge and think, now, what the hell am I looking for?'

'Only one way to know for sure,' Cindy said matter-of-factly. 'An autopsy. After Mark's dead.'

'It's not his fault,' I said, keeping my voice steady, suppressing the urge to scream. 'When Mark started playing football, nobody knew.'

Cindy exploded. 'That's bullshit, Hannah! Total bullshit. They knew it as far back as 1994. That's when the NFL set up the MTBI.'

I'd never heard of the MTBI. 'What's that?'

'The Mild Traumatic Brain Injury Committee.' She leaned forward, closing the gap between us. 'And just to show you how *serious* they were about it, guess who they appointed to head it up? Huh? Huh?'

'Help me out here, Cindy.'

'The team doctor for the New York Jets. A rheumatologist!'

'What could possibly go wrong?' I said.

'Exactly. And it took about two-and-a-half minutes for the NFL Commissioner to label all the hoohah in the press over concussions as fake news.' She flopped back in her chair, apparently exhausted, but before I could sneak a word in, she launched a second salvo. 'And just last year, Congress issued a report that showed how the NFL pressured the National Institutes of Health to strip sixteen million dollars from government-funded research going on up at Boston University. They wanted the money redirected to the NFL's own research team. What a crock! Fortunately, the NIH isn't stupid. They refused.'

Something was niggling at me. Boston University again. The brain bank.

I had a hunch, and I played it. 'Has Mark willed his brain to the brain bank?'

Cindy nodded. 'You guessed. I thought you had. Back at dinner, I saw you staring at him.'

'That's it, then, isn't it? It wasn't Daniel's connection to Big Tobacco that set Mark off, it was learning that Daniel once taught at BU.'

She nodded miserably.

'But, hold on a minute, Cindy. Daniel left BU *years* ago. What could he possibly—?'

Cindy didn't wait for me to finish. 'Saturday night, after Colin disappeared? I came back down to retrieve my stash and Daniel said he was going to tell.' She took a deep, shuddering breath. 'Mark has good years left in him, Hannah, doing what he loves. If Maryland State finds out . . .'

She let me fill in the blank. If Maryland State got wind of Mark's condition, the coaching offer could be off the table.

'But aren't those arrangements supposed to be confidential?' I said. 'If you didn't tell anybody, who . . .'

Again, she cut in. 'Daniel still had colleagues there, I presume.'

While I was tossing that possibility around, she hit me with another zinger. 'And get this. All along the way, the NFL's so-called research team was using some of the same lawyers, lobbyists and consultants as Big Tobacco.'

'Shit,' I said.

Cindy was on a roll. 'And a co-owner of the New York Giants, I forget his name, was also part-owner of the Lorillard tobacco company. The guy served on a couple of the pseudo research boards.'

'The plot sickens,' I said.

'Don't believe me, believe the *New York Times*.' She shrugged. 'Or watch *Concussion* on Netflix.'

'But why, Cindy? Why did he threaten Mark? What was in it for Daniel?'

Cindy's eyes filled with tears. 'I don't know! Daniel had a *thing* about football. He kept ranting on about it, like Mark would be personally responsible for killing kids! It upset Mark so much, he stalked off to bed, leaving me alone with Colin and the sonofabitch.'

'Daniel had no room to talk,' I said reasonably. 'Not when he's working for a tobacco company that spreads disease and death throughout the world. The US market for tobacco has flatlined, you know that, right? Churchill-Mills has a whole division trying their damnedest to hook young consumers abroad.'

'I should talk,' she said. She dug a vape pen out of the pocket of her tunic, clicked several times to switch it on, waited a few seconds for the element to heat up, then took a toke. Then another. She sighed. Closed her eyes.

Had Cindy just pointed the finger at Mark for the murder of Daniel Morecraft-Hill? Or, had she killed Daniel herself to protect her husband's job?

From the speakers, guitars picked out a simple melody. A recorder sang, sweet as a panpipe, performing a folk ballad like they used to write: simple, honest and hauntingly beautiful. *I saw you, saw you comin' back to me.*

My conversation with Cindy seemed hours in the past.

The music faded. Except for Cindy's quiet, rhythmic breathing, silence filled the solarium.

I should have gone to bed, I knew that. I'd promised Claire I'd come up as soon as the album was over, but at that moment it seemed like too much effort. Overcome with weariness, and trusting that Cindy's vape pen had an automatic shut-off, I nestled down in the chair and slept.

I awoke in a panic. The lights were out. I couldn't breathe. I tried to raise my head but something heavy pressed down on it. Desperate for air, I turned my head to the right, but the pressure only intensified, flattening my ear against the upholstery, pinning it there.

I reached up, clawing. At a pillow, at the hands that held it to my face. I grasped one of the hands, dug my fingernails in firm and deep.

'Ouch!' someone cried. I held on, digging harder.

I squirmed, scooting down in the chair, trying to get out from under the pillow, but my only reward was a knee, hard and unyielding, in my stomach. My legs flailed uselessly. My lungs burned, my eyelids stung. If this kept up much longer, my eyeballs would surely burst.

Whttt, whttt, whttt. Whooshing in my ears, gradually growing louder. Was the sound coming from me or my attacker?

Fireworks exploded behind my eyelids, and then everything faded to black.

I felt it first, something pounding on my chest: *one-two-three-four-five.*

A mouth pressed to mine. Air, blessed air, with a hint of hops.

Somebody was calling my name. 'Hannah! Hannah!'

I gasped, took a bite of air, gulped it in greedily. I took several deep, unsteady breaths, delighted to discover that my lungs were still functioning.

Light appeared, around the edges at first, and then a face gradually came into focus, only inches from my own.

'Hello, Colin,' I said.

Twenty-Five

*Persons using this narcotic, smoke
the dried leaves of the plant, which
has the effect of driving them
completely insane. The addict loses
all sense of moral responsibility . . .
While in this condition they become
raving maniacs and are liable to kill
or indulge in any form of violence to
other persons, using the most savage
methods of cruelty.*

Emily F. Murphy, 'Janey Canuck',
The Black Candle, Toronto, Thomas Allen,
1922, pp.332–333.

I was sitting in the chair I almost died in, sipping from a bottle of water. 'Are you OK?' Colin asked. 'Please tell me you're OK.'

'I'm grateful you came back,' I told him. 'For more reasons than one.'

'If I had been five minutes later . . .' He let the thought die.

'The Navy taught you something, at least.' I dredged up a smile. 'Punctuality.'

'Not to put too fine a point on it,' he said, 'but what the fuck was going on here?' Colin bobbed his head to the left, acknowledging Cindy. She huddled on the floor in a corner of the solarium,

229

whimpering, sandwiched between the wainscoting and an antique étagère. A hand oozing blood was pressed against her left eye.

Colin's question stumped me at first. 'What's going on?' I repeated, massaging my temples, trying to pull the scattered threads of memory together. I remembered feeling light-headed after dinner – a mixup, someone said – and then I must have passed out.

'What's wrong with Cindy?' I asked.

'I socked her, I'm afraid.'

Maybe I was still a teensy bit high, but that simply didn't compute. 'Cindy? You punched Cindy? Why?'

'She was trying to smother you, Hannah.'

'Cindy? I can't believe it.' The former cheerleader avoided my gaze, drawing her knees up to her chin, shrinking further into herself.

From her body language, I knew what Colin said must be true.

'You got your licks in first, though, Hannah. Her hand's a bloody mess.'

I winced, distressed by the damage I had done. 'Do you need ice for that eye?' I asked Cindy.

'Waaah!' Cindy wailed, loud enough to draw Dracula out of his coffin, even in broad daylight.

Instead, it was Desiree who burst into the room, barefoot, clad in her nightshirt, her black plait streaming like a banner behind her. 'What the *hell* is going on in here?' She stopped short. 'Colin!'

'Cindy was trying to murder Hannah,' Colin

said almost conversationally. 'I think you better call the police.'

Desiree stood transfixed, her face drained of color, looking shell-shocked.

'The police, Desiree?' Colin prodded. 'We can explain later.'

'Right. The police.' She turned to go. 'Just what we need. The police.'

'And tell Mark we need him down here, too,' Colin added.

'Police. Mark,' she muttered, as if making a list. 'All I want is to run a simple bud and breakfast, no drama, and look what I get.' More choice words ensued, uttering any one of which would have landed my daughter in time-out for life.

At my insistence, Colin fetched a napkin from the sideboard and used it to bandage Cindy's injured hand.

'You'll do well in the Navy, Midshipman McDaniel,' I said, massaging a sore spot on my ribs. 'You get points for being a take-charge kind of guy.'

'That's all well and good, Mrs Ives, but I'd appreciate it if you didn't mention it.'

'What? No letters of appreciation to the Commandant of Midshipmen?'

'Especially to the Commandant of Midshipmen.'

Without taking his eyes off Cindy, Colin edged back the sideboard to fetch me more water.

Fine, I'd told him. *I'm fine.* But my head throbbed, my eyes burned, my throat ached and my ribs felt like someone had used them for batting practice. I shifted in the chair, unable to suppress a moan.

Even though the grand staircase was carpeted, Mark's emergency descent echoed through the house like rolling thunder. Wearing the undershirt and boxer shorts he'd apparently been sleeping in, he burst into the solarium. 'What's happened? Where's Cindy?'

Colin pointed.

Mark's head snapped around.

'He knew, Mark,' Cindy whined when she caught sight of her husband. 'Somehow that horrible man knew.'

'Knew what, sweetheart?' Mark soothed. He leaned over his wife, his hand extended. 'C'mon, let me help you up.'

Using her good hand, she grasped his, like a drowning woman. He pulled her to her feet and folded her into his arms, resting his chin on top of her head, stroking her hair.

'I want you to be happy, that's all,' Cindy sobbed. 'You hated politics – you can't pretend that you didn't. Football is your life. The Maryland job was a dream come true.' She gulped air. 'Daniel was going to take it all, all away,' she blubbered into his chest.

Eyes wide, Mark appealed to me. 'What's she talking about, Hannah?'

'I think Cindy's confessing to murdering Daniel,' I said.

'She'd just tried . . .' Colin began, but I silenced him with a death ray. Mark had enough on his plate to deal with just then. The attempted murder of me would have to wait.

With one beefy finger, Mark touched his wife's chin and tipped her face up gently. 'That's total bullshit, isn't it, sweetheart?' he said, looking directly into her eyes. 'Tell them, Cindy.'

Cindy sucked in her lips, wagged her head slowly.

Mark's face drained of color as the awful truth dawned. 'He suspected I had CTE?'

'Daniel was a biologist,' I explained. 'Before he moved to North Carolina, he taught at Boston University. He had to know about the brain bank and the research going on there. Maybe he maintained his contacts and one of them let something slip about your will. Then again, maybe Daniel simply guessed.'

Mark slumped. 'Is it that obvious?'

'No,' I answered truthfully. 'Maybe to a medical professional, or your nearest and dearest, but to the rest of us, you're just a little forgetful. Early days yet, I'd say.'

Mark led Cindy to a chair. After he'd convinced her to sit down, he stood behind it protectively, gripping the back with both hands. 'It's going to get worse, they tell me.'

I nodded.

'In the time I've got left, I'd like to make a difference.'

'*Carpe diem*,' I said.

After what I'd learned, a good start would be banning football forever. Yet, boxers still squared off in the ring. Cyclists flipped out in motocross. Climbers froze to death on Mount Everest. Cowboys straddled bucking bulls. And a skydiver's parachute didn't always open.

As if reading my mind, Mark said, 'If we're going to fix it, we need to work from within.'

233

'Mark . . .' I began, but Colin, who'd been standing lookout at the door, interrupted. 'They're here,' he said, stepping aside.

This time, Detective Jacobs was not alone. He was accompanied by a rumpled and sleepy-eyed assistant, her hair twisted up in a careless knot and secured with a black plastic claw. In the brightly lit hallway behind them, Desiree and Austin consulted, exchanging worried glances. Desiree gave Austin a gentle shove. Once he was on his way toward the solarium, she disappeared in the direction of the kitchen.

'Sergeant Timmons,' Jacobs said, introducing his sidekick. His eyes scanned the room and alighted on Colin. 'Who are you? Everyone else I know.'

'McDaniel, sir. Colin.'

Jacobs nodded. 'Ah, the prodigal son has returned.'

'Yes, sir.'

'Don't go anywhere. I need to talk to you.'

Colin bowed his head deferentially, then stepped back, as if trying to blend into the wallpaper.

Jacobs executed an about-face. 'Somebody kindly explain why I'm here at this ungodly hour of the morning.'

'Cindy and I had a bit of a confrontation,' I said with a warning glance at Colin. 'She's confessed to killing Daniel.'

Cindy's head sagged. Her body heaved with sobs. 'I, I, I . . .' she began.

'Hush, Cindy,' Mark warned, placing a hand on her shoulder, leaning close and speaking in her ear. 'You don't have to say anything.'

Mark looked up. 'My wife would like to contact her attorney.'

Jacobs shrugged. 'Suit yourself. We can continue this discussion down at the station.'

Mark patted his boxers, his forehead wrinkled in puzzlement.

'You can use my phone,' I said, taking pity on the man, standing there in his underwear. I reached for my handbag, which lay nearly forgotten under the chair I'd been sitting in.

Mark waved the offer away. 'Number's in the phone up in my room. May I get it?'

Jacobs nodded.

Mark bent down and whispered something in Cindy's ear. When he straightened again, he said, 'I forbid you to ask Cindy any questions until I've returned.'

Jacobs shrugged, as if it didn't matter to him one way or the other.

After Mark left, Sergeant Timmons moved into position behind Cindy's chair, keeping watch, remaining silent.

'Now, I'd like to hear what you have to say,' Jacobs said, turning to me. He aimed a finger at Colin and Austin. 'You two, stay here. And give that woman some water or something. I'll talk with you later.'

He motioned me into the sitting room and indicated that I should sit on the loveseat. The same loveseat where he'd interviewed Claire and me – gosh, how could it have been only two days ago? He pulled up a side chair, sat down, whipped out his notebook, pinned me to the loveseat with his sharp blue eyes . . .

And I told him everything. Or, almost everything.

'I'm ninety-nine-one-hundredth's-percent sure that Mark had nothing to do with Daniel's death,' I concluded. 'In her confession to me, Cindy made it clear that she'd acted alone.'

'That fits with what Mark told us earlier,' Jacobs said. 'That he had gone to bed with a headache, leaving Cindy downstairs in the solarium.' He chewed thoughtfully on the retractor end of his ballpoint pen.

'Cindy must have gone nuts,' I said. 'By silencing Daniel permanently, she thought she'd protect her husband's coaching career. Backfired big time, though. It'll all come out now, won't it? And when the disease really takes hold, how is she going to take care of Mark from a prison cell in Colorado?'

'Is there family?' Jacobs wanted to know.

'I have no idea,' I said. 'I met them for the first time this weekend.' After a moment of silence, I said, 'Cindy's confession took me completely by surprise. I'd theorized that the robbery and Daniel's murder were connected, but it seemed clear from my conversation with her that Cindy had nothing to do with robbing the safe.'

Jacobs snorted. 'You're right about that.' He paused, studying me speculatively, as if weighing how much to tell me. 'You'll find out about it soon enough, anyway, as soon as I tell the Nortons. Late yesterday, we made an arrest in the payroll heist.'

He followed this bombshell with a pregnant pause – deliberate, I thought, just to torment me.

I bit. 'Well, Detective Jacobs? Are you going to keep me in suspense?'

'The Nortons should be more scrupulous in hiring security personnel,' he said.

'The Pawlowski brothers?'

Jacobs nodded. 'For a couple of security guys, it was a rookie mistake. We lifted Borys' fingerprints from a drawer inside the safe. That was enough probable cause to get a search warrant. We recovered the money from a suitcase inside the apartment the two brothers shared.'

'I ran into Borys in the hallway that night,' I reminded him, 'but he wasn't carrying anything, so he must have come back later for the money. I wondered if he showed up on the security cameras.'

Jacobs shook his head. 'Being security, Borys knew how to avoid them. That was another thing that aroused my suspicion.'

'The dog that didn't bark in the nighttime,' I said.

Jacobs favored me with a rare smile. 'Something like that.'

'Were the boys in cahoots?'

'Boys? Ha!' Jacobs snorted. 'They're almost forty years old.'

'Sorry,' I said. 'I picked that up from Marilyn Brignole. That's what she calls them.'

'The younger one, Nick Pawlowski, found the combination to the safe. Bragged about how smart he was. Borys did all the heavy lifting, while Nick waited for him in a car parked around the block. Smoking a cigarette,' he added. 'License plate clearly identifiable.' He smiled. 'We picked that up on one of the neighbor's security cams.'

'What a dumb thing to do! They had to know they'd be suspected. Why'd they take the risk?'

'They love their mother,' Jacobs said simply. 'She was getting on in years and was starting to feel isolated out in the country. Had her heart set on moving into a little apartment in old town Ljubljana. Mati had scrimped and saved all her life, Nick told me, so they promised to buy into it for her.'

'Why didn't they simply bring Mati to the States?' I asked.

Jacobs shrugged. 'Mati visited Denver once. Hated every minute. The altitude got to her.'

At more than five thousand feet above sea level, I knew that Denver had seventeen percent less oxygen than cities lower down, but the altitude hadn't bothered me. 'In what way?' I asked.

'Shortness of breath, Borys said, and constant fatigue. She couldn't shake the headaches.'

'What happens now?' I asked.

Jacobs slotted the pen into his pocket and tucked the notebook away. '"The millstones of justice turn exceedingly slow, but grind exceedingly fine,"' he quoted. 'John Bannister Gibson.'

'"We only get the stupid villains. The bright ones are all on holiday in Majorca,"' I quoted back. '*Rumpole of the Bailey*.'

* * *

As dawn was breaking, while the rest of the house still slept, Sergeant Timmons zipped Cindy up in plastic hand restraints and escorted her down the flagstone path from the front door of Bell House to Jacobs' patrol car. Mark followed a few steps behind.

We huddled together on the stoop, watching as Timmons wrenched the door open, placed one hand gently on Cindy's head and eased her inside. After the door closed behind her, Cindy leaned wearily against the window, staring vacantly ahead.

Mark remained rooted to the sidewalk, following the vehicle with his eyes as it, with Jacobs at the wheel, whisked his wife away. After a quiet moment he rejoined us, his eyes brimming.

Austin tugged on Mark's arm. 'C'mon, man. I'll drive you to the station.'

Desiree dangled a set of car keys. 'Take my Beemer, Austin. It's in the back.'

'Thank goodness there are no kids,' Colin said when Mark was out of earshot.

'I wondered about that,' I said.

'Mark's parents are still alive, though, and he's got a bunch of siblings . . .' The rest of Colin's sentence was lost as we turned to follow Desiree back into the house.

We paused in the foyer. 'I didn't know you knew the Kings so well, Colin.'

'That night in the solarium? We had a good talk, Mark and me. I'd seen him play, actually. In the Dolphins Stadium – they call it the Hard Rock, now – when I was a kid.

'After Mark sacked out, Cindy and I shared a joint – some pretty awesome weed called Skywalker, I think. She was in a great mood, singing along with the professor and me for a while, then I thought she'd disappeared. Maybe if I hadn't split when I did, none of this would have happened.'

'You can't know that,' I said, smiling reassuringly. 'Besides, you made up for it tonight.'

'Coffee?' Desiree chirped, sounding artificially cheerful.

I waved the offer away. 'Thanks, Desiree, but I'm desperate for some sleep.'

As I turned to go, she said, 'I'm curious about something, Hannah. Earlier, Colin said Cindy was trying to murder you. When Detective Jacobs was here, you never said a word about that.'

'A figure of speech, that's all,' I said. 'Wasn't it, Colin?'

'That's right,' he said. 'A figure of speech.'

By the time Lisa, Josh and the remaining guests wandered downstairs, dragging their luggage, ready for checkout, I'd crashed, big time, sleeping off the previous evening's ordeal under a down comforter. It wasn't until lunchtime, ravenous and thirsty, that I got an update on the Bell House drama from Claire, running on adrenaline and eager to fill me in. Most of it I already knew, of course.

Before heading downtown with Mark, Austin had instructed Desiree to refund everyone's money. While she kept busy with a checkbook and the credit-card machine, Marilyn managed to deliver breakfast, weeping quietly all the while on behalf of the Pawlowski brothers. In spite of the fact that they'd snatched the payroll, including her own wages, she still thought of 'The Bad, Bad Boys' as sons.

While we caught up, Claire and I relaxed on the patio in side-by-side loungers. Plates, empty of all but sandwich crumbs, sat on the occasional table between us, frosty glasses of cranberry spritzer – low octane – in our hands. One by one, the other guests wandered out to say goodbye. Promised to stay in touch. But would we?

As a kid, I never lived anywhere longer than two or three years. Goes with the territory in a Navy family like ours. Each time I was wrenched from my friends, my late mother used to say, 'The people who are meant to be in your life, Hannah, will always gravitate back to you, no matter how far they wander.'

Sometimes, though, you have to pull them back.

Colin, for example. He'd already left for the airport when I remembered something I needed to ask him. I dug out my iPhone, found his name in my contacts and gave him a call.

'Hey, Mrs Ives,' he said, picking up at once, recognizing my number.

'Daniel's iPhone,' I said without preamble. 'Someone tried to erase the pictures.'

'We did,' he said. 'Lisa and me.'

I thought I'd misheard. 'You and *Lisa*?'

'Yeah. Daniel had passed out and his phone

241

was just lying there on the floor. 'It was Lisa's idea, actually.'

'Don't tell me. So you picked up the phone, used Daniel's thumb . . .'

'That was Lisa. I just erased the pictures. From what I know now, it was win-win for both of us. If Daniel had . . . well, you know.'

Neither of us spoke for a moment.

'Wait a minute,' Colin said, breaking the silence. 'You said someone *tried* to erase the pictures?'

'The police recovered them, Colin.'

'Ah, I should have seen that coming. But it seemed like a good idea at the time. Lisa can be persuasive.'

'You're lucky he didn't wake up.'

'Lisa poked him first. He snorted and mumbled something but, really, the guy was wasted.'

'I hope you mentioned this to the police, Colin.'

'Lisa told that detective what she told me. Her eyes were closed and her hair was a mess, and she'd simply *die* if they showed up on Facebook.' His spot-on imitation of Lisa's diction made me smile.

'No mention of blackmail?'

'It didn't come up, Mrs Ives.'

'I guess it doesn't matter now,' I said.

'Hey, they're calling my flight. Gotta go.'

'Stay in touch, Colin.'

'See you back at the academy,' he said, and rang off.

242

Twenty-Six

If we expect education to result in drug abstinence in the populace then we are doomed to failure. We are a drug using people. From our cigarettes to our vitamins, from coffee to alcohol, from marijuana to heroin – drugs are here to stay.

Marc G. Kurzman, 'Drug Education: Boom or Bust?' in *Report on the Thirty-sixth Annual Scientific Meeting: Committee on Problems of Drug Dependence, Mexico City, March 10–14, 1974*. National Academy of Sciences, Research Council (US), p.967.

'When it comes to fashion, feathers are not exactly my thing,' I complained to Claire.

Several feet away, Claire's designer had decked her out in a strapless gown of cut-up CDs; she flashed and sparkled like a *Saturday Night Fever* disco ball. 'I think you look fab,' she said.

Yasunori Asano, the free-thinking young designer I'd drawn for the Visionary Art Museum charity fashion show, clearly agreed. '*Sugoi!*' he announced with a broad sweep of his arm. 'Gown is awesome!'

Wearing a blank-eyed stare and a perfect pout,

I'd been rehearsing my runway walk down the hallway at home – shoulders back, hips forward, step, step, step, turn – but, sadly, the long, languid strides I'd been practicing would never work with this outfit. The off-the-shoulder, black silk sheath Yasu had designed fit so closely that my knees might as well have been glued together. I'd be mincing down the runway like a fully-kimonoed geisha with an electrocuted guinea fowl strapped to my head.

Final fittings were being held on the third floor of the Visionary Museum's Rouse building, a whitewashed, barn-sized hall where, in two weeks' time, the fashion show would take place. In addition to Claire and me, Tammy from the Reach for Recovery group had secured a spot, as had Bob, who, I could see, was being fitted for a three-piece outfit – kilt, jacket and head-dress – that made him look like an Aztec warrior.

'Maybe you could make the skirt a bit looser?' I suggested.

Yasu's dark eyes flashed behind purple-framed eyeglasses. 'This is original Asano. Worth money someday.'

'I'm sure that's true,' I told him with a concilia-tory smile. 'And I'll take good care of it. But will I be able to sit down?'

A tendril of dark hair, dyed green, trembled over his eyebrow as he pinned me in even tighter. 'Chrissy Teigen doesn't sit down,' he said.

'If I were a top model with her kind of money, I wouldn't need to sit down either,' I said. 'I'd hire people to stand around and prop me up on all sides.'

His lips twitched up around the dressmaking pins. I detected a slight smile.

'Maybe the slit could be higher?' I said.

Yasu stared at me, clearly horrified by the suggestion. 'You are model. *I* am designer.'

'Ouch!' I said as a pin pricked my ankle. 'I'm also a real person, Yasu, not a mannequin.' Jet lag was turning me into a diva.

'Turn, *kudasai*,' he announced abruptly. He made a twirling motion with his finger. I obliged by rotating slowly in place, like a chicken on a spit. He grunted his approval, then dove into the satchel of odds and ends he'd brought to the fitting with him. After rummaging for a few seconds, his hand emerged holding a bouquet of speckled guinea-fowl feathers, dyed every color of the rainbow, leftovers from my headdress.

He considered them speculatively. 'I could put some here,' he said, holding the bouquet over my bustle. 'That could be quite special.'

'Indeed,' I said, surrendering to the inevitable.

'Everyone will be looking at you,' he said as he pinned a multicolored spray of feathers to my silk-enhanced tush.

Yes, I thought, *but not in a positive way.*

'I have a vision,' he said in a low, conversational tone, as if he were afraid another competitor might overhear. 'I see a little Japanese mixed with Hollywood glamour.'

I grinned, feeling somewhat flattered. 'If you put it that way, Yasu, I'll be happy to hobble.'

From the bowels of my handbag resting on a nearby chair, my cell phone began to chime. 'Are we done now, Yasu?'

The young designer nodded, so I made a grab for my phone. I didn't recognize the number and was tempted to let it go to voicemail, but Claire was still being fitted – her pink jogging shoes added a certain *je ne sais quoi* to the disco look – so I had a bit of time on my hands.

'Hannah? This is Josh Barton.'

'Josh! How lovely to hear from you.' Holding the phone to my ear, I waddled out the door to take the call on the museum's iconic Bird's Nest Balcony. 'How's Lisa?'

'She'll tell you herself in a minute,' he said. 'I just wanted to let you know that we're back home and there doesn't seem to be any fallout from our, uh, vacation.'

'That's good news,' I said, smiling. In his voice, I could hear the quote marks around the word 'vacation.'

'In point of fact,' Josh continued, 'the Board of Visitors has just granted me tenure.'

Although nobody could see me, except for two tourists circumnavigating the mosaic egg in the courtyard below, I did a fist pump. 'Go, Josh!'

'But I turned them down.'

I thought I'd misheard. 'You turned them *down*?'

Josh's voice bubbled with excitement. 'Lisa and I will be moving to Baltimore in August.'

'Say that again,' I said. 'I think we must have a bad connection.'

Josh laughed. 'We'll be moving to Baltimore. Lisa's already scoping out houses on Zillow. Seems I'll be joining the biology department at Johns Hopkins as an Assistant Professor.'

'That is the best news ever,' I said.

'Yeah, I'm pretty psyched. And this was all before *The Scientist* picked up my *Drosophila* article.'

'A *New York Times* bestseller for sure,' I teased. 'What will you be working on at Hopkins?'

'Stochastic gene regulation during the development of fly and human eyes,' he said. 'Among other things.'

'Way above my pay grade,' I teased.

'You sound like you're in good spirits, Hannah.'

'Claire and I are at a museum being fitted for a charity fashion show. I'm surrounded by people wearing decks of cards and fur bustiers, all trying to pretend it's the most natural thing in the world to walk down the street wearing a red-and-white checked tablecloth with a picnic basket tied to your head. The student designers take everything super seriously, so don't you dare laugh.'

Josh chuckled. 'I hope there's a video.'

'I hope there's *not!*'

In the background, I could hear Lisa saying, 'My turn, Josh.' After a few more minutes, during which I described the outfit I would be modeling in the fashion show, Josh relinquished the phone.

'I just wanted to thank you, Hannah,' Lisa began.

'For what?'

'Well, I'm not in jail for killing Daniel, for a start.'

'I never suspected you for a minute, Lisa,' I lied.

'I had a nightmare about it last night.'

'Smoke a little Skywalker,' I suggested, 'like the budrista advised.'

'Uh, well, as much as I enjoy it, Hannah, I'm off weed.'

'Ah, right,' I said. 'When it comes to marijuana, Stafford U lacks a sense of humor, as I recall.'

Lisa made a ladylike snort. 'That, too, but . . .' She paused. 'Although I sure could use some Chemdawg about now.'

Chemdawg, if I recalled correctly, came highly recommended for treating nausea and vomiting. Lisa wasn't undergoing chemo, so . . .

On the other end of the line, Lisa began to giggle. 'Not drinking wine, either.'

The penny dropped. 'Lisa! You're pregnant?'

'Yup,' she said. 'We'll be welcoming bouncing baby Barton sometime next March.'

'I couldn't be happier for you both,' I said. 'And with you living in Baltimore, I won't have far to drive in order to spoil the baby.'

'We'll count on it.'

'I suspect you'll be much happier living in Baltimore rather than, where was it, Sulphur Rock, Arkansas?'

'Tell me about it,' Lisa said. 'I wouldn't say the school is sliding down the toilet science-wise, at least not yet, but they've just hired as Provost somebody with the Discovery Institute on his CV, so I fear the handwriting is on the wall.'

I drew a blank. 'What is the Discovery Institute and what does it discover?' I asked.

'They promote Intelligent Design, among other wacko theories, so Josh and I are happy to be moving on before they sail off the edge of the world.'

248

That made me laugh.

'Have you heard from Colin?' she asked.

'He's back at the academy and leading a godly, righteous and sober life, or so he claims. They've assigned him to plebe summer detail. As we speak, he's probably shepherding the Class of 2021 through medical exams, uniform issue and haircuts.'

'Haircuts? The women, too?'

Remembering Lisa's flowing tresses, I could appreciate her concern. 'Hair can't touch your collar. You can tie it up close to your head in braids or in a bun, but a lot of women simply cut it short.'

'Ugh,' Lisa said.

'You should read the regulations. "Multiple braids are authorized, but each braid must be the same diameter,"' I quoted from memory. '"Only two barrettes may be worn at the same time, and they must be the same color as the hair."'

Lisa laughed. 'I'd definitely suck at Navy life.'

'I can't wait for the first guy to challenge the regs with a man bun.'

'Seriously,' she said.

'Anyway, Colin will keep busy being a role model for the future leaders of our nation. After he teaches them how to salute, things get serious. Plebe summer's like boot camp. It's not for sissies.'

Lisa suddenly switched gears, moving on to a more serious topic. 'Tell me what's happening with Cindy and Mark. What's going on in Colorado isn't exactly headline news in the *Texarcana Gazette*. Last I heard, Cindy was out on bail.'

'I had an email from Mark just the other day,' I told her. 'They've charged Cindy with second-degree murder, but it's voluntary manslaughter. Even the prosecutor is convinced that Daniel provoked the attack, so they've reduced the charge to a class-three felony, one of those in-the-heat-of-passion things. If convicted, though, Cindy could still get four to twelve years in the slammer.'

Lisa sucked air in through her teeth. 'Ouch!' After a moment, she added, 'Just grasping at straws here, but can't she claim that marijuana made her do it?'

'The Reefer Madness defense? Not guilty by reason of insanity, because marijuana turned you into a homicidal maniac?' I grunted. 'Not likely. The scientific evidence simply doesn't support it. THC can induce psychosis in some people, sure, but there's no link between that kind of psychosis and violence. If you eat too much weed, the worst that usually happens is you have hot and cold flashes, then you crawl under the covers and pass out.' I paused. 'And I speak from experience here.'

I flashed back to Bell House and the evening of the banquet. How I'd slept off the previous evening's ordeal in an antique brass bed, curled up like a kitten under a down comforter.

'How did it happen?' Lisa asked, snapping me back to the balcony in Baltimore. 'How did you end up stoned? Was it really a mixup, like Claire said?'

'It turned out to be the grapes,' I said. 'I was supposed to eat the green ones but I choose the purple instead. They were infused. That, in combination with wine, my usual drug of choice, did the job.'

'Caution. Drinking alcohol while taking this medication may intensify the effect,' Lisa said, quoting a common prescription bottle warning label.

'A highly dangerous pairing,' I admitted with a chuckle. I could laugh about it now.

'But, I still don't get what motivated Daniel to blackmail Cindy,' Lisa said.

'I wondered about that, too, so after I got home, I made some phone calls. Did a little poking around. For a guy with so few scruples, Daniel was on a crusade. Remember that brother you told us about at dinner?'

'Josh mentioned it, yeah.'

'There was a nephew once, I found out. A smart kid. National Honor Society. A 4.0 GPA.'

'Damn. I know where this is going,' Lisa said. 'You got a healthy mind, a healthy body, a whole life full of promise and then, bam!'

'It happened during a high-school homecoming game. A headbutt on a simple punt return. The kid dropped and never moved. Daniel was in the stands. He didn't need a coroner's report to tell him what happened: a cervical break. According to one of his colleagues at Churchill-Mills, Daniel never got over it. We'll never know for sure because we can't ask him,' I continued, 'but I believe Daniel recognized Mark's condition and pressured Cindy to urge Mark to go public, use it as a rallying cry in a campaign to discourage young people from engaging in such dangerous sport.'

251

'He still can,' Lisa said reasonably.

'For the sake of all the young players at Maryland State, I hope you're right.'

Traffic on 295 South was unusually light for that time of day as we headed back to Annapolis with me behind the wheel. As I slowed the Volvo to take the exit for the Baltimore Beltway, Claire surprised me by switching off the radio and saying, 'Hannah, I have to ask you something.'

'Shoot,' I said.

'I've been thinking about the confrontation you had with Cindy.'

I stole a glance at her sideways, then returned my attention to the road. 'What about it?'

'Desiree described it as a cat fight, but it wasn't, was it?'

'No.' I smiled. 'I'm not the cat fight type.'

'I didn't think so,' Claire said. 'I saw what you did to Cindy's hand. Dirty Harry in a bar brawl did less damage than that.'

'She needed stitches,' I added, trying not to sound boastful.

At fifty miles per hour, the Volvo was practically kissing the tailgate of an ancient Ford F150 pickup, so I pulled into the passing lane and speeded up. So far, only Colin and I – and Cindy, of course – knew the whole story. And I was still waiting for an appropriate moment to fess up to my husband, Paul, about my up-close-and-personal brush with death. Based on past experience, he was going to be singularly unamused. Claire was my friend, though, a sister survivor. I owed her the unvarnished truth.

'She tried to smother me, just like she did Daniel,' I confessed. 'But luckily, Colin showed up and was able to stop her.'

'Judas Priest, Hannah! Why'd she do that?'

'I guessed about the CTE and asked her about it. We actually had a pretty civilized discussion, but she must have realized she'd said too much. When she sobered up a bit, she decided to shut me up.'

'Why didn't you tell anyone?'

It was a fair question – one I'd asked myself hundreds of times since our return from Denver. Why *hadn't* I said anything to the police? I should be furious! Vengeful. Pitiless. Years ago, after a hard-fought battle, I'd beaten breast cancer. I'd won a second chance at life. How *dare* Cindy try to take it away from me?

'What purpose would it serve?' I asked my friend. 'Daniel's dead. I'm not.'

'I don't know how you can be so forgiving,' Claire said.

I managed a smile. 'Cindy wrote me a letter apologizing for what she did and begging for forgiveness. It was quite poignant. Clearly her love for Mark and her concern for their future together overruled logical thought.'

'That's what they all say,' Claire scoffed. 'They're just sorry they got caught.'

I pulled into the right lane and slowed down. 'I didn't forgive Cindy for her sake, Claire, I did it for mine. She's likely to spend a good, long time in prison for Daniel's murder. How much time would a simple assault add to her sentence? Weeks? Days?'

'Don't be silly,' Claire said. 'It wasn't a simple assault. You could have died!'

'Besides,' I added, cutting to the heart of the matter, at least for me, 'Colin would have to testify.'

'Ah, I see,' Claire said.

We drove in silence for a while. As we sped past the exit to BWI airport, I said, 'You know that Chinese proverb that goes: whenever someone saves another's life, he's responsible for that life forever?'

'That's Wookies, Hannah, not the Chinese.'

I laughed. I was no Wookie, but Colin was certainly my hero in a Han Solo sort of way. 'Colin does keep checking in on me,' I said. 'He's convinced there was some sort of cosmic reason compelling him to show up at the critical time. He probably needs to make sure I was worth the effort, that I don't blow my chances for a happy, productive life.'

'Arrgh!' Claire cried out so suddenly that I swerved onto the shoulder, my tires vibrating noisily over the rumble strips.

'Claire!'

'Sorry,' she said, as I eased the car safely back onto the road.

'Jeesh!' I said. 'You scared me half to death. I thought I was about to hit a deer or something.'

'Sorry,' she said again. 'I just realized how close *I* came to getting snuffed out. What if I'd woken up while Cindy was smothering Daniel?' She shivered.

'But you didn't.'

'I feel almost guilty about that.' After a moment,

she laid a gentle hand on my knee. 'Are you all right, then, Hannah? No damage?'

'According to my doctor, no. Nothing permanent, anyway.' I grinned. 'The truth is I still have headaches, but until medical marijuana goes live in Maryland, I'll simply have to make do with aspirin.'

Postscript

DR CARROLL: 'Yes, that happened right here, to your neighbors. It is not too much to say that in your hands lies the possibility of averting other tragedies like it. We must work untiringly, so that our children are obliged to learn the truth. Because it is only through knowledge that we can safely protect them. Failing this, the next tragedy may be that of your daughter. Or your son. Or yours. Or yours. Or YOURS!'

Reefer Madness, Sc. 34 – Int. – Classroom – Night

CPSIA information can be obtained
at www.ICGtesting.com
Printed in the USA
LVHW091518030919
629785LV00008B/63/P